Princess Camion

Princess Camion
and Other Tales
of Enchantment

by
Marie-Madeleine de Lubert

Translated, annotated and introduced by
Brian Stableford

A Black Coat Press Book

ISBN 978-1-61227-796-7. First Printing. September 2018. Published by Black Coat Press, an imprint of Hollywood Comics.com, LLC, P.O. Box 17270, Encino, CA 91416. All rights reserved.
Printed in the United States of America.

TABLE OF CONTENTS

Introduction

Mademoiselle de Lubert (1702-1785) who appears to have been baptized Marie-Madeleine de Lubert, although she was also known as Marguerite de Lubert, was one of the more prolific writers of eighteenth-century *contes de fées*, publishing several long novellas in the genre in the form of booklets. All of them were published anonymously and illicitly, devoid of the royal license required for authorized printing, and advertising false places of publication on the title page.

Mademoiselle de Lubert was the daughter of a lawyer attached to the Parlement de Paris, Louis de Lubert, and his wife Marie-Madeleine, *née* Perrot, who was the daughter of the governor of Acadia. She is known to have exchanged correspondence with Voltaire, who wrote a poem about her in 1732 addressing her by the nickname "Muse et Grace." Otherwise, little appears to be known about her life; Joseph La Porte, in volume 4 of his invaluable *Histoire des Femmes Célèbres dans la littérature françoise* (1769) states that he cannot comment on her character, not having the privilege of being acquainted with her, but describes her as "retiring et studious" and comments that she "has preferred liberty to the engagements of marriage."

Mademoiselle de Lubert's first fantastic tale, published in 1737, was *Tecserion*. Another brief volume advertised as a *conte*, *Blancherose*, was published in 1738. *Tecserion* was reprinted in 1743 as *Sec et noir, ou la Princesse des Fleurs et le Prince des Autruches* (the replacement title unpacked the anagram of the earlier

7

one), along with five other separately published novellas, including the other three collected in the present volume, *La Princesse Lionnette et le prince Coquerico*, *Le Prince Glacé et la princesse Étincelante* and *La Princesse Camion*. The remaining two volumes in the 1743 set were *La Princesse Couleur de rose et le prince Celadon* [roughly, Princess Pink and Prince Blue] and *La Princesse Sensible et le prince Typhon*.

Like other unlicensed publications in the same genre—which were unusually prolific in the 1730s and 1740s—the 1743 volumes appear to have been designed to be sold primarily by *colporteurs* (itinerant salesmen) rather than in bookshops. Treated as ephemeral publications, most of them soon disappeared from view and are now phenomenally scarce; even the Bibliothèque Nationale does not have a complete set.

The author published a few other items similar to the 1743 batch of novellas later in life, but most of her subsequent literary work consisted of editing earlier works for republication, including a four-volume edition of *Amadis des Gaules* (1750), a new version of the Comtesse de Murat's 1710 novel *Les Lutins du château de Kernosy* (tr. as "The Goblins of Kernosy Castle") and a new version of Madame d'Auneuil's 1702 collection *La Tyrannie des fées détruite* (tr. in *The Tyranny of the Fays Abolished and Other Stories*); it was Lubert's version of the last-named title, published in 1756, that was reprinted in Charles Mayer's 41-volume *Cabinet des Fées* in the 1780s, along with *La Princesse Lionnette et le prince Coquerico*, *Le Prince Glacé et la princesse Étincelante* and *La Princesse Camion*.

The version of *Les Lutins du château de Kernosy* that was reprinted in Charles Garnier's parallel set of *Voyages Imaginaires* also seems to be Mademoiselle de

Lubert's 1753 version, as the text is identical to the only copy of that edition available on-line, and it contains one reference that cannot be from the 1710 edition, but no copy of that first version is available for comparison that would enable an estimate of the extent of her editing.

Two further fantastic novellas subsequently reprinted in the *Nouveau cabinet des fées*, one of them signed "histoire traduite de l'arabe par M. Degdacobub" have also been also attributed to Mademoiselle de Lubert, but the anonymity of unlicensed publications often made subsequent attributions dubious, and those may not be reliable. The scarcity of reprints of her works meant that they remained relatively obscure until the end of the twentieth century, when Gallimard reprinted *Tecserion* in 1997. The publication in 2005 by Honoré Champion of a definitive collection of tales attributed to her, simply entitled *Contes*, edited by Aurélie Zygel-Basso, then sparked a flurry of academic interest.

The boom in the production of *contes de fées* in the 1730s picked up the genre after a relative dearth in the production of new works following the initial fad that such stories enjoyed between 1696 and 1700. Mademoiselle de Lubert's works do not appear to have been the most popular productions of the second surge, several of the others being more frequently reprinted, perhaps precisely because hers were among the most adventurous and the most unusual. Her principal model was clearly the work of the Comtesse de Murat, the first of the writers associated with the earlier boom to experiment with novellas between fifteen thousand and twenty thousand words in length, rather than the shorter stories more typical of the genre, and to sustain that length by means of the complication of her plots and the innovative ranging of her imagination. In particular, two of the stories in

Murat's *Histoires sublimes et allégoriques par Madame la Comtesse D*** dédiées aux fées modernes* (1699), "L'Isle de Magnificence" (tr. as "The Isle of Magnificence") and "Le Turbot" (tr. as "The Turbot"), provided models whose themes, motifs and narrative strategies are clearly echoed in Lubert's work, not in a merely imitative fashion but in the sense that Lubert attempted to develop those strategies further and take her work boldly into uncharted literary territory.

In that quest, Lubert succeeded more fully and more extravagantly than any of her contemporaries, with the partial exception of Madame de Villeneuve, whose "La Belle et la bête" (1740), also very obviously modeled on Murat's work, is the classic of the period, although it suffered the ignominy of being overtaken in popularity and renown by a much inferior abridged plagiarism which is the basis for most English versions of "Beauty and the Beast." Villeneuve's other long work, "Les Nayades" (tr. as *The Naiads*), was only published posthumously, in 1765. Like both Murat and Villeneuve, however, Lubert did not receive much encouragement for her ambitious experimentation, and after the striking originality of *Tecserion*—if it was the first story to be written as well as the first to be published—she seems to have reigned in her imaginative exuberance somewhat, although both *La Princesse Camion* and *Le Prince Glacé et la princesse Étincelante* remain flamboyant and intent on defying conventional expectations, and even *La Princesse Lionnette et le prince Coquerico*, which satisfies those expectations in its ultimate conclusion, certainly takes a baroque scenic route in getting there.

There is no way of knowing for sure in what order the later stories reprinted here were written, so it seemed worthwhile to follow Charles Mayer's example in the

Cabinet des fées and arrange those three so that the sequence proceeds from the most nearly conventional to the extravagantly experimental. All four stories were presumably written in a relatively short interval in the author's long life and they must represent a narrow phase in her literary and intellectual development. Unsurprisingly, therefore, they have certain motifs and preoccupations in common, particularly the fascination extravagantly displayed in three of them with metamorphoses of humans into animals, further reflected in the ambiguous naming of realms and individuals—usages carried forward from the two Murat novellas cited above. Such metamorphoses remained a common motif within the genre, as part of its standard repertoire of narrative devices, but no other writer ever deployed it with the same intensity and fascination as Lubert does in *Tecserion, La Princesse Camion* and *La Princesse Lionnette et le prince Coquerico.*

Although *Le Prince Glacé et la princesse Étincelante* is the odd one out in the present collection in its neglect of metamorphosis as a plot lever, it nevertheless has much in common with the others in its employment of erotically-motivated fays and enchanters to harass the young lovers whose awful tribulations provide the core substance of the plots, in the remarkable convolution of its story-line, and in its determination to provide a conclusion in some way distinct from the stereotypical formula. It has particularly close connections with *Tecserion*, carrying forward that story's slightly peculiar fascination with the spoliation inflicted on amorous relationships by coquetry and infidelity.

The "preliminary discourse" of *Tecserion* can serve as a preface to the whole collection as well as the part, but the apology for *contes de fées* (which I have translated as "tales of enchantment" rather than the more usual but misleading "fairy stories") provided by the brief essay is deliberately disingenuous, and it would be probably be a mistake to regard it as if it were an honest reflection of the author's attitude to the genre. The preface claims—as prefaces to works of fantastic fiction are often prone to do—that the story is intended purely for the frivolous amusement of readers, and contains no "mystery" or "allegory" warranting further critical analysis or decoding. No one who reads the story sensitively, however, especially its elaborate description of the strange utopian society of the planet Venus, could possibly believe that claim for an instant.

There are doubtless aspects of *Tecserion*, as there are in the other three stories in the present volume, which are there simply because they are colorful and decorative, delighting in the free play of the imagination for its own sake, but the narrative muscle and momentum of the stories is provided by their celebration of and skeptical commentary on the mythology of amour. The genre inherited that focus at its inception, transplanting it from the novels of Mademoiselle de Scudéry,[1] which had helped to pioneer and to define the fundamental methods and concerns of modern prose fiction, providing elaborate propaganda for the notion that amorous

---

[1] More elaborate accounts of the influence of Mademoiselle de Scudéry on the origin of *contes de fées* in the salons associated with Louis XIV's court, and the development of the genre within that context can be found in the introductions to *The Robe of Sincerity* by Marie-Jeanne L'Héritier de Villandon, *The Land of Delights* by Charlotte-Rose Caumont de La Force and *The Palace of Vengeance* by Henriette-Julie de Murat, all published by Black Coat Press.

relationships provide the only reliable basis for the possibility of happiness in life, and melodramatizing the potentially-tragic effects of everything that might get in the way the formation such relationships, whether external or internal.

Like several of the other leading writers of *contes de fées*, Mademoiselle de Lubert never married—and of those who did, most notably Baronne d'Aulnoy, Murat and Villeneuve, had woefully unsuccessful and exceedingly unfulfilling marriages, which disintegrated long before they wrote their stories—and she clearly had solid experiential grounds for an intense appreciation of the many difficulties involved in the actual rather than the fictitious contrivance of "happy endings." She knew perfectly well that the reason why many of the readers at whom her works were aimed found such stories a delight to read was precisely because they provide parables of the operation of amour, ritualistically affirming convictions that actual experience cannot possibly support: *amor omni vincit*, but only after the most heroic battles, in the representation of which implausibility is a narrative asset rather than an obstacle. In defending *contes de fées* against the frequent charge of absurdity Lubert had no other practical resource than the apologetic claim that their absurdity was essentially unserious, but the actual rhetoric of her work is far more sophisticated than that, and that is what made it genuinely experimental and exploratory, precisely because of its "mystery" and its "allegory."

Because *Tecserion* is the most ambitious of the four stories in the present collection it is also, arguably, the most flawed, in terms of its confusion and its inconsistency; it gives the impression very strongly of having been made up as the author went along, with no certainty as what conclusion she actually wanted to contrive, let alone how to get there, but for that reason it has a unique fascination. The other three stories are more coherent and more competently organized, but the sacrifice of the sheer bizarrerie of *Tecserion* had costs as well as benefits; it is arguable that "La Princesse Camion" strikes the best balance between quasi-surreal extravagance and narrative discipline; there is a certain justice in the fact that it is now the best known of Lubert's works, by virtue of the availability on line of a video of a 2014 dramatization, made by the Théâtre à Bouloire.

The expectation-defying conclusion of *Le Prince Glacé et la princesse Étincelante* is also a strong recommendation, however, and although *La Princesse Lionnette et le prince Coquerico* is the most conventional of the four stories, the unusual elaboration of the character of the aged fay Cornue and her doomed quest to win the heart of Prince Coquerico gives it an exceptional narrative energy. That quest is, in essence, a recapitulation of the confused efforts made in *Tecserion* by le roi des Autruches (the King of the Ostriches) and Ranuncule [Ranunculus, or Buttercup] to seduce Belzamine and Melidor respectively, but the consistency of its obsession in although *La Princesse Lionnette et le prince Coquerico* gives it a greater narrative force.

By virtue of such interrelationships, the collection of the four stories translated herein is a whole greater than the sum of its parts, and it presents a multifaceted insight into the mind and method of one of the most ingenious and enterprising writers of her era. The fugitive publication of her works prevented her from receiving the critical attention and acclaim that she merited in her lifetime, and provided a considerable barrier to subsequent historical interest, but its recent rediscovery has paved the way for a reappraisal that can only work to her benefit. Her work remains very readable—one of the great advantages of *contes de fées* is that they are far less prone to become dated than naturalistic fictions—and the surreal aspects of her works are far easier to appreciate and savor today than they would have been in 1737 or 1743, so, even if they were to be regarded merely as exercises in absurdity, they would have much to recommend them. However, the sharpness of their wit and the skepticism of their moralistic development add a further dimension of interest and potential enjoyment for connoisseur readers.

The translation of *Tecserion* was made from a copy of the Gallimard edition; the translations of the other three stories were made from the versions of the stories contained in the copy of volume 33 of *Le Cabinet des Fées ou Collection choisie des contes des fées et autres contes merveilleux* (1786) reproduced on the Bibliothèque Nationale's *gallica* website. Like the editor of the Gallimard edition I have modified the layout of the eighteenth century texts (which was almost certainly the result of decisions made by the printer rather than the author) in order to adapt them to modern conventions and make them more comfortably readable, without altering their content.

Brian Stableford

TECSERION

or
THE PRINCE OF OSTRICHES

Preliminary Discourse

We cannot ask for mercy for this tale, nor praise it; the former would be futile, at best, and the second evidence of a vanity that we do not have. Thus, the general prejudice that people have against prefaces would be unjust with regard to this one, since its purpose is not the same.

Tecserion is a tale of enchantment, we confess humbly; it is even appropriate to warn that it is nothing more; it is not that one is afraid that it might be mistaken for an epic poem, but intellectuals might search in it for mystery and allegory that have not been put into it, and we would be sorry if the work were to please because of the fine things that might be supposed to be in it, because those fine things would be foreign to it, and we ought not to take credit for what does not belong to us.

People prided themselves once on understanding Rabelais; to confess that they found it unintelligible would have been to renounce the brilliant title of fine mind. In that bizarre composite of the good and the bad, people put themselves to the torture in order to find meaning where there was none, delicacy in the most vulgar things, and mystery in the simplest—in brief, finesse everywhere. In the end, we backtracked; it is agreed today that we were duped for too long by the extravagance of Rabelais, that that true intellectual finesse consists of understanding that which is made to be understood; we ask, therefore, that that general rule be remembered, and that people make use of it, in reading *Tecserion*.

We could say with impunity that the original of this tale was found by the most singular stroke of luck in the ruins of some old château or in some scholar's cabinet, from which a connoisseur had taken it, or even that it has been translated from a foreign language; people would perhaps believe us, as well as a thousand other authors who give their manuscripts an air of adventure that they believe to be necessary, but which is usually only ridiculous.

Judging by the accredited axiom that it is often better to do trivial things than nothing at all, we have amused ourselves writing this tale and would like others to be amused in reading it. We are not embarrassed, by the fact that it might not please some people—geometers and metaphysicians, for instance, for whom it is not intended—but on the other hand, those gentlemen ought not to forbid it to minds of an order different from theirs, for whom it is intended. A philosopher who does not understand that reasonable people can occupy themselves with a tale of enchantment is not a philosopher; he should remember that all humans do not have the good or ill fortune to be one, and only savor philosophical ideas.

We do not pretend that tales of enchantment are a genre of writing comparable to history, or even to the simple novel; however, on the incontestable principle that goodness of different works is relative to different kinds of mind, we believe that such tales can be as good, and even generally better, than excellent books, because they are suitable for a larger number of people.

Even if we supposed them to be devoid of instruction and utility—which is almost impossible—these fabulous stories would not cease in consequence to be good, as soon as they give pleasure, for the evident reason that pleasure is essentially a good in itself, because it is an unsustainable paradox to say that the agreeable is inseparable from the useful. They can be combined as much as you wish, of course, especially because the useful should always be accompanied by the agreeable as often as it has a need to please, but the agreeable can go alone, sure of being welcome everywhere.

That is why good dancers, great actors or excellent mimes are individuals precious to society, more scorned than they are really worthy of scorn, although loved and admired, by way of compensation more, than they merit. They are far below a profound mathematician, a skillful metaphysician, a savant antiquarian or a good orator, but their talents are more likeable and more useful in the ordinary course of life than superior talents. They have the art of giving pleasure, of alleviating boredom, of dissipating chagrin and sadness. Can one pay too much for such advantages, and cherish too much the people who procure them for us?

It is almost the same for tales of enchantment, with regard to a large number of readers. However ridiculous they might be fundamentally, however extravagant the marvels might be around which they move, they are good for those they amuse, whose ennui they relieve, because amusement, as we have already said, is a good thing, and ennui a bad one. Finally, we hold it as certain that there is wisdom to be drawn from pleasure and folly.

And that is enough for an apology for tales of enchantment in general; we shall not add anything in favor of *Tecserion*; if you find pleasure in reading it or criticizing it, we shall, one way or another, have attained our goal, which was to contribute in our leisure to the pleasure of others.

TECSERION

In a country neighboring the realms of Romancie,[2] there was once a wicked king whose name was Tecserion. He was never seen to smile; he knew no other pleasures than that of doing harm; and with that, he had a face that nature seemed to have given him expressly to make him more detestable; in a word, his ugliness equaled the nastiness of his character. No subjects were ever more unfortunate than his; he took pleasure in having them hanged, and found delight in that cruelty.

His name was no less odious to his neighbors; there was no one that he was not capable of taking action against, and nothing was impossible for his magical power, for he was a great enchanter; what is more, if he knew that a neighboring king was in love with some beautiful princess, he changed her into an ostrich and the lover into a parrot, with the consequence that it was not permissible for princes to be in love in their own Estates.

Amour was a crime even more unpardonable for the unfortunate subjects of Tecserion. Either because he could only be sensible to hatred or because he only wanted people to love him, it was forbidden throughout

---

[2] Romancie—which could be transcribed into English as Romancia—is a simple derivative of romance, in the sense of Medieval romances, and refers to a generalized imaginary milieu in which such romances seem to be set. A realm of that name had, however, recently been featured in Guillaume Hyacinthe Bougeant's humorous *Voyage merveilleux du prince Fan-Férédin dans la Romancie* (1735), of which Mademoiselle de Lubert must have been aware.

21

his Estates to be in love; but as it was as impossible for young people of either sex to live without tenderness for one another as it was to love their prince, one saw couples of lovers changed into ostriches and parrots every day—but more often into ostriches, because the tyrant had perceived that in the form of parrots they conserved the use of speech, which could be a consolation of sorts for them in their metamorphosis.

As you can imagine, by forcing his subjects to make a vow of chastity, and changing them into ostriches if they violated it, Tecserion soon found himself the king of a people of ostriches. That might have reduced his horror of amour, but he was unembarrassed by it; he was mad enough to prefer reigning over ostriches than over humans; and, in fact, it suited him better.

He had already been reigning over those birds for a long time when he learned that a queen, the widow of a powerful king, had a unique daughter whose beauty was unequaled. Her realm was named the Empire of Flowers, and the young princess, who was about fifteen years old, was named Belzamine. Since there had been princesses in the world, none had ever been seen as beautiful; the graces had formed her figure perfectly, and nature had given her the kind of intelligence such as is required to make a person accomplished in every way. What a mind! The finest, the most playful, and at the same time, the most solid; in sum, she was the marvel of her century.

There was no place in the world, no matter how remote, where people did not talk about the beauty and intelligence of Belzamine. A thousand kings adored her, but a thousand kings adored her in vain; the insensitive princess was ignorant of the power of amour. Content to please, she did not imagine that anyone could love; however, an oracle threatened her with a violent and unfortunate passion; it had predicted that if she ever left the Empire of Flowers, she would only love a man who did not love her.

What an affront for a beautiful princess, and what a torment for an amorous princess! A more terrible prediction could not have been made for her.

Although everyone knows that the misfortunes announced by oracles are inevitable, people nevertheless try to avoid them, so the queen did not neglect anything to deflect the one by which her lovable daughter was menaced. She took care to hide books of geography from her, in order that the world would appear to her to be contained within the Empire of Flowers, and she would have no desire to leave it. In fact, as its limits were very extensive, in spite of her penetration, she did not think that there was anything beyond it. In addition, her governesses and even the queen preached to her incessantly against amour; at every opportunity, there were stories about the perfidy of men and on the danger there was in listening to them. The poor princess profited from those lessons and, like all young women who have never heard any different, she regarded all men as monsters; she believed what she had been told and made a scruple of even wanting to doubt it.

While the Queen of Flowers was wasting her time inspiring in Belzamine sentiments that nature was bound to disavow sooner or later, Tecserion fell in love with a portrait of the young princess. He assembled the ostriches that formed his council and declared to them that he was absolutely determined to marry her. How surprised they were by that proposition! They could not comprehend how their king, who only knew hatred, had been able to fall in love; but the portrait of Belzamine that he showed them explained the prodigy; they were dazzled by the charms of the princess, and applauded Tecserion's choice unanimously.

An important ostrich was immediately delegated to go to ask for the princess on the king's behalf, and speech was rendered to him for that purpose. He had orders, however, to tell the Queen of Flowers that if she refused her daughter, the King of Ostriches and all the ostriches in the world would fall upon her realm and put it to fire and blood. The ambassador got ready to carry out that impertinent commission, and departed with several of his companions, who formed a rather lively retinue.

Informed by the ambassador of Tecserion's intentions, the Queen of Flowers found herself in a strange embarrassment. Instead of assembling her council for an affair that required more enlightenment than human prudence, she thought it more appropriate to address herself right away to the cleverest fay there was at the time. That was the Fay of Myrtles, who lived in a province of her empire. The queen counted on her amity no less than her science, and she was received as she desired.

The compliments having been made, the Fay of Myrtles took a great book and, after having read it, she said: "Queen of Flowers, Princess Belzamine is menaced by a greater misfortune than that of marrying Tecserion. She will, however, avoid it if she can deliver herself without repugnance to that marriage."

"O gods!" cried the queen, "my daughter is going to be Tecserion's wife! Have I raised her with so much care to render her worthy of that monster? And how can she vanquish the repugnance that a face so frightful is bound to induce in her? Can the heart acquire sentiments that are not natural to it?"

"Queen," said the fay, interrupting her, "Destiny is stronger than nature; dispose Belzamine's mind, therefore, to the marriage that frightens you, and only think about diminishing the repugnance that alarms you, or prepare yourself to see her the unhappiest person in the world."

At those words, the queen, seized by dread, did not have the strength or the presence of mind to reply to the fay; fully occupied with the fate of her daughter, she took the road back to her capital diligently. She arrived there at the same time as the ostriches, who immediately requested an audience with her. She listened to their speech, and asked for time to respond. She summoned Belzamine to her apartment immediately, embraced her a thousand times, like a victim she was about to sacrifice, and told her that it was necessary for her to resolve herself to marry Tecserion.

How much it cost her tenderness to pronounce that cruel order, for she loved her daughter recklessly! It was not a political interest that made her sacrifice her; she was less affected by the king's threats than the misfortunes predicted for the princess if she refused. Belzamine, who had not yet been in love, did not have the consequent determination. She loved her mother more than she hated the King of Ostriches, so she decided to obey her in order not to cause her to despair, and promised her more than she could deliver.

The queen was charmed by that obedience, but the fatal prediction passed through her mind repeatedly that if Belzamine left the realm of Flowers she would love a man who could not tolerate her. She could not imagine that her daughter's heart could become sensible to Tecserion, even less that Tecserion might not adore her. That oracle, which she thought she ought to hide from the princess was, therefore, a mystery for her, which gave her cruel anxieties, but she flattered herself that it might be devoid of effect if Belzamine could marry Tecserion without leaving the Empire of Flowers.

By virtue of a brutal stubbornness, however, or an order of Destiny, the king did not want to come to the Empire of Flowers to make his marriage; all that could be obtained from his complaisance was that he would come to the frontier. Belzamine was therefore obliged to depart with her mother for the Field of Anemones, and go in search of a husband there who ought to have made her flee to the farthest ends of the earth.

The province in question was the smallest in the Empire of Flowers, and adjacent to that of Topazes. A great river separated the two Estates at that point, and served them as a natural boundary. On the banks of that river stood a vast porcelain building; it was that palace that was destined for the marriage ceremony.

A magnificent hall, which advanced as a projection over the river, was ornamented for the meeting with everything imaginable of the rarest and most beautiful; the walls were in white porcelain covered with beautiful anemones and precious stones, attached to branches of emeralds that emerged from vases or were embedded in the porcelain; the whole formed an arbor equally rich and brilliant. The windows, of a single piece of rock crystal, opened on to a balcony, whose golden staircase ended in a shell on the river, which bathed the steps of the hall and the walls of the palace. A thousand decorated boats, painted in a thousand colors, presented a charming spectacle on the water to divert the princess; races were organized, and even a naval battle.

In the midst of those amusements she waited for three days for Tecserion, doubtless with more dread than impatience. On the fourth day, ostriches sent to announce his arrival, declared that he was about to appear. Immediately, young Belzamine was ornamented with all the crown jewels, but the magnificence of her garments could not add anything to the splendor of her beauty.

She received the compliments of the ostriches with mildness and good humor. At times, sadness and fear surprised her, but in order not to augment the affliction of the queen, who was in tears, she made a violent effort, and appeared content with her lot.

Finally, someone came to tell her that Tecserion's litter had appeared on the other side of the river. The Prince of Topazes, who was accompanying Tecserion, his uncle, had had a magnificent tent erected on the edge of the water in order to receive the princess in her passage. The King of Ostriches stopped there, and, taking a telescope, he examined the princess, who was on the balcony of her palace. He nearly fainted with surprise, she was so beautiful; but for an ostrich who was serving as his squire he would have fallen over.

"Someone fetch me Belzamine," he said, abruptly, to his ostriches. "I want to marry her right away; I can't wait any longer."

"What are you doing, Sire?" said the Prince of Topazes. "You can't think so; the queen and the princess won't suffer being abducted thus. Violence...."

Tecserion did not give him time to finish; furious at that remonstration, he darted a fiery gaze at him, and said, in a menacing tone: "How dare you contradict my will? Is it made to be contradicted? Look at that Belzamine—and although I forbid you to find her as beautiful as I do, I ask you whether the river crossing, which would be long and troublesome, ought to be an obstacle to my desires, when I can pass over the ceremony and have the princess instantly?" Addressing his ostriches, he said: "Go on, then; bring me the Queen of Flowers and her daughter, by consent or by force, or I'll wring your necks, as well as that of my nephew, whose advice offends me."

Tecserion spoke with an urgency that put him beside himself, and that agitation immediately caused him a violent fever, which was redoubled, and he was seized by a fit so furious that his nephew the prince, whose name was Melidor, was constrained to have him tied up. At the same time he dispatched one of his confidants to the queen to tell her to remain tranquil where she was—but he was too late; the ostriches, frightened by Tecserion's threats, had already abducted the princess, without even explaining the reason for their arrival, and brought her a few minutes thereafter to the tent, where the king's life was in great danger.

Melidor was a very amiable young prince, mild, generous and benevolent—in a word, the complete opposite of his uncle. In addition, he was no less powerful than him. An amorous chagrin had caused him to go to Tecserion's court, where he hoped to be able to forget more easily a coquettish young fay, to whom he was still attached in spite of her cruel infidelity to him. Given his uncle's character, his conversation and company had appeared to him to be a remedy appropriate to the recovery of his tranquility. He had thought that by means of speaking evil of women with him, he would be able to get his mistress and her treason out of his mind; and, in fact, Melidor's amour and hatred had diminished every day, and had gradually given way to scorn. On the other hand, while he was working so fortunately to forget the infidel fay, he gained the amity of Tecserion, who, charmed to find his sentiments so much in conformity with his own, had taken him in affection and regarded him as his son.

Things had reached that point between then, and no one at the court of the King of Ostriches had any other occupation than tearing apart the fair sex, when Belzamine's portrait had arrived there. At the sight of that portrait, all the king's hatred abandoned him; he felt amour for the first time, and resolved at the same time to marry the princess, who pleased the Prince of Topazes no less. Prejudiced as he was against the perfidy of women, from the very first day, for his own part, he formed the design of making himself loved by her, in order to break the chain of the fay whose had deceived him so unworthily. He had a handsome face, and knew it; and that knowledge answered for the success of his concerns. The glory of prevailing over his uncle and avenging himself on his infidel mistress flattered him agreeably, for there was more vanity and vengeance than amour in the desire that he had to please Belzamine.

Tecserion had no suspicion of his nephew, so he accepted with pleasure the proposition the prince made of accompanying him, all the more so as it was necessary to pass through the realm of Topazes in order to get to that of Flowers. Melidor even got his uncle to promise to remain in his Estates for a few days, where, he said, he wanted to render him, on his return, the honors that were due to him and to the princess that he was going to marry.

Tecserion, in fact, was delighted by his nephew's attentions throughout the journey, and did not recognize in his conduct or his speech anything that could give him the slightest suspicion, until they had arrived opposite the porcelain palace, on the bank of the river where we left Tecserion very ill, and the Queen of Flowers and

Belzamine in the tent, very annoyed about their abduction.

Melidor therefore found himself responsible for receiving the princesses and doing them honors on behalf of his uncle, and, as can be imagined, he did not forget his own interests in circumstances so favorable to his amour. He presented himself before the Queen of Flowers and the young princess in a respectful manner, and eager to please. He begged their pardon for the violence that had just been done to them, and excused himself gallantly, putting the blame on Belzamine's charms, which Tecserion had wanted to see before dying.

"The beauty of the princess is so marvelous," said the prince, darting a glance at her full of tenderness, "that the king will be only too happy to expire before her eyes, and to soften her heart at that final moment, for," he added, "the fact is that he is in despair for his life."

Belzamine only responded with a modest silence, and a timid and embarrassed expression, which Melidor was able to interpret in his favor,

He conducted them into a cabinet of the tent, where the king was in a lethargic torpor. If art could correct the face of a monster, the magnificence of his clothing and the richness of the bed on which he lay would have rendered him less frightful, but under the adornment one still found Tecserion—which is to say, the vilest man in the world. Imagine a small figure, about two feet tall, half of which was a face, but so thin and narrow that one almost lost sight of it in a bonnet with ermine-lined earflaps. A beard so white that it seemed to be made of the same hair as the fur of his bonnet hung down below the knee. A crown a foot high, in which a single diamond glittered, had a ridiculous effect on his head, and his crimson and black velvet robe, attached by diamond clasps, was, in truth, the most beautiful thing in the world, but also the most futile to render the King of Ostriches handsome.

As the richness and magnificence of clothing did not yet have the magical power to beautify apes, Belzamine found Tecserion as frightful as he was. "That's your uncle, Sire?" she said to Melidor as she approached the king's bed. "O Heaven, that's the husband destined for me!"

The astonished queen did not know how to excuse those offensive exclamations to Melidor, who, with a candle in his hand, was maliciously illuminating all his uncle's ugliness. "Sire," she said, "you can see that my daughter is a little surprised to find such a husband, but it's necessary to hope that the king's intelligence and manners will compensate for his great age, which is always a revolting fault in the eyes of a young person."

That fine excuse was quite unnecessary; Melidor was not shocked by the aversion that Belzamine had for his uncle; on the contrary, he was grateful to her for the lively and ingenuous fashion in which she had just expressed it. He therefore replied to the queen with an easy politeness, and when they left the king's chamber he conducted her to his tent.

There, after some discussion of Tecserion's illness, he represented gallantly to the princesses that they could not remain in such an uncomfortable place, and that they would be much better off on the Isle of Turquoises, which was not far away. They accepted the prince's proposition with pleasure, and immediately set forth for that island, which was the capital of the realm of Topazes. Tecserion was also transported there; neither the physicians nor the journey could extract him from his torpor.

The Queen of Flowers and the princess were lodged in a palace made of a single turquoise of a perfect blue. The doors were diamond, as well as the balconies and the windows. That brilliant edifice was in the middle of a lake of pure water, and communicated with the island by means of a bridge of rock crystal, garnished with gold and enriched with the most beautiful turquoises. They entered the palace at the moment when it had just been ornamented from top to bottom with letters of light, which caused he named of Belzamine to shine everywhere. An apartment furnished with blue and gold fabrics was given to the princess, and from then on she was served as the Queen of Ostriches. She had a numerous staff, which was rather brilliant, although only composed of ostriches. It is true that Tecserion had rendered them all the power of speech, so they were talking and reasoning ostriches.

Tecserion's lethargy lasted for forty days, which were forty days of continual fêtes, agreeably diversified in order to cheer up the sadness of the young princess. In fact, Melidor spared no effort to please her and to dissipate her sadness, but the latter was more difficult than the former. The odious image of Tecserion followed her everywhere, plunging her into the cruelest reflections, and increasingly inspired an aversion that was not diminished by the sight of the amiable Melidor.

What a difference there is, she said to herself, *between those two princes! Why has unjust fate taken the liberty of choice away from me?* She lamented incessantly the fatal oracle so contrary to her wishes, for the queen had revealed it to her in order to warn her about the danger she was running in seeing Melidor.

How dangerous it is continually to see an object that one dreads loving! Belzamine, in combating her penchant for the young prince, only caused the arrow that had wounded her to embed itself more deeply. Amour and Melidor's attentions made her silence the oracle and forget the threats; and the princess feared no other misfortune than that of not marrying Melidor.

One evening, when she was taking her sad reflections for a walk in the palace gardens, accompanied by a young ostrich who was one of her maids of honor, she asked her a few questions, less out of curiosity than to stifle the chagrin that was overwhelming her. Among other things, she asked her about the laws of the realm of which she was about to be the queen, and why there were only ostriches there. This is what the ostrich replied:

"Our realm, Madame, has not always been as it is today. It was only a little more than a hundred years ago that the father of King Tecserion, annoyed with his wife, the queen, because of certain chagrins that she had caused him, acquired such a strong prejudice against amour and against women in general that he resolved to prevent his son from running the same dangers as him by preventing him from being able to fall in love. To that effect, he changed Tecserion's face, which was as handsome then as it is ugly now; but that imprudent father did not think that his son, without being able to give amour, might acquire it, and that his metamorphosis would then render him doubly unhappy.

"However, Tecserion soon acquired the sentiments that his father expected of his. Distressed by seeing that he was so ugly, he communicated the metamorphosis of his body to his mind, and became as somber and as malevolent as he had previously been cheerful and mild.

The king repented subsequently of having made a monster of his son, but destiny did not permit him to return him to his original form; he merely assured him as he died that he would recover it one day, if he were able to find a princess who would marry him without repugnance.[3]

"Tecserion sensed how futile it would be for him to undertake any such research, and thus, becoming increasingly insupportable to himself, he only occupied himself with means of avenging himself for the hatred and scorn that he believed that he inspired in everyone by his ugliness. His sister, the mother of Prince Melidor, died two years after her husband, the Prince of Topazes. Tecserion had loved her very much, and that loss further embittered his character, and brought his misanthropy to a peak. From then on, dedicating himself entirely to hatred, he swore to banish amour from his realm, and even from the world, if he could. He tried, in fact, for he changed all his subjects into ostriches, and those of his neighbors whose amours he discovered. However, he left them the choice of resuming human form at sixty, or of remaining ostriches if they preferred. I have not seen many at that age, which is no longer that of amour, requesting a return to their original condition, especially women; they content themselves with recovering the liberty of their tongue, of which they make use until death, and with even more frivolity, in the form of ostriches.

_____

[3] The present story was published three years before "La Belle et la Bête" by Madame de Villeneuve, which undoubtedly took its primary inspiration, as Mademoiselle de Lubert did, from the work of the Comtesse de Murat, but Villeneuve probably read *Tecserion*.

"In solitude in the middle of his depopulated States, Tecserion started to study destinies; that of Prince Melidor was the first that he discovered…."

"Oh! What does that destiny promise him?" the princess interrupted, swiftly.

"A misfortune without equal," replied the beautiful bird, sadly. "The loss of his life, by the fault of the woman who loves him the most."

"O Heaven!" cried the princess. "Is it necessary, then, never to love anyone but Tecserion?"

At those words, realizing that she had said too much, she pretended that she felt ill, and went back to the palace. Immediately, in spite of the remonstrations of the queen and the pleas of Melidor, who wanted her to appear at the ball, she went to bed and asked that she be left alone, saying that she needed to rest. The poor princess was, however, far from being able to get any, and it was not for that reason that she retired. As soon as she found herself alone with the ostrich who had already talked to her, she ordered her to continue the story of Prince Melidor. The ostrich obeyed, in these terms:

"I had the honor of telling you, Madame, that destiny threatened the prince with losing his life, by the fault of the woman who loved him most, and that his uncle the king had divined that deadly secret by means of his science; that is why he resolved to keep young Melidor away from all the women in the world, but with the intention of rendering him human form at sixty years of age; but he could not metamorphose the prince against his will. He employed all kinds of stratagems in order to obtain his consent, but always in vain; Melidor replied to him that he would rather die of the pleasure of being loved than the chagrin of not being.

"His uncle, obliged to be content with his reasoning, good or bad, no longer thought about anything but inspiring sentiments in him that would have the same effect as the metamorphosis. In order to succeed in that, he took him out of the hands of women and put severe tutors in charge of his education, who repeated to him gravely from morning until evening that he ought never to love or seek to be loved. Melidor was not very attentive to those lessons; his naturally tender heart abandoned itself with pleasure to the sweet flattery of thinking that true happiness consists of loving tenderly someone who loves us in the same fashion.

"Meanwhile, he grew up and finally became his own master. He remembered the kindness that the Fay of Myrtles, who was known for her prudence, had shown him, and thought that he ought to go and pay his court to her and show his gratitude for the good advice that she had given him. That fay was then putting all her cares into raising the young fay Ranuncule, her cousin, but her cares had been futile, for Ranuncule had been born a deceitful coquette, incapable of any other attention but that of hiding her petty coquetries from her cousin.

"So, Melidor went to see the Queen of Myrtles, and chanced to arrive there on a day when she was giving a grand ball in her palace; when the prince arrived the dancing ceased, and all the fays, surprised by his grace, arranged themselves in a line to let him pass. There and then, Ranuncule formed the design of pleasing him, not because she had any penchant for him—she did not know what it is to love—but because her vanity was flattered by the idea of stealing the conquest of Melidor from all the other fays who might aspire to it. She therefore never ceased making eyes at him and provoking him, in spite of the signs of the Fay of Myrtles, who begged her to contain herself. Seeing that the young prince, exceedingly timid, was responding nonchalantly to her advances, she took him to dance, and whispered to him, while squeezing his hand: 'Great God, is it possible that your eyes respond so poorly to what mine have been saying to you for more than a hour?'

"At those words, Melidor woke up, as if from a profound torpor, and, looking at the fay with great blue eyes that marked nothing less than indifference, said to her: 'Madame, how can I believe that for which I dare not hope? Is my good fortune not a dream?'

"'Keep your voice down,' the fay said, interrupting him, 'and come to the labyrinth of myrtles this evening; you'll see what I can do for you if you love me.'

"With those words she quit him in order to go and mingle with the fays who were dancing, and continued her coquetries with all the princes composing the assembly, in a manner capable of driving Melidor to despair. Entirely occupied with the conquest of Ranuncule, however, and not daring to doubt her sincerity after what she had just said, the inexperienced young prince imagined that she was only behaving thus in order to deceive her cousin's gaze.

"The ball came to an end, and after having escorted the Fay of Myrtles to her apartment. Melidor flew to the labyrinth. He waited there for two full hours, with as much impatience as anxiety, for the flighty Ranuncule. She finally arrived, and immediately made him forget, by means of all the tenderness she showed him, the cruel moments he had just endured. Delighted by the fervor of his mistress, he thought that she felt at least as much amour for him as she inspired in him for her.

"She continued to arrange rendezvous with the young prince, who was becoming more infatuated every day, thinking himself the most fortunate of men; he only lacked a pretext for remaining at the court of the Fay of Myrtles, and his amour rendered him industrious in giving birth to one.

"The two lovers had been living in a perfect intelligence for six months when Ranuncule promised Melidor to give him her portrait in the same labyrinth that had witnessed the commencement of their amour. That evening, the Fay of Myrtles retired later than usual, with the result that the prince, unable to quit her with decorum, allowed the time marked by Ranuncule to pass. As soon as he was free, however, he ran to the labyrinth with the urgency of the tenderest of lovers; but he was very surprised, on approaching the cabinet where Ranuncule ought to have been alone, to hear voices. He stopped, less to listen than to avoid compromising her, for he thought that she might be taking to one of her companions, who had followed her, and of whom she was unable to rid herself.

"He was soon undeceived. 'I don't like Melidor at all,' said the flirt, 'and the sacrifice of my portrait ought to prove it to you. I've amused myself with him for a long time, in order to put the Fay of Myrtles off the track, who wouldn't have forgiven me for trying to please you, but since you love me enough to forget her, I promise you that I won't see Melidor anymore.'

"'No,' cried the prince, advancing into the cabinet, 'undoubtedly you won't see him anymore. And you, traitor,' he said, addressing Prince Romarin, who was still at the young fay's knees, 'won't enjoy your perfidy; I'll avenge the Fay of Myrtles and my tenderness at the same time.'

"With those words he drew his sword, with which he was about to run his rival though; but Ranuncule seized him with her arm in time, and made a sign with the other hand to Prince Romarin to withdraw, which he did very rapidly. 'What were you going to do?' she said to Melidor then, looking at him tenderly. 'Ingrate that you are, do you want to drive me to despair by a jealousy that has no foundation?'

"The prince, more astonished by that effrontery than by what he had just heard, put away his sword rather coldly and, looking at Ranuncule with a scornful expression that disconcerted her, he said: 'I'm not jealous; I would even be quite wrong to be. I'm departing, in order not to leave you in any doubt regarding my sentiments, and I shall try to efface even the shame of having conceived them.'

"He quit her at the same time, in spite of the efforts that she made to retain him, and the following morning, having taken his leave of the Fay of Myrtles, he returned to his Estates. He only traversed them in order to go to the abode of his uncle, the King of Ostriches, and tell him of his despair.

"For her part, Ranuncule, scantly embarrassed by the loss of Melidor, consoled herself easily with Prince Romarin, whose conquest flattered her heart less than her vanity; she did not really love him, but she wanted to steal him from the Fay of Myrtles, who loved him, and she succeeded in doing so.

"The fay, sensitive to that affront, avenged herself on Ranuncule by expelling her from her court; Prince Romarin went with her, but soon afterwards, weary of his mistress's coquetry, which nothing could fix, he abandoned her. The fickle fay then recovered her initial sentiments for Melidor and resolved to bring him back to her; it was with that design that she came to the Isle of Pearls, which one can see from here."

"What! Ranuncule is so close by?" Belzamine interjected. "Has Melidor seen her?"

"No, Madame," the ostrich replied. "He even appears to be occupied with something else."

"That's enough," said the princess. "Go to bed, my dear ostrich, for I sense that I'm falling asleep. Your story has delighted me, and I confess that you tell it perfectly."

The ostrich withdrew, after a profound reverence, and left the princess to her own devices, to her amour and her jealousy.

You will easily guess how she spent that night; she doubtless wished a thousand times that the Isle of Pearls and her dangerous rival were at the other end of the world.

What rights a first inclination has over a tender heart! Belzamine recalled them with an exactitude that made her despair. In addition, she was not yet sure of being loved by Melidor. That night appeared to her to be eternal, although she was unable to spend it entirely in her bed, where the silence and tranquility augmented her agitation. Finally, she found herself in the gardens at sunrise; but the walk could not dissipate her troubles, and the daylight, on the contrary, only aggravated them, by means of the objects that it enabled her to see. From an elevated terrace she discovered the Isle of Pearls, and the entire island presented nothing to her mind except the redoubtable Ranuncule; her eyes paused upon it, and she leaned on a lapis balustrade that circled the terrace in order to abandon herself to the most bitter reflections.

For his part, Melidor, anxious about Belzamine's health, had not slept tranquilly; he was already up and about, walking in the gardens outside the princess's windows, waiting for her to wake up. He perceived her

40

on the terrace, and was quite astonished to see her so early; she appeared to him to be so occupied that he hesitated to interrupt her in her reflections, but amour prevailed over that consideration.

"What are you doing here, Madame?" he said, approaching her respectfully? Do you prefer solitude to the pleasures that we try to procure for you? Do our efforts displease you? Are you scornful of our cares?"

"No, Sire," the princess relied, looking at him with a mixture of sadness and languor. "I do not flee amusements that ought to please me, but sometimes one likes to relax in solitude for a while from the tumult of fêtes."

"Alas, Madame," said Melidor, "how glad one would be if you would permit him to imitate you! How agreeable these moments of retreat would be for the person who had the good fortune to share them with you." Kneeling down, he continued: "I adore you, divine Belzamine; all the respect that I owe to my uncle cedes to the pleasure of telling you so. I shall die if you consent that he marries you."

The embarrassed princess had to make an effort in order to reply. "I have not chosen Tecserion for my husband," she said. "Princesses are ordinarily the victims of the Estate. However, my faith is engaged, and although I had no part in that engagement, my duty obliges me to subscribe to it."

"Oh, cruel woman!" the prince cried. "What is duty, when amour speaks? Say rather that Melidor's tenderness has not touched your heart, and that you accept without difficulty the crown of the ostriches."

"I ought at least to let you believe that," said Belzamine, moved by the prince's dolor, "But alas, I do not have the strength to resist that reproach. You are unjust, Melidor; however, flee from me if you love me, make that sacrifice to my glory; I sense, and I make you the confession, that it has need of that aid in order to be sustained. Yes, believe that it is with an extreme dolor that I consent to wear the crown that is offered to me. Alas, without the oracle that menaces your life...."

With those words she quit Melidor abruptly, and went to shut herself in her apartment.

The prince remained motionless. It would be difficult to say what was passing through his soul: surprise, hope, dread and joy caused sentiments in his heart that he had difficulty distinguishing himself.

What! he thought, when his emotion had calmed down somewhat. *I am loved by Belzamine! That beautiful princess is interested enough in my days to be afraid that her love might be fatal to them! Oh, princess! Is there a fate more beautiful than that of dying for you? Is the most beautiful life worth as much as a death so fortunate?*

The more he recalled Belzamine's words, the happier he found himself. The knowledge that she had of the menaces of the oracle, and he care that she had taken to tell him so, assured Melidor of the interest that she took therein, and that first assurance of being loved by a princess whom he found adorable caused him to savor the delectable transport that lovers only experience once, which is the purest and perhaps the most solid of their pleasures.

He stayed on the terrace for a long time, recalling the sweet moments that had he had just passed there. The amour that was maintaining his reverie interrupted it; he desire to please his princess and complete her conquest caused him to return to the palace.

Belzamine was shut away in her cabinet. The shame of having told Melidor that she loved him caused her an extreme pain; her virtue criticized that confession of crime and weakness. Amour only made it a slight fault, easy to repair; she resolved, therefore, to do so, but amour mocked her resolution. She strove, in truth, to constrain herself, but that effort only augmented the violence of her penchant; in any case, the imperious reason that orders us not only to dissimulate but also to stifle sentiments that are dangerous to follow, had scarcely any part in the pride with which the princess ornamented herself; it was really a pride necessary to assure herself of Melidor, by making him buy her conquest more dearly.

She set about getting dressed, and gave her adornment all the care and complaisance of a young woman who wishes to please; in fact, she was adorning herself for Melidor, although she wanted to hide that design from herself. She had never been more content with her cares; amour seemed to be arranging her hair, so easy was it to place it graciously. In the end, her mother found her more beautiful by half, and the ostriches paid her compliments with admiration and surprise. Belzamine felt a secret joy in consequence that she dissimulated with difficulty; the eulogies of the queen and the ostriches answered to her for the impression that her beauty would make on the eyes of her dear Melidor, and that agreeable thought triumphed over the importunate reflections of reason, the tyrannical scruples of her duty, and all the secret reproaches made to her, futilely, by her own glory and that of her sex.

Melidor came into Belzamine's apartment as she was putting the final touches to her adornment. He remained nonplussed on perceiving her, and stood in the doorway, motionless, more surprised than if he were seeing her for the first time. I leave you to imagine whether the princess was sorry to see her charms acting do force-fully.

"Come in, Sire," the queen immediately said to Melidor, "and see whether my daughter has put on suitable attire for today's fête. She has imagined dressing as a nymph, and I think that it suits her very well."

"Madame," said Melidor, "the princess is always so beautiful that art cannot give her anything; it is true that her beauty seems to lend itself to all attire, since she cannot change clothes without acquiring new grace."

In fact, a garment of blue and gold gauze, garnished with embroidered networks of diamonds, clung to her figure lightly, allowing all its finesse to be seen. Her beautiful ash-blonde hair was naturally curly, negligently attached by blue plumes, which gave her face a brightness difficult to sustain. Her necklace, bracelets and belt were wrought gold, garnished with turquoises and diamonds. Those three pieces were a gallantry on the part of Melidor, who had had them put on her dress-ing-table.

After a moment of silence caused by admiration, Melidor offered the princess his hand in order to pass into a gallery of the palace where a theater had been set up for the performance of a ballet.

"But Prince," she said to him, as she gave him her hand, "I think that I ought not to take so much pleasure in the diversions that are offered to me, since the King of Ostriches is not responsible for them."

"Is it to make me sense my misfortune more keenly," said the prince, "that you are making me party to that reflection? Oh, Madame, my uncle is too fortunate; he has your faith and your tenderness; at least give me your pity."

Belzamine lowered her eyes on encountering those of the prince, and said to him in a faint tone: "I would like to be sure of only feeling pity for you, Prince; alas, I am not so fortunate. Why have you taught me to know other sentiments?"

At the same time, she took her place, and the spectacle commenced. As everything speaks to lovers of their amours, Melidor and Belzamine found a great deal of resemblance between the subject of the ballet and their situation. They recognized themselves everywhere therein, and said so to one another with their eyes. Their hearts, especially Belzamine's, made more progress that evening than either of them imagined.

A grand ball followed the ballet; Belzamine stole all suffrages therein, and no one tried to dispute them, for never has anyone danced with as much grace and lightness as they showed.

In the middle of the night, as everyone was preparing to retire, and while Melidor, intoxicated by amour and joy, was at the feet of the princess, a cloud the color of fire and gold suddenly filled the entire hall, and, opening suddenly, allowed the sight on huge nacreous seashell of a ravishing beauty surrounded by twenty ladies, who would have appeared beautiful anywhere but by her side.

The Queen of Flowers thought that the spectacle was another gallantry on Melidor's part, but the young princess was not deceived. She was gripped by fear at the sight of that redoubtable beauty. She had no doubt that it was Ranuncule; and indeed it was. For his part, Melidor went pale, but he advanced nevertheless in a disconcerted manner toward the chariot in order to offer his hand to the fay, in spite of a movement that Belzamine made to retain him.

Ranuncule saluted the queen with a pride that completed the prince's disturbance, and addressed herself to him. "Why," she asked him, "did you leave me in ignorance that these illustrious persons are here? Do you not know that it is an honor for my sisters and myself to have an opportunity to serve them?" At the same time, she said to her companions: "Bring the presents destined for the Queen of Ostriches."

Immediately, a huge basket made of pearls appeared, strung with gold filigree, which formed miraculous designs; first, a yellow and silver scarf was pulled out of it, then a golden shuttle and a brooch of diamonds.

"This scarf," the fay said to Belzamine, "will render you invisible whenever you wish; the shuttle will save you from a great danger; and the brooch can grant a wish."

The princess was not curious about those presents; she found it humiliating to receive them from the hand of a rival. While she received them, with chagrin painted in her eyes, a loud burst of laughter emerged from the bottom of the basket, which astonished the whole assembly. The ribbons and jewels there were still in it were thrown to the floor by a violent shock, which allowed the sight, on a small mattress of white satin, of Tecserion, more monstrous and more frightful than ever. What an apparition for the princess!

"I doubtless wasn't expected here," said the resuscitated monster, immediately. "Ha ha! So, Princess Belzamine, this is how you passed the time while I was asleep? From what I can see, you were not very anxious about my health; but let's see whether you want to marry me right away, for I fear no longer having the same desire tomorrow."

That strange compliment completed the distress of the princess; her beautiful eyes were flooded by tears, and her dolor scarcely permitted her to respond.

"Sire," she said to him, "I am ready to obey the queen, if she orders me to marry you, but I hope that she might give me some time to resolve myself to it."

"Frankly, Sire," the queen said then, softened by her daughter's tears, "your first appearance seems to me to be a trifle singular."

"Frankly, Madame," said Tecserion, "it is necessary to do as I wish, and you scarcely seem to me to be disposed to do that. Someone lock this beautiful damsel in my parrot cage immediately, and we'll see what it pleases her to decide. And you, Prince Melidor, is this how you serve your uncle? One more day asleep and you'd have played me a fine trick! Come on, bring me my cage, and let there be no more resistance."

An ostrich brought a magnificent cage then, from which the king's parrot was taken out and in which Belzamine, in spite of her resistance, was imprisoned.

The queen protested loudly about that fashion of acting, but she was not heeded, and Melidor, who feared irritating his uncle further, did not say a word. He advised that princess to return to her Estates, promising to employ all his art and all his credit in order to have liberty rendered to the unfortunate Belzamine. The queen departed immediately, after informing Tecserion that this violence broke all engagement between them, and that she would never consent to the marriage.

Without responding to the queen, Tecserion commanded that the cage containing the princess by suspended in one of the palace towers, which was executed immediately. The cage was very large, since it contained a cot in blue taffeta, a seat, a table and a dressing table.

All that, however, only made a frightful little prison, in which Belzamine, outraged to see herself treated in such an undignified fashion, expressed all her despair by means of an obstinate silence. Her eyes, which were turned toward Melidor, and Ranuncule, who was present, were the only interpreters of the sentiments that agitated her, and she allowed herself to be carried away without deigning to complain into the tower, where ostriches were ordered to guard her day and night.

Melidor, all the more afflicted because it was necessary to dissimulate his dolor, escorted his uncle and the fay to their apartments, and then retired to his own. What a night he passed! It would be necessary to have been in his situation in order to be able to depict it. Amour, despair, fury, indignation and a thousand different passions agitated him equally. Ranuncule occupied him as much as Belzamine; he could not forgive her for the cruel trick she had just played on him. He did not understand what had happened at all.

Finally, tormented by all his reflections, he got up very early and went into a cabinet which looked out in the direction of the tower in which the unfortunate Belzamine was imprisoned. He learned on the window-sill and started dreaming profoundly.

Scarcely an hour had gone by in that sad occupation when the door of the cabinet opened and he saw Ranuncule appear. She was dressed magnificently, and even more gallantly; her garment was nothing but a tissue of pearls embroidered with ruby buttercups. In order to leave her figure more liberty, it clung to it lightly, and a diamond clasp attached her loose robe negligently over one knee, in such a way that it allowed the sight of a leg covered by a brodequin similar to the dress; her arms were bare and her cleavage was only covered by jet black naturally curly hair. Pearls and rubies artfully placed on her head composed her entire coiffure.

Sure of her charms, she entered with a conquering air and, without waiting for him to speak, she said: "I've come to justify myself with you and to bid you adieu at the same time, for I want to spare you the confusion of seeing someone that you always accuse so lightly and who has so many reasons to complain about you, No, no," she continued, seeing that he wanted to speak, "what you have to say to me is nothing at the price of what I can tell you. Know, Melidor, that in spite of your injustices, I have not cease for a moment to love you; I know that I was wrong in the form, but my tenderness justifies me fundamentally, for everything that you heard was merely to test you; but let's pass over that adventure, as I blush at making excuses to the most ingrate of men. Know, then, that this amour has caused my jealousy, and that I woke Tecserion up in order to serve my vengeance. Punish me for that crime, it is the only one for which you can reproach me, or, rather, continue to offend my tenderness with the one that touches you today; that is a punishment I deserve, and of which I don't complain. However, my heart, which is always yours, in spite of your cruelty, will only ever avenge itself by loving you more. Adieu; you will never see me again; I'm leaving in order no longer to importune you with my tenderness, which I cannot vanquish."

With those words, accompanied by a gaze of which Melidor still recognized the power, she made as if to withdraw.

"Stop, cruel woman," cried the prince, retaining her by the robe. "Come and enjoy once again the woes that you have caused me. It isn't that still love you; after your infidelity, nothing ought to remain in my soul but indignation...."

"Go on," said the fay. "Boast to me about your tenderness for Belzamine; nothing more remains but for you to confess it to me. O Heaven" she cried, with an appearance of dolor. "It is to see myself sacrificed to a new passion, then, that the ingrate wants to retain me? Have you not punished my pride enough? Is it necessary to render me witness to your indifference? Alas, have I not already suffered enough in learning that your heart belongs to another?"

Then, pretending to feel a sharp dolor, she let herself fall into an armchair, and covered her face with a handkerchief, as if to hide her tears.

Melidor, torn between an object that was renewing a passion of which he had sensed all the charm and by his new amour for Belzamine, remained immobile at that spectacle. The artifice of which he knew Ranuncule to be capable, the frankness and the mildness of the young Belzamine, her naïve beauty, the tenderness that she had shown him almost in spite of herself, and the fact that she was suffering because of him in Tecserion's irons, all spoke in favor of the young princess, and the fay coquette sensed that clearly; that is why, in order to triumph more surely over the prince, she had pretended to fall ill in her armchair. She appeared to make an effort to get up, and went to throw herself on a bed that filled the back of the cabinet.

As Melidor hastened to help her, she said "Let me die. This is the day of the year when I can lose my life; the cruelest death is preferable to the woes I am suffering; you would be less barbaric to pierce my heart than to tell me that you no longer love me; in spite of the certainty that I had of it, I still pleased myself in doubting it, because you had not said it to me, but now…yes, pierce my heart, strike, behold what will fly before your blows…."

As she said that, the deceitful fay uncovered a breast that would have disarmed the most ferocious of men. In fact, vanquished by that seductive sight, Melidor sensed his anger and courage abandoning him, and Ranuncule appeared to him more lovable than culpable.

"No, Madame," he cried, throwing himself on his knees, "I don't want your death; is it not rather you who wanted me to lose my life, when I heard that fatal conversation?"

"Oh, let's leave that adventure," said the fay. "I detest it, since it has taken away your tenderness from me, when it was only concerted to conserve it for me."

"Eh! Why so much art" said Melidor tenderly, "since I loved with so much frankness? Was such a cruel proof necessary to convince you of it?"

"Perhaps," said Ranuncule, hotly, "and since you want to talk about it, I proved that it was necessary, since it convinced me that you did not love me enough to find me innocent; you departed abruptly, without even doubting, and I know that you already have a new amour…in sum, it's certain now that you love Belzamine; you couldn't deny it. What shame for me! But what am I saying? The shame is only for you; you've betrayed me, and at the same time you've betrayed a king who confided his tenderness to you. Are you not frightened, Melidor, by the blackness of those sins? Without you, without your passion, would the Belzamine that you're lamenting be so unfortunate? She would only have known her duty, she would be tranquil, and you have exposed her, by loving her, to the most terrible misfortunes. Save her—there is still time. Is it necessary for it to be me who urges you? Your uncle the king, irritated as he is against her, and against you, might, by virtue of your repentance, suspend, and even forget, the anger that animates him. Say the word, speak, and I'll take charge of the rest."

"Well," said the prince, "what is it necessary to do to save her?"

"Renounce her," said the fay. "And it isn't me who asks that of you: it will be your glory, and I am forgetting at this moment any other interest. For after all, what trust could I have in future in your fidelity? It would be necessary to be very weak to add any faith to your oaths."

"Renounce seeing her, and loving her!" cried the prince, getting up precipitately from the fay's knees. "Oh, cruel woman, impose another law upon me if you want me to follow it."

"Well," said the fay, "continue to love her, since nothing can detach you from it, and you do not sense the offense you are doing to her glory and yours."

"What tells you, Madame," said Melidor, "that I am wounding the glory of the princess in loving her? Can I not hope, then, to receive her hand? And can that love, as pure as the fire of her beautiful eyes, which ignited it, ever…"

"That love that you believe to be so delicate and pure, ought to make you tremble, since it is by the blackest treason that you are stealing Belzamine from your uncle the king. Is she not his? And has he not trusted you? But it's futile to say anything more to you, you're so smitten with that beauty, who charms you. Go, prince, go, if you can boast to her of that constancy, which will seal her misfortune. I blush to have been able to love you, to the point of taking a step so unworthy of me, but I repeat to you again that in making it, I have listened less to the interests of my amour than those of your happiness."

With those words she stood up and, striking the floor with her wand, she caused a winged griffin to appear, flame-colored and white, which she mounted; it flew away with her through the window, in spite of the efforts of the prince to stop it.

In what a state he found himself after that conversation! If Belzamine still seemed to him to be lamented, Ranuncule justified seemed to him more lovable than ever; he found himself the author of the princess's misfortune, and culpable toward his uncle of the treason that the fay had exaggerated so cleverly. When he believed, out of delicacy, that he ought to forget Belzamine, his heart, out of weakness, returned to Ranuncule; or, rather, he loved them both without perceiving it.

While the unhappy prince experienced all that uncertainty and amour have of the most cruel, Tecserion sent word to him that he was returning to his Estates for a few days in order to settle a disagreement that had arisen between the ostriches and the parrots, and that he was leaving him his prisoner to guard.

That news frightened Melidor, for he dreaded seeing Belzamine as much now as he had wanted it two hours before. In any case, the commission that the king had given him was very delicate; so he spent the rest of the day in his cabinet, without knowing what to do. Finally, by virtue of abstraction, or the necessity of making a decision, he directed his steps toward the tower. The door was closed, but the ostriches, who had orders to let him in, opened it immediately.

As he advanced toward the cage, he saw Belzamine through the bars, lying down negligently. As soon as she saw him she raised herself up on to her elbow.

"Frightful monster!" she cried. "Barbaric king, have you come again to heap me with reproaches as cruel as they are vain? How does it serve you to afflict me further with your presence? Flee from my eyes; I shall never love you, and if it is necessary, in order to increase your rage, to confess that I am sensible to Melidor's amour, I dare to tell you that, and I shall only speak again in order to assure you of it."

The prince was in the utmost astonishment to see her loving and hating simultaneously. "What!" he said. "You mistake me for Tecserion, and I learn in the most cruel fashion that you have been touched by my tenderness?"

"It is in vain, barbarian," said the princess, "that you try to tear Melidor from my heart; he alone can reign there, and your projects of vengeance against that unfortunate prince and against me cannot shake either of us. I can, if necessary, brave them by my death, for I prefer that to the liberty you offer me on conditions so unworthy of me."

That tenderness on the part of Belzamine returned to the prince all the amour that he had felt for her. "O Heaven!" he cried. "She can't hear me. Belzamine, beautiful princess, recognize your lover, see Melidor desperate, transported by amour and fury, suffering all torments at once, and dying of dolor and pleasure at the same time."

The princess made no reply, and, merely making a gesture of scorn and indignation, she let herself fall back on her bed and turned her head in another direction."

Melidor lost patience then, and, beside himself addressed himself to the ostriches.

"What has happened, then," he said to them, "between Tecserion and the princess? Great gods! I can no longer doubt it; why did I not know sooner? His blood would have washed way this insult. Too unfortunate princess, is it me, then, who has caused your misfortune?"

"Sire," said one of the ostriches, who had been in Belzamine's court, "don't accuse the king of such a vengeance; a more powerful force is acting upon the princess; that scarf you see is enchanted, and it is that, in spite of Tecserion and the efforts we have tried to take away from her, which is responsible for the change that astonishes you. The princess, in the confidence that the scarf would render her invisible, put it on this morning in order to hide from the king's eyes, but it is her intelligence that has disappeared instead of her face, for she mistook the king for you and said the most tender things to him; he took them for as many piquant ironies and left immediately, but with the design of marrying Belzamine as soon as he returns, in whatever fashion. We fear that the other presents are equally dangerous, but we cannot take them away from her without injuring her; the diamond brooch is attached to her hair so forcefully, and the golden shuttle to her hand, that dexterity and force have thus far proved impotent to take them away from her."

"I recognize the hand from which that vengeance departs," said Melidor, "but my dear ostrich, does the princess not have lucid intervals?"

"We have not yet remarked any, Sire," said the ostrich. "Since she put on that fatal scarf, we have always seen her the same. If we remark any change, you will be informed."

"And in the meantime," said the prince, "I shall go in search of aid for her, and to avenge myself in my turn on the wicked Ranuncule."

With those words he left the tower, and, mounting a blue eagle, of which he made use on great occasions, he went to the abode of the Fay of Myrtles in two minutes. He found the Queen of Flowers with her, overwhelmed by dolor, and fully occupied with the measures she had to take in order to see her daughter again and avenge herself on the King of Ostriches.

He went up to them abruptly, without pausing for any ceremony, which dolor and danger have the right to suppress. "The strangest of all misfortunes," he said to them, in a troubled manner, "has happened to Princess Belzamine...."

"I know," said the fay, gravely, interrupting him, "and I was talking to the queen about it when you came in, but she has greater things to fear if she makes use of the other presents. You know only too well that it is your tenderness that has attracted all these woes to her, and that Ranuncule's presents will only have power for as long as you feel love for the princess. The more you love her, the more unfortunate she will be, for such is the force of the charm that she has been given."

"What, Madame!" cried the prince, penetrated by the sharpest dolor. "I am the cause of this frightful adventure, and I can only save the princess by abjuring an amour that is dearer to me than life? And even if I wanted to, alas, could I?"

"Sire," said the fay, "one can do anything one wishes; the power of the amour only comes from your weakness; try to vanquish it, and you will be victorious."

"Oh, cowardly Ranuncule!" cried Melidor. "It's necessary, then, to try no longer to love an adorable princess? But it will only be on quitting life, rather than render you a tenderness that you do not merit."

"Ranuncule is not as culpable as you imagine," said the fay. "It is true that she woke Tecserion and told him about your love for the princess, but it is the king himself who enchanted the three presents, and Ranuncule only contributed to it by the malign pleasure of bringing them."

"Is that nothing, then Madame?" said the prince. "And can I forgive her for that blackness? But I must think, for the present, about something other than avenging myself on her. My uncle will profit from Belzamine's error and marry her in my name. That thought makes me shiver; can I suffer that the King of Ostriches will abuse, by means of unworthy artifices, a tenderness that is only given to me? In addition, as Tecserion has made the charm, he can destroy it. What regrets, what dolors will my beautiful princess not have when she sees…?"

"Have no fear of that, Sire," said the fay. "Tecserion, it is true, made the charm, but as soon as Ranuncule gave it to her, he was no longer the master if making it cease. As for the fear you have that he will marry the princess, that is just, for he can, and if he marries her, as is Ranuncule's plan, you will lose her forever. But what is more terrible still at this moment is that the princess, in her despair, might remember to invoke the brooch and the shuttle. Fly to her aid, if there is still time. Here, prince, this is a glass hazelnut that can ward off the evils that we fear. Be careful to break it before going into the tower; it will enable your projects to succeed, in the case that they are not forestalled, for afterwards, I cannot do anything. Go, don't lose a moment; but I repeat to you again that it would be wiser and surer for Belzamine and for you to renounce your amour!"

"Oh, Madame," said the prince, "order me to die; that order would be a thousand times milder for me."

The Fay of Myrtles sighed, and she embraced Melidor with tears in her eyes. "All our power," she said, "is very feeble compared with the power of amour. Why is it necessary that such a beautiful passion should be subject to so many woes? Go, prince, I fear that you might arrive too late."

Melidor remounted his eagle immediately, in order to return more rapidly than he had come.

In the meantime, Ranuncule was not idle; she had been triumphant at first at having shaken Melidor, but since she had learned that he had seen the princess, and that he had recovered more love for her than he had ever had, she had gone to find Tecserion and had engaged him to go back to Belzamine and advise her to make use of the brooch and the shuttle.

Tecserion, passing for Melidor by virtue of the charm had only to speak to her to persuade her. The princess, touching the brooch, wished to be freed from her prison, and immediately, the cage and the tower disappeared. Then she touched the shuttle, and asked that her enemies should no longer have any power over her. Immediately, she disappeared, and was transported a hundred leagues away.

How surprised Ranuncule and Tecserion were! Neither of them had expected a similar effect of the shuttle, to which they believed they had attached another charm, deceived, one by her amour and the other by his jealousy. Melidor arrived at the moment when the princess had just disappeared. He asked his uncle for her, and the fay, whom he found equally consternated. He abandoned himself to all his fury and exhaled his anger in the bloodiest reproaches, but Ranuncule soon stopped him; she struck him with her wand and changed him into a dragon with wings and ruby eyes; he was, however, animate and even reasonable; for fear that he might fly away, therefore, Ranuncule attached him with diamond chains to the foot of the palace walls.

Tecserion took change of tormenting him until he had renounced Belzamine, and to begin his vengeance, he declared to him that he would be a dragon until he had shed Belzamine's blood himself. At that frightful prediction, the dragon uttered howls the echoed of which resounded for a hundred leagues around. The cruel Ranuncule saw without emotion the bitter tears flowing of a prince she had loved. When the King of Ostriches had been a spectator for long enough of the dolor he had caused the unfortunate prince, he withdrew with Ranuncule, who applauded herself for all the harm she had caused.

What became of the unfortunate Melidor? He should have died of dolor; the torments that he was made to suffer, his frightful form and the usage of speech of which he was deprived all afflicted him less than having lost Belzamine.

Why not take reason away from me, barbarians? he cried, in his heart, for he could only express himself by means of shrill hisses that even frightened him. *But I shall soon lose it, with life, for the dolor that I feel is unsustainable. Admirable Belzamine, perhaps you are suffering as much as me; how do I know whether you are not accusing me of your misfortunes? Alas. that would be the completion of mine, since I cannot help you.*

Those reflections threw him into a despair so excessive that he vomited flames, which ravaged the countryside for a considerable distance and made the frightened inhabitants run away.

Tecserion returned to the kingdom of the ostriches, where Ranuncule sought to please him, because of her liking for coquetry and her self-interest. Her design was to engage the King of Ostriches to pursue his vengeance and make Melidor suffer woes that would constrain him finally to abandon Belzamine. In fact, the king, having become subject to the most violent passions, and having lost all hope of possessing Belzamine, who had escaped him and over whom he had no more power through his own fault, did not resist Ranuncule's artifices; he became fanatical, and his heart was divided from then on between amour and the cruelest hatred; those two passions fortified one another.

Meanwhile, Ranuncule had a secret chagrin at seeing Melidor constant; every day she was witness to the torments that he suffered, but also to his courage and the fidelity he conserved to the princess.

As for Belzamine, on emerging from the cage she found herself in an uninhabitable desert. She immediately demanded her dear prince in that frightful solitude. "Melidor!" she cried. "Dear Melidor, what has become of you?" But only the echoes responded to her voice

"What! Melidor has abandoned me after showing me so much love! Can a passion so tender finish so promptly? Is this, then, the recompense for mine? No, Melidor, I know you better, pardon me that injustice; it is our enemies who are retaining you. And how can they not be jealous of my happiness? You love me, and I can only love you."

Although the beauty she had seen in her rival gave her a few moments of anxiety, Melidor's tenderness and the virtues that she believed she had remarked in him reassured her; she convinced herself that without the cruelty of Tecserion and he jealousy of Ranuncule, she would see the prince in her desert.

She walked for a long time through the brambles and thorn bushes; finally, night being imminent, she perceived an old tree, the hollow trunk of which offered a retreat of sorts, but common with all the owls of the region, which made it their dwelling. She retired therein, not without great fear, although it was soon dissipated. The owls, awakened by the darkness, commenced to shake their feathers and to converse together before separating.

The princess, surprised to hear the birds talking, listened to their discourse, and heard one old owl saying to a younger one: "The cries of that dragon won't inconvenience us tonight—which is to say, our day—for it must be a long way away from us."

"Not as far as you think, Sire Owl," replied the young one, "but what will surprise you is that the monster isn't malevolent, for I took it some cherries on the part of the Fay of Myrtles, and, far from devouring me, as I had feared, it caressed me gently and made me a sign of gratitude."

"Is it a dragon from the fay's menagerie, then?" said the old owl.

"I don't know," replied the other, but I believe she favors it, at least, for I'm going to take it more to eat on her orders."

The princess, very surprised by that conversation, emerged from the hollow of the tree and addressed the owls. "My dear friends," she said to them, "would you

61

be kind enough to tell me what I need to do to see the Fay of Myrtles? Can you, who know her, not direct me to her abode, or at least tell her that Belzamine desires very much to see her? You would not be obliging an ingrate."

"Madame," said the young owl, what you ask of us is not difficult; I will serve you with pleasure. Since you know the fay, I will go to her abode immediately. It's a long way from here, but I'll come back soon. Wait for me, and don't take the risk of going there, for it would be necessary to pass close to the dragon, which might well devour you."

"Oh, great gods! Where is this dragon lodged?" said the frightened princess.

"A hundred leagues from here, Madame," said the owl, "and I still shiver when I think about its frightful form, although it's true that I've approached it without it doing me any harm."

"Might it not come here, good Owl?" said the princess.

"I don't believe so," it said, "for it's securely chained. But Madame, do you not need to eat? We can offer you something."

"I accept with great pleasure," said the princess, "for I confess that I'm very hungry."

Immediately, the owl brought her a little basket full of figs, which she ate with a god appetite. After the princess had thanked it, the owl flew away, and she remained alone in the desert, delivered to all her reflections.

What astonished her was that she no longer had the scarf, the shuttle or the brooch; she supposed, however, that those things had lost their virtue because of the wishes she had made. She could not imagine, however, why she was separated from Melidor. She reproached herself for not having named him in her wish when he asked to be free of her enemies; it was not dread or shame that had prevented her from doing so, for she was no longer hiding her passion for him then, and she believed that to be justified by Tecserion's cruelty.

While the princess was racking her brains for a means of rejoining her lover, or at least obtaining news of him, the owl came back. "Great Princess," it said to her, the Fay of Myrtles exhorts you not to be anxious about your fate. She has to go and consult Destiny, and try to soften it in your favor; continue on your way, but always go straight ahead without deviating either to the left or the right. Provided that you do not fear the obstacles to which your enemies can give birth, they have no further power over you; if you arrive at the Talking Forest without being frightened, you will vanquish them and you will be happy. Here is a pomegranate that will nourish you throughout the journey. I cannot tell you anything more. If I were not occupied elsewhere I'd guide you, but with these instructions you can do without me."

"Generous Owl," said the princess, "what can I do to show you my gratitude?"

"Nothing, Madame," replied the bird, "except follow my advice; I am sufficiently recompensed by the pleasure of obliging you."

It flew away at the same time, and the princess set forth, but the desert was so sandy that she could only walk with difficulty, and she soon felt a great thirst. A single seed of her pomegranate refreshed her perfectly, and gave her new strength.

Finally, after having walked for several days, her pomegranate always furnishing her with enough to eat and drink, she arrived on the edge of a flowery meadow, the sight of which caused her to rejoice, and on the far side of the meadow she saw a mountain, the foot of which formed a spacious cavern.

As night fell, she went into it in order to rest there until daylight, but she did so trembling, in the fear that it might be the den of some wild beasts.

By groping, she found a little bed of moss, on which she lay down, and having supped on a pomegranate seed she went to sleep quite profoundly, so fatigued was she.

At daybreak, a shrill hiss that made the cabin resound woke the princess. As the daylight was already bright enough, she saw a frightful dragon lying on the ground ten paces away.

"O Heaven!" she cried. "What a horrible monster! But why hasn't it devoured me?"

Immediately, the dragon, which was staring at her, opened its wings, as if to testify its joy, which the poor princess interpreted quite differently, for she believed that her life was over. She uttered a piercing scream, which caused the dragon to recoil and rendered it motionless.

It was then that the unfortunate Melidor—for it was him, and the cavern and the mountain were also the palace and the Isle of Turquoises, changed by Tecserion— felt very keenly the harshness of his destiny. He uttered hisses so dolorous that the princess thought that he was about to die.

Doubtless, she thought, *some protective fays want to help me, since the monster is expiring.*

However, she dared not emerge from where she was, because the dragon was chained up near the entrance, so that Belzamine, having gone deeper into the cavern, could not get out of it without passing close to the dragon.

It was no longer moving, and its languid eyes, attached to the princess, gave her hope that it was about to die and deliver her from her fears, when she saw Ranuncule arriving on a flame-colored camel.

Neither of them had expected such an encounter, and it would be difficult to say which of them was the more astonished.

"Is it to do me yet more harm," said Belzamine to the fay, "that you have come here? Will I never be delivered from your persecutions, then?"

"Great gods!" replied the fay. "I've come to render you a great service. Will you always take my cares for offenses? Come, beautiful princess, mount this camel; it will take you to the Isle of Turquoises. Since it's necessary that you marry Melidor, I want you to have that happiness from my hand."

"I would refuse it," said the princess, "if it were necessary only to take it from you, and I would prefer never to be happy. Go, Madame, leave me prey to your dragon; it will be less frightful for me to be devoured by it than to make you the arbiter of my fate."

"Well," said the fay, "if your fate can be even more unfortunate by virtue of what I can tell you, know, imprudent princess, that Melidor, touched by my tenderness, has finally surrendered to me. I am triumphant, and your despair completes my happiness. Stay with this dragon; it hasn't eaten you today, but you will serve as its fodder, and we shall finally be delivered of your importunities."

"Melidor is unfaithful!" cried the princess, dolorously. "Well, what do I now have to hope for or to dread?" Immediately, she threw herself furiously between the dragon's claws, in order to find a death there kinder than the life she could no longer support.

At that moment the glass hazelnut that Melidor had at the moment of his enchantment fell to the ground and broke. A sound emerged from it similar to a clap of thunder. The dragon's chains broke, he recovered his strength; he picked up the princess and rose into the air in the presence of Ranuncule, who fled on her camel, very frightened by that prodigy.

Meanwhile, Belzamine, who had fainted between the dragon's feet, was no longer possessed of sentiment or consciousness. He perceived that, and set her down in a great forest in order to help her. The cool air brought her round, but it was only to fall into a state a hundred times worse than the one from which she was emerging. Consciousness is beginning to return to her? The infidelity of her lover is the first idea that presents itself to her mind. She opens her eyes? The first object she perceives is, once again, the miserable dragon.

"Finish, then, taking my life," she said. "I no longer fear you, frightful monster. Come and terminate days that are too unhappy, since Melidor has forgotten me. Oh, barbaric Ranuncule! Is it by a refinement of cruelty that you let me live after that fatal news?"

The dragon was suffering as much as the princess; her condition rendered him desperate. He could not speak and the least of his movements made Belzamine shiver, even though she was demanding death. What a sad situation! In the midst of his pains, though, he savored a delightful pleasure: he had the strongest and the most touching proof of the beautiful Belzamine's tenderness, and few lovers have savored a pleasure so delectable.

Finally, he made the decision to move away in order to take away her fear, and to show her that he even dreaded causing it. What more could he do to have himself recognized as Melidor? But would that suffice?

He therefore advanced into the forest, and even went quite a long way.

The princess, seeing him draw away, only wanted not to see him again, and continued her regrets regarding Melidor's infidelity. A soft murmur, like that of a zephyr agitating the leaves of the surrounding trees, punctuated her laments.

After quivering for a long time, as the daylight faded, the trees opened up and from the middle of each one little men of a sort emerged, covered in light green bark, with hair of leaves. Their feet were only roots, but their faces and their hands had human form, so some of them were handsome and some ugly as among humans.

A large number of them assembled some twenty paces from the princess and sat down in a circle; one of them, who seemed to hold a distinguished rank in his nation of oaks, spoke in these terms:

"A linden was born this morning in our empire, and it is to inform you of that event that I have assembled you here this evening; but ought we to suffer it among us? It has been planted by a human hand, and you know, my dear citizens, that that is against our laws. It is certain that it is a foreigner, and has come here from anther Estate, but that same quality of a foreigner also seems to forbid us to use violence against an unfortunate who asks us for a refuge. In addition, it is beautiful and promises good shade, but should we trust that appearance, which is often deceptive? Or should we follow the law of the empire, which is only founded on the same law that expressly forbids us to suffer among us any tree of a species different from ours? The affair is embarrassing, and has need of your enlightenment."

"Illustrious and venerable Oak," said one of those making up the circle, "your speech is full of wisdom; it is by just title that you bear the glorious title of protector. We owe you the conservation of our liberties; but what will become of us if we once receive foreigners? Our charges and our prerogatives might pass to the vilest trees; our shoots would be deprived of them, and the least shrubs would want to establish themselves in our abode. Is it, in fact, our empire if it is shared thus? Let us therefore make a terrible example of this imprudent and reckless linden; let us cover it with our shade in order to prevent it from growing; let is extend our roots to stifle its roots, and no longer suffer...."

"Oh, what are you proposing?" interjected a young oak. "Is it necessary to prevent by your cruel and unjust means evils that might never happen? Why cause the death of an innocent tree that has only come into the Empire of Oaks because a human has planted it here? After all, can the strength of our Estate be weakened by strangers who might establish themselves here? Is it not evidence of our power to be able to give them a refuge? Oh, Oak, adopt milder sentiments. And you, protector Oak, who gives wisdom, glory, beauty and other gifts that depart from you, take this unfortunate linden under our protection; it will publish your clemency and your grandeur. Do not blacken the memory of your name by a harshness for which you would be punished by remorse. I am the Oak of Justice; listen to it, for that is what is speaking through my mouth at this moment."

"Well, then," said the protector oak, "let us follow the path of mildness and generosity, and tolerate this stranger among us; may it please the gods that we never repent of an action of which they ought to approve. But now," he continued, "let us talk about the dragon that has arrived in this place. It is, my dear citizens, a frightful monster. You must have seen it, or at least heard its frightful hissing. What has it come to do in this empire? Has it come to trouble the peace? Does it intend to fix its residence here?"

"No, Sire," relied another important oak. "it is only seeking a refuge against the persecutions of a cruel fay, and this morning's oracle—which is to say, a zephyr that passed over the Oak of Truth—has enjoined us to serve it with our power, because it is protected by the Fay of Myrtles. It has brought a young woman with it, apparently to serve as nourishment. When it has devoured her, we ought to permit it to hunt in our forest, in order for it to live here until further notice from its protectress."

Then Belzamine, who had listened in a profound silence to the speeches of the oaks, rose to her feet precipitately and went to throw herself at the feet of the protector oak.

"Divinity of this forest," she said, with a touching grace, "you who dispense the law in their redoubtable refuge, deign to order that the dragon devour me right away; I ask you that as a favor, because, in the situation that I am in, death has become for me a desirable good. Do not leave me, therefore, to languish any longer; hasten the end of my woes."

"Get up, my daughter," said the oak, touched by Belzamine's beauty and affliction. "It is into this fortunate abode that the gods send their favorites; if they have ordered your death, it will be given to you without our cares; it is good not to fear it, but also, you ought not to wish it; for after all, without entering into mysteries that only interest you, can no relief be found for your pains?"

"Alas, Sire," said the young princess, "my woes are without remedy, and your pity can only augment them. I do not blush to tell you that I have loved the most lovable of men, but my shame is extreme in telling you that he is infidel."

"Infidel!" cried all the oaks at once. "Infidel! Can a man loved so tenderly become so?"

Those exclamations astonished the princess; she raised her beautiful eyes, bathed with tears, slowly, toward the little men, and she waited in silence for what would follow those murmurs.

"Feeble mortals!" cried the protector oak. "By what vanity do your believe yourselves to be the masterpiece of nature? How can you boast of being perfect creatures, since crime scarcely costs you anything and even virtue often renders you unhappy? Unfortunate princess, your lover has no shame in his ingratitude and his perfidy, while your tenderness and constancy cause you your misfortune. But why punish yourself for that lover's crime? Rather forget him; it is poor reasoning to die because he is guilty."

"Eh! Without him, what shall I do with my life?" said Belzamine. "Since his inconstancy, I find myself alone in the world, and the daylight is odious to me; once again, deliver me to the dragon; it alone can terminate my troubles."

As she finished those words, the dragon arrived. She sensed, at the sight of it, that the life to which she was attaching such scant value, was still dear to her, and she threw herself for a second time at the knees of the protector oak.

"It is not," she said, "in order to resist the decrees of Heaven that I am seeking a refuge near you; forgive the weakness of my sex the instant of fear that has gripped me; it is a last effort of nature. Help me, generous protector, to complete the sacrifice."

This speech alarmed the oaks who were present, and rendered the dragon immobile, who shed a torrent of tears. However, he made a sign with his paw that the princess should approach him. The protector oak took her by the hand and led her to him. Then the dragon seemed more tranquil; his tears dried up, and his eyes, attached to Belzamine, expressed his languor and his tenderness.

The surprised oaks looked at one another; even the protector admired that prodigy in silence. Finally, he turned to the assembly and spoke. "Immortal gods," he cried, "and you, divine fay, who reign over these forests, it is doubtless you who enlighten me at this moment. This dragon is a man, thus changed by the order of Destiny. He loved the princess, and he still loves her. Gods, who have revealed this mystery to me, you are inspiring me to unite them together; that is doubtless your will. Come, then, to honor with your invisible presence this strange marriage; you ought to render it happy, since it is your work." Addressing Belzamine, he went on: "And you, Princess, do not resist the orders of the gods; complete rendering them favorable to you by means of this sacrifice. This dragon ought not to frighten you, for he is only a dragon in appearance, and I guarantee that by marrying him, you will change his destiny and yours into a fortunate fate."

"O Heaven," cried the princess, "what are you proposing to me? O august Oak, do not be blind to the will of the gods; it is my death that they are demanding rather than this abominable marriage. Their inspirations are always obscure; do not give them an interpretation unworthy of them. Melidor has abandoned me, but in spite of his ingratitude I want to remain faithful to him; or, rather, I cannot forget him. I feared death a moment ago, but at present I prefer it, not only to marrying a monster, of which I no longer want to hear mention, but even to anything the gods might offer me more desirable. Alas, can there be anything more desirable than Melidor? O gods, return him to me; it is by that evidence that I would recognize your protection."

The protector oak, seeing Belzamine in that resolution, did not want to embitter her dolor. "Well, my daughter," he said, "we shall see tomorrow whether the gods wish to explain themselves more clearly. In the meantime, calm your affliction. And you," he said, addressing a few young oaks, "take the dragon into the sacred grotto, so that he may repose there until tomorrow, and let the princess be lodged in the palace of moss, where the Fay of the Woods holds her court. As for us, let us reenter our somber dwellings, and let us merit by our prayers that the gods enlighten us tomorrow, in order to obey them."

Immediately, six oaks led the dragon, and six others the princess, to where the protector oak had ordered, and they gave each of them wild fruits for their nourishment.

The linden of which here had been question in the council of oaks was near the tree under which the princess had been placed. As, in the horror of the night, she only found relief from her dolor in tears and sighs, she abandoned herself to them, but she suddenly heard the branches of the linden colliding violently and producing a muffled noise that surprised her, for the air was calm. She listened to it, and her surprise increased further when she heard it say: "Come closer to me, Belzamine; I want to talk to you."

The princess rose to her feet, trembling, and approached the young linden.

"I know you, young Belzamine," it said to her. "I know your troubles, and I feel sorry for you; if you were capable of resolution, I might even be able to help you."

"And what can you do?" she said. "Are my woes not complete?"

"No," it said, "But they might become so if you are not careful. You love Melidor, and what further woes are you preparing for yourself in loving him?"

"Alas," said the princess, "I am no longer the mistress of my heart. Melidor is fickle, but he is still lovable; in sum, I love him, because I cannot hate him."

"Try his constancy," said the linden, "and if he merits yours, it will be permitted for you to render him happy; but if he renders himself unworthy of your tenderness, permit that your hand be disposed in favor of the one who has adored you for such a long time."

"What are you saying?" said Belzamine, sharply, interrupting. "Don't you know, then, that Melidor loves Ranuncule?"

"I know everything," said the linden, "and your Melidor is not yet unfaithful. I cannot tell you anymore, but go find the dragon; command him to bite your little finger; come back immediately, and I will speak to you."

The princess, accustomed to prodigies since she had been in the forest, thanked the linden, and without hesitation, she went to look for the dragon. At any rate, she had been assured that her dear Melidor was not unfaithful, and that news had poured a sudden joy into her soul, which did not permit her to reason about the inconvenience there was in going to get herself bitten, without knowing what might happen in consequence.

It was the most beautiful night; the moon illuminated the forest paths, and its silvery rays passed through the bushy oaks, forming a more agreeable light than that of the sun. By the favor of that beautiful night, Belzamine arrived with a light step close to the dragon; she found him lying down, and, believing that he was asleep, she tugged one of his paws quite forcefully. The dragon got up immediately and started to lick the beautiful hand that she held out to him.

"Bite my finger," she said to him, "and don't importune me with your caresses."

The dragon recoiled at first, and refused that strange service for some time. Finally, she pressed him so much that he squeezed the princess's finger gently between his teeth. She was afraid then, and as she snatched her hand away she scorched it sufficiently to draw blood, which fell on the dragon; at the same moment he vanished from Belzamine's sight.

She remained frightened by that prodigy for some time, but she retraced her steps and went to find the linden.

"I've done what you wanted," she told it, "but the dragon disappeared. What do you have to tell me? And what do you want me to do?"

"Nothing, until tomorrow," it said, "except to listen to me. Know, then, that that dragon was Melidor...."

"Melidor!" she cried. "What! You've separated me from him, baleful divinity? If you wanted to help me, why did you leave me in ignorance of that secret? What! Melidor wasn't unfaithful? It was for me that he was suffering. I refused to marry him. He has seen my tears flowing, he was not unaware that it was or him that I was shedding them, but I was able to misunderstand him and fled from him! O, barbaric fay, you are well avenged for his scorn, and you, cruel Tecserion, for my indifference. O Heaven! I have doomed you, Melidor, and perhaps I have doomed you without resource."

The linden let Belzamine talk without interrupting her, and when her surge of emotion had given way to a gentler dolor, it resumed speaking. "Princess," it said, "do not attributed to ill will what I have done; it was necessary that that adventure be accomplished, and that your blood put an end to Melidor's metamorphosis. Console yourself for his absence in thinking that he regrets you no less. Know, too, that in the form of the dragon, he conserved the usage of reason, that all the movements of your heart were known to him, and that he was equally afflicted by your dolor and his impotence to give you evidence of his gratitude and his amour. But beautiful princess, Melidor was unfortunate then, and he only saw you before his eyes...."

"Don't offend him," the princess interjected, "with insulting suspicions. I know his tenderness, and I know of what he is capable."

"But do you know men well enough," said the linden, "to be able to answer for your lover when he no longer has anything to desire

"Even if it is true that men are unjust enough no longer to love as soon as they are happy," said Belzamine, "I believe Melidor to be incapable of such cowardice; his tenderness, his virtue and my glory determine me to make an exception in his favor."

"Credulous princess!" said the linden. "Lovable Belzamine, only too worthy to fill alone the heart of a virtuous lover! I lament your destiny; deliver yourself to your error, since it pleases you; if you experience the misfortunes that I fear for you, I have warned you, and I can do nothing more. Remember too that a tender and faithful heart rarely encounters one that resembles it. Tomorrow you might know more, for today I have nothing more to say to you."

With those words, the linden sighed and fell silent.

The princess returned to the oak that she had initially chosen and waited there in an inexpressible anxiety.

What! she said to herself. *I refused to marry Melidor! Will he pardon me for that injustice? Yes, doubtless, since he knows that I did not know him, but is it possible that he might not love me forever? Oh, Melidor, you could not become fickle, and why would you, since I will love you forever?*

Daylight surprised her in those sad reflections, and the protector oak appeared before her, accompanied by twenty of his companions.

"Princess," he said to her, "Sovereign orders are taking you away from this place, and the zephyr, the minister of the gods, is going to take you to the star Venus; it is there that the penitence imposed upon you must be concluded. Here is one of my leaves"—he took one from his head—"which can tell you the most important thing in your life, but do not make the trial of it lightly. Go, Princess, since the Immortals are accomplishing your wishes, and rendering you as happy as you merit."

With those words he withdrew, leaving the princess motionless, so great was her astonishment. She wondered whether he protector oak's words were a dream; she let herself fall down again at the foot of the tree under which she had spent the night, and plunged back into new reveries. Then, either by virtue of fatigue or the effect of a power that she could not resist, she fell into a profound slumber.

Sometime later she woke to the songs of a thousand birds; Belzamine opened her eyes and found that she was lying in a charming arbor on a bed of grass strewn with flowers that she did not recognize, any more than the place where she was. However, she remembered what the protector oak had said, and understood that she was on the planet Venus, although she did not know how she had had got there, or how long she had been there.

She emerged from the clump of trees, and darted admiring glances at all the objects that the new world offered her. The first thing that struck her was a forest of myrtles, though which spacious paths formed as many magnificent promenades, where bushy trees always maintained a delightful coolness by means of their shade. Those myrtles were somewhat distant from one another, but palisades of roses and jasmine filled the intervals they left between them, and everywhere there were fountains of clear water, which sprang up higher than the myrtles and fell back with a murmur appropriate to stimulate reverie.

In fact, Belzamine, enchanted by everything she saw, intoxicated by the perfume of a thousand choice flowers and soothed by the amorous songs of birds caressing one another in the branches, sensed that she was in the empire of Amour.

"Oh, my dear Melidor!" she cried, "if only you were here! Even if you had become insensible, you would love me in this charming abode."

Meanwhile, she advanced through the forest, without taking any path, and she had almost arrived in the middle when she perceived, by the edge of a vast fountain, which was falling in a cascade into a huge white marble basin, a large number of young and beautiful individuals of both sexes. They were so occupied in their conversation that they only perceived Belzamine when she was close by, so she had the leisure to examine them.

They were all clad in long gauze robes of various colors, with diamond belts; they all had faces so beautiful and so young that Belzamine mistook them at first for a hot of beautiful girls; however, she remarked that some wore a brilliant star on the head and the others in the knot of a ribbon under the chin, and she judged that that was what distinguished their sex. In addition, as those who had the star under the chin were a little taller, and had a slightly freer attitude, she judged that they were men.

Meanwhile, they finally perceived the princess, and were dazzled by her beauty. "Who is this beautiful young woman who seems to be coming to us?" said one young inhabitant.

"O gods, don't deceive us!" said all the others, in unison. "It's doubtless Venus herself, who has come to preside over the choice that we must make tomorrow."

The troop of shepherds and shepherdesses stood up immediately,[4] and advanced with a respectful air toward Belzamine, singing hymns to Venus. Her confusion was as great as her astonishment to begin with, but, recognizing their error, she said: "Stop, blind shepherds, cease to profane the name of your goddess. I am a mortal, seeking a refuge among you; only deign to accord it to me."

---

[4] Because the planet Venus was known in Classical times as "the shepherd's star" it would be perfectly natural for an educated writer of the eighteenth century to refer to its hypothetical inhabitants as shepherds and shepherdesses, even in the manifest absence of sheep.

Those words, pronounced with so much modesty by the most beautiful mouth in the world, filled all the inhabitants with admiration. The shepherdesses agreed that she had the charms of Venus, and the shepherds were delighted that she was only a mortal, with divine beauty. They assured her with vivacity that they were happy to have her among them, and that they would not neglect anything to render her sojourn on the plant agreeable.

At the same time they conducted her to a little cabin of myrtles, the artfully interlaced branches of which formed admirable designs.

"Beautiful shepherdess," said one young inhabitant, "we have no palace to offer you; our lodgments have a simple and perhaps rustic appearance, but we live happily there." He continued: "You do not know our laws as yet; the first is to love; doubtless you will not be rebellious to it as soon as you have seen the handsome shepherd who has been here since yesterday; all our shepherdesses are already disputing his heart...but here he comes, advancing toward the fountain."

Belzamine turned her head in that direction, and immediately, abruptly quitting the shepherds, she flew toward him. For his part, Melidor—for she was not mistaken—launched himself like lightning toward his dear princess.

What did they not say to one another as they came together? What transports! Sighs, tears, even silence: everything was employed to express their amour, and the pleasure they felt in rediscovering one another. Melidor threw himself at the feet of the princess; he embraced her knees a thousand times, and confirmed by the most tender oaths and amour of which she was already convinced.

When the agitation of their senses had calmed down somewhat, they sat down on the edge of the fountain and recounted to one another everything that had happened since their separation. How many new reasons for loving one another more they found in their common misfortunes. Belzamine did not believe that all her tenderness could repay her lover for the woes that he had suffered in his metamorphosis, and Melidor wanted to equal by his ardor the constancy of the princess, of which he had had such strong proofs.

Meanwhile, the day was advancing, and the fortunate lovers only perceived it because they would have liked it to be even longer.

"How quickly the time flies for lovers, my dear Melidor," the princess said. "It seems to me that it was only a moment ago that I saw you; however, when I think of everything that we have said, it was more than a day; it must be the case that the sun shines for longer here than it does on Earth."

"Alas, adorable Belzamine," the prince replied, "I wish that the days here were as long as a year; with you, they would still appear too short to me. But I do not know as yet either the seasons or the days of this new land. I do not even know how I was transported here; your blood, which spilled upon me, put an end to my metamorphosis, and I found myself here immediately, where your presence has just terminated my woes. As yet, I know nothing about the planet where we are, but we can be informed of everything we need to know by the young inhabitant who has just drawn water from the fountain."

As he spoke, Melidor got up, approached the shepherd in a civil fashion, and asked him to tell them where they were, and how the sun measured its course there.

The young inhabitant responded to the prince obligingly, and immediately commenced speaking in these terms:

"The land that you are inhabiting, Madame, is the planet Venus, called by the name of the goddess that we worship here. Everything that respires here knows her sovereign power. The women here are beautiful and tender, the men well made and amorous, with the consequence that among us, living is nothing but loving. Our years are about eight months long, but our days are at least double the length of yours; the sun, which, it seems, ought to render our planet uninhabitable because of its heat, absorbs its rays in a vast atmosphere that surrounds our upper air, so we only feel a temperate heat, which is always even, for we have a continual spring, and that which reigns in our world is only an influence of our globe, since the inhabitants of Earth almost savor our good fortune then.

"Night, too, does not envelop us with thick darkness, because it is almost entirely divided between the evening and morning twilights, which take the place of the moon here. We also draw great advantages from that; often, a rigorous beauty, after having driven her lover to despair during the day, becomes more tractable in the seductive darkness of the night; often, too, the commencing dusk has seen more than one amour die to which the dawn had given birth; for amours of six long months, which are sometimes seen among you, are unusual prodigies here. We love from birth, but we are born inconstant, and change is not a crime here, since it is not against our laws. However, we admire constancy, when we chance to see examples of it; in any case, the fundamental law of this land is to love, and we observe it exactly by always changing the object, since breaking one engagement for another is not to cease loving.

"All that will surprise you less, Madame," he added, "when you know that the god Hymen is unknown here, as are his respectable chains, and that Venus, our goddess, laughs at the oaths and perjuries of lovers."

Belzamine lowered her eyes during that speech, which caused her virtue to suffer; that is why she interrupted the shepherd. "Permit me," she said, "to ask you a question. By virtue of what charm can I understand your words, although your language is unknown to me?"

"Amour," relied the young inhabitant, "that omnipotent god, that sovereign intelligence, whom we serve with such a pure worship, is the inventor of our language; although it is not regular, we make ourselves understood without difficulty and persuade without eloquence. In what place in the universe is 'I love you' not understood? It's a familiar phrase in our idiom; the rest is as easy for those whom Amour inspires. We speak the language of the gods, therefore, since it is that of Amour, the master of the other gods; it is a universal language, for every mortal can understand it, and the most amorous are those who speak it best.

"Our Academy, composed of the most spiritual lovers, is not occupied with enriching or reforming; it respects usage, applies itself to conserving it, and takes it for granted that fine language is that which is generally received. That august tribunal also administers justice, and judges the culpable. Here, form never prevails over foundation, for we detest quibbling and its formalities; our judges, although young, are luminaries and integrity personified. In any case, our laws are so simple and so few in number that it is sufficient to consult them to pronounce a verdict in every case.

"We scarcely know any other crimes than jealousy, coldness, indifference, infidelity and coquetry; the latter two, especially, are the most unpardonable. I have told you that inconstancy is permitted, but infidelity is not. A shepherd can quit his mistress in order to attach himself to another, but, at the same time, he loses his rights over the heart of the first. A shepherdess has the same right to change, provided that she too only has a single lover and does not betray him while he believes that he possesses her heart. That law is founded on the rectitude and probity of which all humans must profess, so the amorous senate shows no mercy for that crime; it also punishes the others in accordance with their genre and the circumstances, and the guilty are sent forever to the planets Saturn or Mercury.

"In the past year," he continued, "I saw two winged vessels departing filled with criminals relegated to those two planets: a thousand infidels, as many coquettes, and ten ingrates departed for Mercury; five jealous men and one young woman convicted of obstinate coldness were sent to Saturn. That insensitive beauty was not afflicted by her banishment; she even dared to mock Psyche, and she said that Venus, our goddess, was only a fine name that we have given to the passion that animates us; she even took scandal as far as saying that she would merit altars more, since she had vanquished the same passion that our goddess had been unable to resist. I only dare to repeat those blasphemies tremulously. In any case, that shepherdess is the only one that I have seen accused of indifference.[5]

---

[5] Mademoiselle de Lubert, at the age of 35, was presumably convinced by the time she wrote *Tecserion* that she would never marry, and might well have thought of her character as contentedly saturnine.

"You should also know," he went on, "that we are governed by a high priest, who is simultaneously a king; his authority lasts for ten years, and he shares the honor of the hierophancy with a shepherdess who is similarly declared to be a priestess of Venus. They are both elected by a general assembly; particular attention is paid to their beauty and their tenderness, for although they can quit one another, the question of whether they have at least loved one another in good faith is examined.

"Don't be astonished at only seeing young people here; no one here has ever been seen to die or even to grow old. As soon as men reach thirty-five and women thirty they quit our cheerful empire in order to pass on to the planets that suit them. Thus, Jupiter, Mars, Saturn, Mercury and even the Moon share our cast-offs. Tomorrow, for example, we shall elect a new high priest and a new priestess; the old ones will depart with the colony, and if they want to unite themselves by the laws of marriage before leaving, the ceremony is performed in the temple."

Melidor interrupted the shepherd then to ask whether it would be permissible for him and the princess to witness the ceremony.

"Of course," said the young man. "Your presence would honor us greatly, and as soon as tomorrow's dawn appears I will come to fetch you and take you to the temple myself. But night is approaching and you must need to take some nourishment. Don't disdain a frugal meal that I offer you with the greatest pleasure in the world."

Melidor and the princess expressed their gratitude to the shepherd for his kindness and his generosity, and accepted his offer. The meal was only composed of fruits, but so delicious that it did not allow them to regret the most exquisite meats. The shepherd's mistress heaped Belzamine with honors and asked for her amity. The conversation only concerned amour, but who could expect anything else of lovers?

Finally, Melidor, yielding to the pressure of his host and the shepherdess, recounted his adventures and those of Belzamine, and the misfortunes they had both suffered. If the most tender amour and the most fervent ardor were painted in Melidor's story, his lover's eyes were no less eloquent. Their hosts, astonished to see a couple of lovers so constant and so tender, gazed at them with admiration. When the meal was over, they took them to a small cabin nearby and returned home, swearing to one another, and promising Venus, to imitate the piety of the amiable strangers.

As soon as Belzamine was alone with Melidor, she no longer constrained her dolor. "In what country are we?" she said, gazing tenderly at the prince. "Inconstancy passes for a virtue here; am I going to lose you, then?"

With those words, she sighed, and her beautiful eyes filled with tears.

Melidor threw himself at her knees, and swore a thousand times over that the vices of the climate would never seduce his heart. "I have for guarantees of that," he said, "your charms and my amour, divine Belzamine."

The princess held out her hand to him, and begged him to pardon her tenderness for the weakness it had shown him. "If your amour," she said, "is the price of mine, dear prince, it must be eternal. Could I witness your inconstancy without dying?"

Melidor spent the night reassuring Belzamine, and the princess giving her lover evidence of all her tenderness.

The following day, at dawn, several inhabitants, accompanied by the shepherd who had told them about Melidor and his lover, came to their cabin and conducted them to the temple of Venus. It was a great hall of evergreen myrtles. In the middle of which the statue of the goddess appeared, elevated on a pedestal. She was naked, sitting in a shell, as the poets depict her at her emergence from the waves, and seemed to be regarding with a tender gaze the shepherds who laid their presents at her feet, on an altar set up to received them. Grass dotted with all sorts of flowers covered the hall and served as seating for all those attending the ceremony.

The high priest and the priestess entered the temple, both clad in long robes of white gauze sown with blue flowers. At the foot of the statue of Venus they deposited the crown of myrtle and he ring that were the marks of their dignity. Then they burned ten grains of incense, and asked to depart together for the planet Jupiter; they were married immediately and they were conducted in pomp to the vessel that awaited them. Their departure excited the regrets of the whole planet and the tears of numerous inhabitants.

"Beautiful Coronis," cried a few shepherds, "we are losing you, and you are not even sensitive to our dolor!"

She did not reply; she was talking to her husband and only seemed to see him; at the same time, they embarked, to the acclamations of all the people. Two young shepherdess seemed no less touched by the departure of the high priest; their sighs and their gazes expressed their dolor, and they returned to the temple with a trouble that augmented their beauty.

Then they proceeded to the election of the new hierophants; the names of the beautiful Myrrha and the amiable Armidor had already been heard in the temple, but all of a sudden, the eyes of the assembly turned toward Melidor and Belzamine. The shepherd who had conversed with them the previous evening had exaggerated their tenderness so much that he had gained the majority of the suffrages in their favor; their beauty drew the rest. At first they refused an honor that he had not expected. But, in spite of their resistance, they were proclaimed by a unanimous voice, and clad in the marks of their dignity

The laws of the planet were read aloud to the new hierophants, who swore to observe them. A sacrifice was made of two turtle-doves and two sparrows, birds cherished by Venus; a frugal meal was served then, after which the assembly broke up.

Melidor and Belzamine, heaped with honors and intoxicated by tenderness, finally found themselves as happy as they had previously been unhappy. They would gladly have abdicated royalty and hierophancy in order to have no other cares but that of loving one another. Belzamine only had eyes for her lover, and Melidor only adored Belzamine. They were both revered and cherished in the amorous empire; lovers disputed as to who could equal the ardor of Melidor, and shepherdesses proposed the tenderness of Belzamine as a model for themselves; thus, Venus was better served there than on Paphos or Cythera, such was the force of the examples that the tender hierophants gave their people.

They spent a year in that happy state; but what happiness is durable? Deceitful felicities of amour, you are only a shadow, or similar to a dream; you have that lightness, and only leave lovers the memory and the regret of what they have lost!

Myrrha, the inconstant mistress of the tender Armidor, conceived amour for Melidor, and neglected nothing in order to give it to him; seduced by her artifices, and ceding to the lack of appetite that naturally follows a placid possession, the prince loved Myrrha, and became infidel.

Belzamine still continued to testify her tenderness to her lover in thousand new fashions; she saw without jealousy the complaisances that he had for Myrrha, and dared not believe them criminal, but she eventually obtained exceedingly cruel proofs of what she did not even want to suspect. One day she surprised him with Myrrha in a honeysuckle arbor; he was nonchalantly lying on the grass and his lover, with a teasing expression that testified to her contentment, was braiding his hair.

What a sight for the princess! She took two steps back, but, reflecting that they had seen her and that she would offend the prince by giving evidence of suspicion, she determined to go in. The mild and serene expression that she had been able to compose reassured the guilty couple.

"I was looking for you," she said to Melidor then. "Your people are asking for you, to know from you whether a linden that has been exiled from the forest of oaks, and which the zephyrs have just brought here, can be put into the wood of myrtles."

"Oh, are you not the mistress here, Belzamine?" said Melidor, without getting up. Your orders are mine; speak, and let everyone obey you; my presence would be an obstacle to your rights. Go, dictate my will, and I shall always be content with whatever you have ordered."

Belzamine did not reply, and went out promptly in order to hide the tears that were about to flow from her beautiful eyes. "O gods!" she cried. "Is it thus that you recompense my constancy?"

With dolor in her soul and sadness panted on her face, she went to give her orders in the name of the high priest, and the linden, ornamented with garlands, was placed at the door of the temple. The ceremony lasted all day; Melidor did not appear; he left to Belzamine honors that did not compensate her for the tenderness that he had taken away from her.

The next day, she saw her infidel lover, but he appeared so preoccupied that she could scarcely get two words out of him. She did not make him any reproaches. The presence and the triumphant expression of Myrrha completed her dejection. Instead of getting carried away against her rival, she hid her agitation, resolved not to oppose any other weapons to it than her virtue and her tenderness.

However, she often went to see the linden; it was the same one that had said so many things to her in the forest of oaks, but it did not speak to her any longer; it only agitated its branches when Belzamine wept beside it, and seemed to testify by means of violent shaking that it was sensible to her troubles. Sometimes she even saw the linden distil drops of water while she shed tears.

One day, when the princess was delivering herself to the full excess of her dolor at the foot of the sensitive tree, she heard it sigh with her, quite distinctly.

"Who are you, then," she said, "who seem so interested in my troubles? You spoke in the forest of oaks; what enchantment forbids you speech here while leaving you sentiment? Can I not know whose compassion my fate excites?"

The tree trembled, and made futile efforts to respond; nothing emerged from its branches but a confused murmur, to which the princess listened in vain.

She was holding in her hand the mysterious leaf that the protector oak had given her, and she thought about the usage that she ought to make of it.

If I touch the linden with it, she thought, *will it talk to me? Will it tell me the important secret that the oak mentioned to me? I know, alas, that Melidor no longer loves me, can anything be revealed to me that touches me more? Or can this leaf, by means of a supernatural power, render me the tenderness of my lover? I've lost all hope of that. Go, futile leaf....*

With those words she threw away the leaf. Hazard carried it against the linden, which shivered at first, and then inclined its branches as if to thank the princess. Finally, it spoke in a distinct voice that emerged from its trunk.

"Adorable Belzamine," it said, "you have just rendered me life, and although I only owe it to your chagrin, I am no less obliged for it. Take back your leaf; it has not lost its virtue for you, because you did not have the design of making the proof of it for me. Guard it carefully; it will be necessary to you on another occasion."

The princess immediately ran to pick it up. As she bent down to grasp it, the wind pushed it further away, and made it pass over a clump of parsley and a marjoram plant, which were very close together. Belzamine went forward and bent down or a second time, but as she picked it up she was very surprised to hear the parsley and the marjoram talking.

"Charming Zamire," said the former, "what prodigy is rendering me speech? Ought I to make use of it to talk to you about an amour that has caused your misfortune? I have doomed you with me, and I must be odious to you."

"No, Calistandre," replied the marjoram, "far from blaming you for my woes, I am sensible to yours. I only blame fate and amour; one scarcely loves when one is not able to be unfortunate with the person one loves; but we have no more to lament now that we have the liberty to tell one another that we love one another, and that commencement of happiness gives me great hopes. Perhaps the fay Diablotine is weary of persecuting us; perhaps her power is reaching its terminus; perhaps the king, our father, has repented of his wrath, what do I know? Someone has rendered us speech; perhaps they will soon weary of seeing us plants."

"Adorable Zamire," replied Calistandre, "the hopes that you give me flatter me less than the happiness that I enjoy at present; you love me, you pardon me for your metamorphosis; mine no longer has anything harsh. What does it matter in what form or what figure I am happy? And I am, since I can savor the pleasure of being loved...."

Belzamine, entirely occupied with Melidor's infidelity, which rendered her insensible to anything else, did not have the curiosity to listen to that conversation any longer. She returned promptly to the foot of the linden, which resumed its speech thus:

"So, what I predicted to you has arrived; the ingrate Melidor, weary of his happiness, has abandoned you. O Heaven! He was too fortunate. You have followed blindly the first prejudices of your heart, and nothing has been capable of deflecting the misfortunes with which the oracle threatened you."

"Eh! what good does it do to remind me of that fatal prediction," said the princess, "since it was necessarily accomplished? When my heart was given to Melidor in spite of myself, that prince was worthy of all my tenderness. His amour and mine reassured me against the menaces of the oracle; or, rather, enabled me to forget it. Could I have done otherwise?"

"It was necessary to test Melidor for longer," said the linden. "His initial tenderness for the fay Ranuncule ought to have warned you that he was incapable of a great constancy. Charming as you are, he has forgotten you today, and less powerful lures have drawn him, because of the lightness of his character."

"Oh!" cried the princess. "If only the gods had made that prince less lovable, since he has ceased to love me! But in spite of his perfidy, he is no less charming."

"What, Belzamine!" said the linden. "Would you try to make Melidor return to you? That is a weakness that offends your glory; take a nobler resolution and more worthy of you; avenge yourself on your lover's infidelity, and suffer that a heart that knows the full price of yours...."

"Stop," said the princess. "Don't force me to go away from you, to flee the sole consolation that remains to me."

"No, no, Madame," said the linden. "You ought not to fear me. I am the unfortunate, the frightful Tecserion; my misfortunes interest me in yours. Permit me at least to feel sorry for you. I am only a tree at present, and my metamorphosis is the work of Ranuncule; it is thus that she has recompensed my amour. But what am I saying? Can one profane the beautiful name of amour for another, when one has once sensed it for you? That barbaric fay overwhelmed me with all her power, at a time when mine was useless; for you know that our power ceases as soon as we are amorous for a fay. She therefore profited from the advantage she had over me, and, to punish me for having loved you, she changed me into a linden, as you see.

"The oaks received me in their forest at first, but afterwards I became the subject of a thousand quarrels. In order to end them I condemned myself, and easily renounced a place where you no longer were. I asked to been transported here, and they dared not refuse me that. I had, however, no hope of speaking to you about my tenderness because, in leaving the forest, I had lost the power of speech. I have been more fortunate that I had hoped; your presence, and the pleasure of sharing your troubles, initially softened the harshness of my fate, and you have just rendered me speech.

"You know the sharpest of my pains; do not overwhelm me, charming princess, with your rigors; at least do not take away from my shadow the advantage of protecting you from the sun. Never will the respectful amour that you have inspired in me be expressed in your eyes other than by my cares and my obedience; deign not to refuse them. I know only too well that I must be odious to you, but Belzamine, remember that if I have caused your first misfortunes, my nephew is even more criminal than me. Your tenderness, which I have bought with immortality itself, has made him an ingrate. You still love him, however, although he is infidel, and I know hatred, and always constant. What a difference, beautiful princess! Will your eyes always be dazzled by a beautiful face? You ought to be above vulgar prejudices, but I pardon your blindness, by the gods who gave me such a poor share of external advantages. You have only ever seen me ugly...."

"Well," said the princess, in a more tranquil tone, "were you not the cruelest enemy that I could have?"

"I was jealous and frightful, beautiful princess; that was more than enough to be hated. But did you not learn from an ostrich that I could change appearance?"

"That's true," said Belzamine, "but my heart, prejudiced in favor of Melidor, did not give me time to examine the motives of your cruelty; I only saw in Tecserion an unjust tyrant, who wanted to force my inclination, who opposed my happiness, and who persecuted my lover. In fact, what right did you have over my heart, to set out to obtain it in spite of me? I loved Melidor, I was adored by him; what permitted you to oppose our amours, to employ the most unworthy treatments against us? But what am I saying? Your cruelty ought not to have prescribed itself any limits; you should have prevented my misfortunes by taking my life, and I would not have seen Melidor infidel today."

"Here he comes," the linden interjected. "Go, lovable princess. He is doubtless looking for you; your joy announces to me what I must expect; you're going to tell him who I am, and he will sacrifice me to his anger; if it's only for love of him, I forgive you for all the woes he is preparing for me, only too happy to be able to expiate by my death the crime of having cost you so many tears."

With that, the linden fell silent, and the water that his branches immediately distilled left the marks of his dolor on the ground.

Softened by that spectacle, Belzamine reassured him. "No," she said to him, "you have nothing to fear; treason will never serve my vengeance."

At the same time, she advanced toward Melidor, who brought her back to the foot of the linden and said down there beside her. "Why do you like this tree so much?" he asked her, first. "Why do you prefer its shade to all the other trees with which the gardens are full?"

"Is it not sufficient to please me, Sire," she said to him, "to have contributed to the happiness of finding you again? I remember continually under its shade the time that I spent in the forest of oaks, the dolor that I felt then at your absence; in sum, I find pleasure here in the memory of what I suffered for you. But it seems to me," she continued, looking at him tenderly, "that you have some anxiety? You're not saying anything? You're not listening to me? Can Belzamine not enter into your confidence? She is still the same; speak, Sire, perhaps I can serve you."

"Madame," said the prince, "of what are you accusing me? I have no mystery to make you, and I don't doubt your sentiments for me; but I confess to you that I'm embarrassed, and what brings me here might cause you some pain."

"No, Sire," she said. "Speak, and have no fear of displeasing me; are you not yet sufficiently convinced of that?"

As she pronounced those words in a passionate tone, she took Melidor's hand and squeezed it between her own. The prince was shaken at first, but, sensing that he was about to allow himself to be touched, he turned his eyes away from Belzamine and became bold in that forced countenance.

"I have come," he said, to ask you for your crown. "Myrrha would like to put it on tomorrow, and I have promised to bring it to her."

"You have promised her?" Belzamine exclaimed, sadly. "But do you know," she continued, "whether the people will suffer that she wears without their consent the marks of my dignity?"

"I've foreseen everything," said Melidor, coldly. "Besides, am I not the master? My will makes the law, and you also know that you only derive your power from mine."

"That's enough," said the princess, sharply penetrated by the harshness of those words. "I finally see that I have nothing more to oppose to your injustice. Well, here it is, this fatal crown; take it, then. I did not desire it; it only flattered me because of you. Go, ingrate, take it to the one you love; a crown will please her; for myself, I would have refused it if it had been offered to me alone, and I shall not regret it if, in losing it, I have lost your heart at the same time. But I blush at my weakness...."

With those words, she quit him, in order to go and hide her tears and her despair. Melidor also drew away, taking away Belzamine's crown.

The princess dared not return to the linden; he had been the witness of the affront she had received from Melidor; he would have exaggerated it, and in spite of her despair, she did not feel strong enough to hear evil spoken of her lover; everything, even her anger, made her sense how dear he still was to her.

Oh, doubtless, she thought, *he has been drawn in spite of himself by the power of the planet. No, Melidor, if you were not here, you would love me with the same tenderness that once made your happiness and mine.*

Thus, always ingenious in flattering herself, she spent the rest of the day regretting and justifying her lover. The next day, pretending to be indisposed, she asked to be permitted not to appear at the fête.

"What, you want to dispense with it, Madame?" he replies. "Since the games are in your honor, it's necessary that you be present; furthermore, I desire that you appear there, and I believe that you won't refuse me that favor."

"I cannot refuse you anything," replied the princess, "but I thought that I was unnecessary at that fête."

"I do not see, Madame," he said, "that you can dispense yourself from attending it, unless you want me to nominate Myrrha to take your place."

"I consent to that," replied Belzamine, "and I beg her to do the honors of the fête for me. Go," she said to several young priestesses who were with her, "go tell Myrrha on my part that I have chosen her to take my place."

"I'll take charge of that myself," said the prince. "I'll go immediately to inform her of the honor that you're doing her."

As he pronounced those words, he went out.

It is easier to imagine the situation that the princess found herself in then than to describe it. She shed a torrent of tears; a thousand times she wanted to die, a thousand times she formed the design to do so, but the image of Melidor, and the hope of regaining his tenderness, dissipated her violent resolutions. Finally, in spite of the dejection into which dolor had cast her, she dragged herself toward the linden in order to consult him.

On approaching him she was astonished to see that he was almost dead; instead of their natural verdure, his leaves had a yellow color, similar to that which the end of autumn gives forests.

"Whence comes the change that I perceive?" she said to him. "What misfortune can have overtaken you?"

"Alas, princess," replied the linden, in a faint and tremulous voice, "I hope that Heaven is finally relenting in my favor, that today will be the last of my life, and that it will finally put an end to your hatred. I implore you by your charms, adorable Belzamine, since I am dying of the dolor that is overwhelming you, to forget that I have persecuted you. You are sufficiently avenged, and I am sufficiently punished."

"You're dying," cried the princess, "and you're leaving me even more unfortunate that you! Oh, deign to help me, live in order to console me. The unjust Melidor has abandoned me; I cannot hate him, but I no longer want to love him; he has offended me tenderness by procedures that are too cruel; he no longer merits it. What am I saying, alas? If he no longer merits it, what will become of me? Can I live and not love him?"

With those words, the princess, overwhelmed by dolor, fell almost motionless at the foot of the linden. He seemed keenly afflicted by that.

"If you were capable of a veritable resolution," he said to her, "I would tell you what it is necessary to do to avenge yourself; but beautiful princess, your amour is stronger than your anger. If Melidor told you himself that he is infidel, you would not believe it. He has taken away your crown, and he has given it to another; can you still doubt his perfidy and remain insensible to his outrages? Examine yourself; I can serve your vengeance, but your resolution, once taken, must be followed with constancy."

"Well, then, avenge me this instant," said the princess, "for if I see him again, my amour will no longer leave any strength to my anger."

"Take the protector oak's leaf," said the linden, "And rub the foot of my tree with it; that is all I ask of you."

The princess took the leaf from a golden box, into which she had put it, and with a tremulous hand, she did what the linden had said.

Then, the tree gradually took on human form before the eyes of the princess. She saw the metamorphosis operate, the linden finally disappear, and a man take its place. He did not bear any resemblance to the frightful Tecserion. He appeared to be about fifty years old; he was well made; his feature had nothing but amiability and majesty. He was magnificently dressed, and his appearance inspired respect.

"Now, beautiful princess," he said to her, "I am in a state to avenge you on my perfidious nephew. I hold his life or his death in my hand; order it as you will, and be sure that you will be obeyed, from this moment your orders are the rules of my will."

The princess had not ceased looking at him, and her surprise had not diminished.

"What, Sire!" she said to him, finally. "You are the same king that I saw under the features of Tecserion?"

"Yes, Madame, I was your tyrant and the cruelest of your enemies. Today, thanks to your goodness and the power of the mysterious leaf, I am Orcanor, King of Ostriches, your subject and your most submissive slave."

"I implore your generosity, then," she said, "for my fickle lover; do not punish him for the injury he had done me. I am not the mistress of my sentiments, can he be the master of his? Perhaps my heart is not worthy of Melidor; leave him his life, Sire; sooner or later, he will recognize his fault and the price of my tenderness."

"Feeble princess," said Orcanor, "you love him still, since you fear seeing him punished, but I can only grant you his life. He is about to be dispossessed, and the hierophancy given to me. Master of sovereign authority, I could still, if you wish, make your fortunate rival repent, by means of an exemplary punishment, of having stolen Melidor from you."

"Heaven preserve me," cried the princess, "from avenging myself thus! What has Myrrha done to me? She has ceded to a penchant of which I know the danger; if it is a crime to love Melidor I am the guiltier, since I still love him in spite of his ingratitude. I would rather consent that she should be loved and that the prince should hate me than punish her for being lovable."

As she finished those words she saw the inhabitants of the planet appear, who came to throw themselves at Orcanor's feet; they conducted him to the temple, and proclaimed him king and high priest. He was placed on the throne, and Belzamine was made to sit down next to him, in spite of her resistance.

Then ten priests brought Melidor into the assembly, with a chain of myrtle. Myrrha followed him, chained in the same way and conducted by ten priestesses. In that humiliating state, at the foot of the throne where he was accustomed to sit, Melidor dared not raise his eyes, and the confused Myrrha dared not look at her rival.

"Look at me, Prince," said the king, "recognize Orcanor and see your judge and your master. I permit you, however, to defend yourself and justify yourself, if you can, with the princess, for the injustice of your procedures."

Intimidated by his uncle and by his own conscience, did not say a word in response.

Orcanor ordered the senate, which was present in full, to judge Melidor in accordance with the laws of the land, and to pronounce its judgment. Then the first senator addressed Belzamine, and spoke to her in these terms:

"Great Princess, Melidor is convicted of ingratitude and infidelity; the rigor of our laws cannot be softened in his favor, for we never grant mercy, in order to take away all hope of impunity. He is therefore condemned to depart for the planet Saturn, and the coquette Myrrha will deposited for a year in a desert on the planet Mercury. But before then she will spend a year in the Sun, in order to expiate in that burning world the crime of having seduced a heart that should only have burned for you. Such, great Princess, are our conclusions, or, rather, those of justice itself; it is for you to have them carried out."

Then Belzamine, who was sitting on her throne, stood up in order to respond to the senate. "I know the severity of your laws," she said, "and I do not want to criticize their equity; but Melidor is not culpable; he is only so toward me, and I pardon him. Myrrha is beautiful, the Prince is amiable, how could they help loving one another? I therefore ask that neither one of them be punished. Permit me, at the same time, to return to the Realm of Flowers and to enjoy there the tranquility that I sense reborn in my soul; all the woes that I have suffered have enabled me to know today the price of my liberty, so it is necessary that I quit you. I know your maxims; you ought not to suffer among you an insensible heart, which would attract the wrath of Venus to the nation. If my esteem and amity can content the king that you have just chosen, I offer them with all my heart, but I can do no more."

Having said that, Belzamine fell silent, and a confused murmur immediately rose up in the assembly.

Orcanor demanded silence, and spoke thus:

"Admirable princess, you know that I have always been unhappy, and I shall be even more so if I lose you, but will you not allow yourself to be touched by the rigor of my fate? And you, amorous people, can you suffer that your king has the dolor of seeing the princess depart who alone can make his happiness? Can you also consent to lose a queen whom you love?"

Orcanor was interrupted in his discourse by a prodigy that he had not expected. Myrrha unfastened her belt and placed it on her head; her features changed immediately.

The king, Belzamine and Melidor recognized her as the fatal Ranuncule.

"King of Ostriches," she said, in an assured tone, "Prince of Topazes, and you, tender princess, listen to me. I will terminate your disputes. I have come here in the guise of a young shepherdess; I have tempted Melidor's heart again by means of artifices that he could not resist; I have rendered him as unhappy today as I desired, to punish him for the infidelity that he committed against me. I am content to have taken him away from Belzamine, and ashamed of having pleased him with a borrowed face. At present I am abandoning him forever; let him live happily if his natural inconstancy permits him to do so. Belzamine can continue to love him, but let her take this ring and pass a needle through it; destinies have attached her happiness to that ceremony."

As she said that she passed Orcanor the ring that she held, for the princess, and disappeared, without even casting a glance at Melidor.

Then Orcanor threw himself at Belzamine's knees, and implored her, in the name of the assembly, to conclude everything by doing what Destiny ordered. He also assured her that that what would happen would enable her happiness, and that she would be able to enjoy it without obstacle, even if he were forbidden ever to see her again.

The princess, pressed by the king and the senate, took the ring from the king's hand, tremulously, and passed a needle through it.

At that moment, Melidor uttered a piercing scream, and fell to the ground, bathed in his blood, which was emerging in floods from a profound wound beneath his heart.

Belzamine ran to him, and found him unconscious; then pity reawakened her amour, which was not extinct. The dying Melidor did not appear to her any longer to be culpable; she shivered with horror when she realized that it was her who had stabbed her lover by piercing the malevolent Ranuncule's enchanted ring. She could not retain her tears, and hastened to help him.

However, Melidor's blood stopped; he opened his eyes, and paraded them for a long time over the king and the assembly; finally, they paused on the princess "I am dying, Madame," he said, "and the oracle has been accomplished all too fully, since I am dying at the hands of the person who was most interested in my life. My unique regret is not having had the time to show you my gratitude for everything that you have done for me; I recognize my errors and I repent of them sufficiently to attract your compassion in this last moment. Forget them, Madame, and be assured that I am dying the most amorous and the most repentant of all men."

With those words he took Belzamine's hand and bore it to his mouth; the chill of his lips made a vivid impression on the princess; then her dolor no longer knew any bunds; she threw herself on the body of her lover and said, hugging him in her arms: "You shall not die alone, my dear prince; I shall follow you! No, Melidor, you have not betrayed me. You have ceded to the cruelty of Destiny. I only remember your tenderness, and since you loved me enough, I shall die content with you!"

She leaned her beautiful face over Melidor's, and only her sobs permitted the belief that she was still alive.

"O Heaven!" cried the prince, in a faint and dying voice, "can it be that I am finding this felicity at the moment when I am losing it? Oh, Belzamine, how cruel your tenderness is for me, and how unhappy I am in dying without being able to show you my gratitude!"

Orcanor, who had remained motionless throughout that time, descended from his throne, and, with dolor painted on his face, he approached the two lovers, who seemed to have no longer than a moment to live.

"That is too long to persecute you," he said. "Faithful Belzamine, take the leaf of the protector oak; it can serve you to restore life to your lover."

The princess immediately touched Melidor's wound with the leaf; he was cured immediately and he got up, with as much strength as if he had not lost a single drop of blood.

What were Belzamine's pleasure and astonishment at that moment! Accustomed as she was to prodigies, she feared that the one she was seeing was only an illusion of her amour. Melidor picked her up himself, and gave her evidence of his tenderness by means of transports so fervent that she began to believe that he was really alive.

After the first astonishment, Orcanor took Belzamine by the hand and made her sit down on the throne. He mounted the throne beside her, and with the scepter he was holding he made a sign that he wanted to speak. Silence fell, and he commenced.

"The spectacle that we have just witnessed no longer permits us to separate these two lovers; they would be too unhappy apart from one another. Their destiny is accomplished; it would be to unjust to trouble their happiness. You have chosen me for your king, and as that honor can compensate me for the loss of the beautiful Belzamine, I shall keep it, and I put into the hands of my nephew the prince the Kingdom of Ostriches, with the Princess of Flowers.

"Suffer, then, fortunate people, that I crown the Prince of Topazes King of Ostriches here, and that I give him his princess for a wife, since her heart cannot accept the homage of mine. That action, which might appear generous to you, does not merit your admiration. Although the effort that I have made has cost me, I have sensed at the same time that it was necessary; I could not have been happy with the princess, whose happiness I could not have enabled; I render myself justice regarding my age and I recognize the merit of Melidor; thus, in renouncing Belzamine in his favor, I am only ceding him a benefit that I could not have enjoyed."

Orcanor had not yet finished speaking when Melidor embraced his knees. The princess, following his example, did likewise, and swore to him a thousand times that she would never forget that she owed her life and her happiness to him.

Orcanor lifted them up and embraced them both. "Go, my children," he said to them, "go and enjoy a felicity that I no longer envy you; forget, in loving one another, the harm that I have done you, and pardon my injustices."

Then he put a crown on Melidor's head and a ring of inestimable value on Belzamine's finger, and had their marriage celebrated with an infinite pomp.

The Fay of Myrtles, informed that the destiny of the lovers she protected had finally been accomplished, immediately carried the news to the Queen of Flowers, and took her with her to the planet Venus. They spent a year there with the royal high priest, who strove to repair in regard to the queen, by means of the honors with which he heaped her, the harshness of his former procedures.

When the year had gone by, the Fay of Myrtles brought the queen and the two lovers back to the Kingdom of Ostriches. The new king commenced his reign by returning human form to everyone, and instead of punishing lovers there, as Tecserion had done, in consideration for his love for Belzamine he published severe laws against the indifferent.

They lived for many years, always amiable and always amorous.

Orcanor reigned with great wisdom on the planet Venus; he spread from there the gentlest influences over his nephew and Belzamine. It is believed that when the ten years of his reign were over, he asked to depart for the planet Jupiter.

PRINCESS LIONNETTE AND PRINCE COQUERICO

In the mountains of Circassia lived an old man and his wife who had retired from society; weary of having endured its caprices, they had made a comfortable retreat in a cavern that extended a long was under one of the mountains, and their solitude was only troubled by the dread of seeing one another die.

They had lived in Courts and knew all their falsity; far from regretting the brilliant position that they had occupied, they felt sorry for those whose ambition or lack of experience rendered them susceptible to desire it. Their life was quiet and tranquil; fruits served as their nourishment; a vast pond on which the old man went fishing furnished them abundantly with fish, and a flock of ewes of which the old woman took care gave them the most beautiful wool in the world with which to dress themselves.

The old man was named Mulidor and his wife Phila; they prayed incessantly to the gods at least to be kind enough to send them someone to console whichever of them remained on earth last, or to close their eyes, but, thus far, their prayers had not been heard. It is necessary not to believe, however, that the gods had rejected such pure and reasonable desires; they wanted to test the constancy of those good people in order to compensate them subsequently with interest.

The old man had gone out one day to catch a few fish, and having brought his boat back to the bank he was laying his fish out on a rock in order to dry them in the sun when a lion emerged impetuously from one of the cavities in the rock and came to drink from the pond. Mulidor was afraid at first, but then, seeing the proud beast roar because it could not reach the water, which was too far from the bank at that point, he went into his boat and, having filled a bowl with water, he presented it to the lion, which approached and emptied it several times.

After the lion had slaked its thirst, it raised its head and contemplated its benefactor with eyes that were so lacking in hostility that the good man dared to stroke it. The lion enjoyed that, and accepted a little bread and cheese from the old man, which he took from a basket he had over his arm. As that company was not safe, however, the old man thought about going back to his cavern, fearing that his wife, anxious at not seeing him, might come to look for him.

That anxiety was tormenting him when the lion, after having licked his hand, went home itself, and left the old man the freedom to withdraw. He went back to the cavern, where he found his wife already alarmed by his lateness. He told her about his adventure; she shivered on hearing it, but they talked about it, and drew the conclusion from it that humans could take lessons from animals in humanity and gratitude.

"Don't expose yourself any more, however, to the indulgence of that cruel beast," she said to him, tenderly, "or expose me with you, for I don't want to live in the idea of having seen you so close to danger; you've been returned to me, but can I flatter myself that the gods will always be as favorable to me?"

Touched by that tenderness, the old man promised her to avoid that encounter henceforth. That conversation had taken them rather far into the night; they went to sleep, and were only woken up by the dawn, the gilded rays of which came to strike their eyes.

Phila went out in order to feed her ewes, but she was very surprised to find at her door a lion of prodigious size and strength, with a lioness equal in strength and beauty. The latter was carrying a little girl of about five or six years old on her back, who got down as soon as she saw the old woman and came to embrace her.

The good woman, surprised by fear and admiration, remained motionless, and the lions, after having kissed the little girl—who responded to their caresses—fled and disappeared in an instant, leaving her in the hands of the good woman. The latter recovered from her fear then, and gazed at the child, who did not cease to embrace her. She took the child in her arms and went back into the cave in order to show her to her husband.

They both admired the child's beauty and her mildness. She was stark naked, but her blonde hair descended over her shoulders, and on her right breast she bore a clearly marked crown. The good people thanked the gods for that present, and they dressed the beautiful little child in a light white dress girdled with a rose-colored ribbon. They also put up her hair. She allowed them to do it complaisantly, and did not say anything. They caressed her and gave her milk freshly drawn from a ewe. She smiled at that sight, and, while gazing at them, she uttered a cry similar to the roar of a lion.

She became accustomed to them easily, however; she had nothing of the lion about her but her cries. For that reason they called her Lionnette; she responded to the name, and the vivacity of her intelligence soon enabled her to understand what was being said to her, and, eventually, to speak herself.

She had been with the good folk for a year, who loved her passionately and were loved by her in the same way, when Mulidor, in order to accustom her to their usages in case she lost them, took her fishing. He had been on his own several times without encountering the lions, but little Lionnette was no sooner at the foot of the rock on which the old man put his fish to dry than she uttered a little roar, which woke the lion and the lioness and caused them to run to her. The animals flattered and caressed her in competition with one another. She embraced the lioness affectionately, which allowed her to do it, and then leapt on to her back, and the lions drew away in a moment.

The poor old man was consternated. He threw himself on the ground face down and desired to die, because he had lost Lionnette; finally, after a long time, seeing that his despair was not doing him any good, he went back to the cavern, bearing desolation with him, and told Phila about Lionnette's adventure.

"Lionnette, my dear Lionnette," the good woman cried, "can it be that we have lost you? Alas, why have the gods shown you to us only to steal you away so cruelly? Of all the things that we have lost, we only regret you."

She was immoderately afflicted, and poor Mulidor scarcely had any more courage to sustain that misfortune. The night passed in laments and tears.

At daybreak they got up in order to go and look for her; they no longer feared the lions or their fury; their tender amity for Lionnette made them desire to be devoured if she had suffered that terrible fate.

They were both running toward the rock where the lions had established their dwelling when they saw little Lionnette, whom the lioness was bringing to them. As soon as the lovely girl saw them she got down and came to throw her arms around them; then, taking from the back of the lioness a roe deer that she had killed while hunting, she said: "Here, this is what my lion mother is giving you; she took me hunting for you."

The good folk were dying of the delight of seeing her again; they could not stop weeping and washing her pretty face with tears. "My dear daughter, my dear child," they cried, "you've been returned to us!"

Lionnette was moved by that spectacle. "Is it because you're forbidding me to see the lioness that you're not saying anything, and that you're weeping while embracing me?" she said.

"No, no, my dear child," the both cried, "but we feared that you might have abandoned us."

"Mother Lion doesn't want that," said the child. "She wants me to be your daughter." She turned round then, to take the lioness as a witness, but she was already no longer there, and Lionnette went back to the cavern with them cheerfully.

Mulidor and Phila found much that was marvelous in that adventure. They discussed it in private, and decided not to refuse the child to the lioness when the whim took the latter to take her for a walk. At the same time, however, Mulidor had his wife approve the desire that he had to consult Tigreline about Lionnette's destiny. Tigreline was a very knowledgeable fay.

"I've already thought of that," said Phila, and it's not too late to go and seek information."

It was agreed that he would leave early the next morning.

The good woman had prepared a present for the fay in order to render her more favorable; it was not something precious—the fays have no need of those—but a piece of sky-blue ribbon and a little basket of hazelnuts, of which Tigreline was passionately fond.

Mulidor set forth, and headed for the fay's dwelling; she had chosen for her residence a corner of an immense forest that was full of tigers, and it was from that circumstance that she took her name. When anyone went to ask her for just things, the tigers did not do them any harm, but if anyone took it into their head to go there with evil designs, the tigers tore them apart avidly, and they did not reach the fay's castle.

Having nothing to fear in that regard, the good man did not arm himself with any defensive weapon, and reached the castle without difficulty at the moment when the fay had just got up. He found her occupied in stringing large pearls on a golden thread; she received him quite graciously, and removed her spectacles from her nose.

"Approach, wise old man," she said to him. "I know the subject that brings you here, and I'm very pleased to see you."

Mulidor bowed profoundly and kissed Tigreline's robe. He offered her his little present; she received it kindly, and then, inviting him to sit down, she told him that she would consult Destiny in her large book, in order to reply to him on the matter that had brought him.

After having read for a long time, she raised her eyes to the heavens and then fixed them on Mulidor. "This," she said, "is what I have discovered about Lionnette: it is necessary for her to avoid loving the man who will be presented to her directly, for great misfortunes might arrive, and she might even lose her life. If she reaches the age of twenty years without experiencing that destiny, I can answer for her happiness."

Then she told the old man that Lionnette was a great princess, who had been exposed to the lions almost immediately after birth by the malevolence of a queen; but she did not want to say any more, and exhorted the old man to continue to bring her up with the sentiments of which he was capable. She left it to his choice whether to tell her who she was, confident in his sagacity to render her happy. Then she gave him, for Lionnette, the string of pearls that she had just finished.

"As long as she never loses it or gives it away," she told him, "it will preserve her from many evils, and perhaps it might serve her happiness, if she guards it faithfully."

The old man thanked the fay and went back home toward evening.

He found his wife and Lionnette; the latter made him a thousand caresses. He attached the fay's pearls around her neck, and recommended her to conserve them carefully. Lionnette was delighted by that new ornament, and when she drew away the old man told Phila what the fay had said to him. They hesitated as to what decision to make, and resolved to say nothing to Lionnette about her birth, in order to spare her the regret of an ambition that might be futile.

"There will be plenty of time to tell her what we're hiding from her," the prudent wife added, "and we might have to reproach ourselves, only being able to give her the education of a simple shepherdess, if the mild character that we know her to have today were to change by virtue of the knowledge of her estate. Let us form her heart and her mind; princesses don't have time for that; this one will learn from her own experience that they are subject, like anyone else, to the caprices of fortune, and perhaps she'll be happier for it,"

Mulidor agreed with that verity, and they applied themselves more than ever to the education of the lovable child, whose excellent nature left them nothing to desire.

Lionnette was twelve years-old, and still going hunting frequently with the lioness, carrying a little quiver on her shoulder and shooting skillfully at wild beasts, when she came back later than usual one evening, and the cavern resounded with the roars of the lioness.

Mulidor and Phila both went out, and found the lioness at the door. She had brought Lionnette back, who lay on the ground in order to caress the poor lioness, which was in despair.

"The lion is dead," cried the child, "and my mother is inconsolable. A hunter has killed him with his arrows."

The lioness was rolling on the ground, shedding torrents of tears. The old man, his wife and Lionnette did their best to appease her grief, but in the end, when they had spent the night without succeeding in that, the lioness died in the morning. Lionnette's cries and grief were extreme; she could not quit the body of the poor beast; she embraced her and dissolved in tears. Finally, they took her away from that frightful spectacle, and while the old man buried the lioness, the tender Phila helped Lionnette, who was in the cruelest affliction.

Mulidor came back in and was moved by the child's dolor; he tried to console her, but, seeing that he was only irritating her distress, he said to her: "But my daughter, what would you do if it were to one of us that this misfortune had happened? It isn't possible for me to believe that you would be any more sensible to it."

"Oh, Father," she cried, opening her arms to embrace him, fearing that he might be offended by the scant attention that she was paying to his consolations, "if the gods have such misfortunes in reserve for me, I pray them to enable me to die right away; I could not bear them."

"The gods, my daughter," said the old man, "do not always grant such reckless prayers; it is an offense to the decrees of their providence not to submit to them. Do you think, then that you are alone in suffering the pains of life? Is this the courage of which I thought you capable?"

Lionnette lowered her eyes, and the severity of that remonstration, which had brought a modest blush to her cheeks, rendered her even more lovable. Mulidor thought that he had said enough; he went out, and left his wife the care of softening the excessive harshness that the remonstration might have had.

Phila embraced little Lionnette. "In fact, my daughter," she said to her, "you ought not to have made us think that you no longer had anything to regret; undoubtedly, we praise the amity that you had for those poor animals, but it's necessary to be consoled and to thank the gods for not sending you greater misfortunes."

"Oh, Mother," cried Lionnette, embracing her, "How obliged I am to you for speaking to me thus; don't permit my father to be irritated with me anymore; I sense that I wouldn't be able to bear his anger."

Mulidor came back in; Lionnette ran to embrace him. He responded to her caresses with a tenderness that consoled the charming child. He and Phila never ceased to admire the generosity of the child, her sensibility, her docility and her frankness, so they loved her dearly.

Lionnette was sad after the loss of the lions; a foundation of melancholy appeared in all her actions; she dared not to give in to it before Mulidor, but she was less constrained with Phila. They talked about it several times; but, alarmed by her condition, they sought to distract her. They often went out for walks; they allowed her to go hunting and fishing; they gave her birds, flowers and shells; but her taste determined her to hunting more them all the other amusements.

The region in which they lived was so deserted that it was necessary for someone to come to it expressly, or to go astray, in order to be found there. They had no fear of evil encounters, but the adventure of the lion killed by a hunter came back to Mulidor's mind. He had not been able to understand how a man who had come all that way had not penetrated as far as their retreat, and why he had not been surprised to see a young woman on the back of the lioness, who did not separate from the lion when they went hunting.

They dared not question Lionnette about that, for fear of renewing her grief, but not did they dare to forbid her to hunt, the good folk thinking that it would be cruel to deprive her of that amusement; they only begged her not to go far.

After a few months, Lionnette recovered a little of her gaiety. The old man and his wife were delighted by that; they applauded themselves for having helped to console her by their complaisance, and judged that she must finally have forgotten the lions.

She was growing up, and beginning to take form; she was ravishingly beautiful in her exceedingly simple clothing. Phila had made her a garment out of tiger skins, the most beautiful in the world, and a little bonnet of the same material; when she put it on, one might have taken her for Diana herself, she had so much grace and majesty. Her beautiful dark eyes further heightened the brightness and vivacity of her complexion, which the most ardent sun and the strongest wind dared not attack, any more than the whiteness of her arms and throat.

She was not aware of her beauty, the strength of her mind and that of her education put her above the advantages of nature; she spoke well and thought even better. The good folk were astonished to see her, at such a tender age, capable of such just and sage reflections. She was then approaching the age of fifteen.

For some days, Phila had noticed that she took care when going to bed to put her hair in curls, and that when she went out, she looked at herself with a sort of complaisance in the water of a spring adjacent to the cavern. She informed Mulidor, who was as astonished by it as she was; they did not want to say anything about it to her, but they resolved to examine her carefully in order to discover the reason for that attention, and recalled that for some time she had seemed pensive and anxious, and that things that had amused her previously seemed to have become indifferent to her.

Lionnette came back to the cavern quite early that day; she brought back two wild grouse that she had killed. The good woman asked her whether she was too tired to help her thread a distaff that she wanted to finish.

"If you'd care to dispense me of it," said Lionnette, "I'd be greatly obliged to you; I'd like very much to rest."

Phila permitted her to do that, and let her go into a little corner of the cavern, which served her as a sort of cabinet. She had ornamented it with the rarest things she had found: the plumes of singular birds decorated its wall, and flowers placed in shells that she filled with fresh water provided the pretty retreat with vases. Mulidor had taught her to paint, and she had made some pretty pictures; with the wool that she had found in the cavern she had embroidered cushions, of which she had made a little bed of repose. She lay down on that bed; and there looked more like a goddess than a mortal.

The good woman, anxious because she did not come back, went to look for her. She found her as I have just depicted her, lying back on the cushions, with her eyes closed. A few tears that seemed to want to emerge from between her eyelids made Phila understand that the beautiful Lionnette had some chagrin. She stood there for a time, considering her. She had never seen her so beautiful. Finally alarmed by her condition, however, she approached her and took her hands, which she held in her own tenderly.

That action woke Lionnette, and, turning her eyes toward Phila, she threw her arms around her neck and said: "Oh, Mother, how ashamed I am of appearing to your eyes like this!"

"Why, my dear daughter?" she said. "Why hide your troubles from me? Do you not know how interested we are in them? What's the matter with you, my dear child? Don't hide your distress from me; perhaps I can soothe it."

It was some time before Lionnette dared to respond; she kept her head lowered in the old woman's hands, which she kissed ardently. Finally, she made her resolution, and raised herself up, with a modest blush that suddenly covered her cheeks. "I'll tell you what has been tormenting me for a long time; at least that confession might serve to merit my pardon."

"Speak, my dear daughter," said Phila, "and have no fear; I'm more anxious about your distress than annoyed because you've hidden it from me."

The Lionnette, recovering a little courage, told her that about three months before, when she went into the forest, she had seen a young shepherd asleep, who had only been awakened by an arrow that she had loosed, which, instead of piercing the bird at which she had aimed, had pierced the young man's hand. Attracted by the cry that he uttered, she had approached and had aided him to stem the flow of blood.

"That wound," she added, "caused me to feel and unknown emotion. I trembled as I applied to it the herbs I had collected, the properties of which you had taught me. As for him, far from being annoyed with me, he said that he would never complain about the wound, but only of the one that my eyes had just caused him. That language, utterly unknown to me as it was, delighted my soul, and I would have liked not to quit him.

"He wept as he looked at me, and kissed my hands in order to retain me. I proposed that he come with me, in order that my father could finish curing him. 'I cannot, beautiful Lionnette,' he said—I had told him my name—'a destiny that is too severe makes me seek solitude; but promise me to come and share it sometimes, and I shall ask nothing more of the gods; I shall believe that their rigor has softened.'

"I promised him that; he had asked me so tenderly. In the end, I was afraid that you would be anxious, and I quit him, with a regret so sensible that I shed tears in consequence, and I went away abruptly, in order that he would not see them, for I was ashamed, I think, of my compassion. I came home anxious and afflicted; the next day I went to look for him. I don't know what shame

119

prevented me from telling you that; but I opened my mouth a hundred times to say it, and a hundred times I sensed that it would be impossible for me. Perhaps it was because he had begged me to keep the secret to myself alone. In the end I went to find him, in order to ask him for permission to tell you.

"As I approached the place where we had seen one anther the previous day, I stopped; I sensed an emotion that reproached me for having hidden what I was doing from you; furthermore, my heart was so agitated that I feared coming to harm. 'What am I doing alone here?' I said to myself. 'I'm devoid of help, and the man I might find might be very dangerous. Unfortunate Lionnette, where are you heading? Flee, return to your duty; for it's impossible that this isn't failing in it, since my tranquility is so disturbed by this secret step; the gods are warning me; this state of mind isn't natural.'

"I had sat down in order to reflect; I got up and was retracing my steps when a dolorous thought made me stop. 'Alas,' I said, "perhaps he hasn't been able to come to the rendezvous because of the wound I inflicted on him. And if that's so, what will his despair be in not seeing me there? Doubtless he has only me for a resource in this savage abode; to refuse him my aid would be too inhumane; let us just see whether he has need of me, and only see him for that.'

"I therefore went back to the fatal place where I had wounded him the day before. He wasn't there. I was gripped by fear; my legs gave way and I fell on to the moss that covered the ground; I could still see traces of his blood. It would not have taken much for me to succumb to my dolor; my tears flowed abundantly; that relieved me, but I was cruelly afflicted in thinking that I might have caused his death. I took out my arrows and I broke them one by one to punish them for my cruelty. The one that had wounded him by chance was offered to my sight; it was on the ground and still stained with blood.

"My tears were redoubled by that frightful object, and I could not retain my cries; they were interrupted by the young shepherd himself, who came running precipitately. I could not get up; he knelt down beside me, so fearfully that I was frightened myself by his pallor. He asked me what was wrong at the same time as I asked him the same question; we both reassured one another. I told him the reason for my tears; never has anyone been thanked so tenderly.

"His words had a charm that passed all the way to the depths of my soul. I listened to him with a pleasure that I had never felt before; I almost forgot his wound, so fearful was I of interrupting him. I was surprised, however, to hear him saying that he loved me so much, having hardly seen him, and I was even more astonished to comprehend that he had become so dear to me, for he was telling me what I dared not say to him, and I thought that he was reading my mind, since I was thinking the same things as him, except that he was giving it an appearance that I believed I would never have been able to give it.

"Finally, he told me that he wanted to be mine. 'Are you not already?' I said to him. 'Could you be any more so? That would delight me.' He smiled at my words; I thought I had spoken badly; I blushed at the coarseness of my expressions.

"I don't know what he thought, but he said a thousand things to me even more tender, and told me that he was the son of a great king, and that he wanted to be my husband. 'I can't be yours, then,' I said to him. 'People wouldn't want me to be your wife,'

"'Who could oppose it?' he said, 'if you wanted it?'

"Then I told him that my father and mother had always told me that a crown was an obstacle to the happiness of life, and that they surely wouldn't consent to that alliance. 'Let a few days pass,' he said, 'and I'll tell you the means of softening their rigor. If you love me, you'll help me to vanquish it; but don't stop coming to this place; my life depends on that complaisance. Have no fear with me, beautiful Lionnette, nothing is as pure as my tenderness, and I attest here by the divinities of these woods that I will always respect your virtue.'

"He gave me his hand, and I gave him mine, and I swore, like him, to love him forever, if you consented to it. I wanted to see his hand; it was healed; I was overjoyed by that. I quit him, promising him to return, and only to talk to you when he wanted it. I came back so occupied with the idea of him that it seemed that I had only started living at the moment when I saw him approaching. Nothing pleased me any longer but him; the more I saw him, the more I desired to see him. He was the same.

"He is charming, Mother, and if you had seen him you wouldn't be able to help loving him. Three months have passed in that sweet union, and now misfortune has come. This morning, he told me that it was necessary for him to go away for a few days, for indispensable affairs that would only tend to ensure our happiness. I didn't know what it was to lose sight of him; I sensed a distress equal to his. He was immoderately afflicted, but he told me that he would come back soon, and that he was even more eager than I was to come and complete his happiness. I was in tears.

"Finally, the time to separate came; I unfastened my necklace and attached it to his arm…."

"O Heavens, what have you done, my daughter!" cried Phila. "We're doomed and without resource!"

With those words, she let herself fall to the ground, and filled the cavern with her cries.

Frightened by that spectacle, Lionnette got up to help the good woman. "What's wrong, Mother?" she cried. "What connection can a necklace of such little consequence have with your distress?"

"It's for you that I'm weeping, my daughter," said Phila. "Your happiness was attached to the conservation of that wretched necklace." Then she told her what the fay Tigreline had said to Mulidor, and did not hide it from her that she was a princess, but she told her that she did not know anything else.

Lionnette, who had a naturally elevated soul, was not astonished by that news.

"Well, Mother," she said to the good woman, "the more you confirm me in the high idea you have of my birth, the more I ought to support with courage the deadly events that are predicted for me, although, to tell the truth, I scarcely believe in them and I don't see anything unfortunate in this except the absence of the shepherd that I love, and his unfortunate name, which has made me flee him, without being able to help myself. That's the only misfortune that I know."

"What are you saying, my daughter," said the old woman. "His name has made you flee him? Explain that enigma to me; I don't understand it at all."

"Alas, that's what is making me despair," said Lionnette. "I had no sooner attached that necklace to his arm than he kissed my hand with an ardor that suspended my dolor momentarily. 'Yes, beautiful Lionnette,' he said to me, 'it's for life that you have enchained the fortunate Prince Coquerico.'[6]

"Scarcely had he pronounced that name, which he had never said to me—he always wanted me to call him my shepherd—than I felt a horror that made me flee as fast as I could. He followed me, and called out to me, but I could not turn round. An invisible power seemed to constrain me to draw away. 'My dear Lionnette!'" he shouted, where are you going? It's your shepherd, your Coquerico, who is calling to you!'

"I ran even faster; finally, I lost sight of him, either because I had taken detours that he did not know, or because he was afraid of displeasing me by following me any longer. I arrived here in a distress that I had great difficulty in hiding from you, and I beg your pardon a thousand times for having obtained such little profit from your sage lessons, and although I owe my birth to seemingly powerful princes, I shall never remove myself from your obedience."

Mulidor came in as Lionnette was finishing that speech; he was told about the adventure. He remained in an extreme dread of what might happen because of the loss of the necklace; he dared not even go to consult Tigreline, to whom they had been so formally disobedient. They decided to wait for whatever fate ordered for the princess; they exhorted her to forget the young man. They succeeded in consoling her somewhat for his ab-

---

[6] *Coquerico* is the conventional French representation of a cock's crow, a more dignified equivalent of the English "cock-a-doodle-doo." One of Aesop's fables, recycled and popularized in French by Jean de La Fontaine, asserts that lions have an intrinsic fear of a cock's crow, which obliges them to run away when they rear it.

sence, and in spite of her sadness, she yielded to the pleasure of their conversation.

Two months passed thus.

One night when they were sleeping profoundly, a clap of thunder woke them up with a start and made them think that the cavern was about to collapse. They got up, but they did not have time to reassure themselves; a hideous fay, very richly dressed, touched them with her wand and transformed them into two lionesses and a lion; then she transported them into the forest of tigers, where she left them, and disappeared.

Who could express the astonishment of the sage old man and the dolor of his wife? That of the princess was even crueler; she reproached herself for being the cause of the misfortune of those good people, and what afflicted her even more was that, because she no longer had the usage of speech, she could not console them. That present misfortune had suspended momentarily the idea of Prince Coquerico, but when she thought that she would not see him again, being frightened of what might happen, or of no longer being known to him, she uttered roars so frightful that the forest resounded with them, and her poor companion came toward her to try to console her.

It was a redoubling of their distress to see that they could no longer understand her or speak to her; they bemoaned that. In the end, all three of them came together, in order to go to see the fay, without communicating that design to one another, being unable to do so. The lion set forth first; the two lionesses followed him.

The tigers barred their way, but without doing them any harm, and seeing that their design was futile, they understood that it was an order of the fay. They plunged into the heart of the forest and lay down very sadly on beautiful green grass, which served them as a bed.

They spent a considerable time there without the fay showing herself to them; she had, however, taken care to send them something to eat via one of the tigers, which brought them nourishment every day.

It is now time to tell the reader who Prince Coquerico was. That young prince was the son of a king, who had been very powerful and had reigned in the Fortunate Isles. That king had died, and because he had left his son at a young age, the queen had become regent. The ambition to reign as sovereign mistress had closed her heart to natural emotion. She had her son raised in a castle on the edge of the sea, in an unequalled laxity and indolence, giving as a pretext for that education a prediction made by fays at his birth, which had said that he would risk his life if he had the misfortune to bear arms before the age of twenty. He had therefore been forbidden everything that might have given him a desire to do so, and the art of war had been depicted to him in colors so frightful that, however valiant the young prince had been born, he shivered when he saw a sword in a painting.

His father, the king, who had died in battle, was represented to him as a king so sanguinary that he swore that he would never imitate him. He had been called Coquerico in derision of the fact that one day, against the advice of his tutors, he had amused himself pleasurably watching a cock-fight. He spent his life walking and having amorous romances read to him, in which the heroes were enfeebled in order not to give him the desire to become one. He learned to play musical instruments, to paint and to do tapestry work. The queen came to see him quite often, and depicted the fate of kings to him in such dire colors that he regarded as an unequaled penalty the moment when it would be necessary for him to mount the throne.

He was approaching his tenth year, the time when the queen was supposed to cede the crown to him, when, while walking on the sea shore some distance from his retinue, he saw a great whirlwind rise up, which swallowed him and caused him to disappear instantly. His tutors, surprised by the fact that it was taking him so long to return, went to look for him and could not find him; the most scrupulous searches were futile; it was necessary to inform the queen.

She would have consoled herself without difficulty for that accident if the people of the island, weary of her government and indignant at the education their king had been given, had not revolted. After having torn her ministers apart, they constrained her to flee to the home of a neighboring king, who welcomed her. The king had been a widower for two years, having no children except for a daughter who has caused her mother's death. He married her, and the people of the Fortunate Isles appointed a council to rule the kingdom while awaiting news of their Prince Coquerico, whom they imagined to be still alive.

They were correct. The whirlwind had been whipped up by a fay who, delighted to see such a handsome prince and annoyed by seeing him so badly brought up, had resolved to remove him from a mother so unworthy to have brought him into the world, in order to cultivate a natural beauty spoiled by such a wicked education. Another motive, less generous and more natural, had guided the fay in question: the prince's beauty had touched her; she imagined that gratitude would one day give her a dominance over the heart of young

Coquerico that her few charms never would. She was already old, and had a horn in the middle of her forehead, but her soul was sensitive, and she had always complained that she had only ever known ingrates.

In bringing up the young man, she said to herself, *he will become accustomed to my face, and perhaps my cares and my amity will enable him to find within himself what I have not been able to find in men: the union so sweet and the tenderness so perfect of which I have heard so much talk, and of which I alone have found myself capable thus far.*

Cornue—that was her name—reasoned thus as she transported the handsome prince to her dwelling, which was in the wilderness in which the old man and his wife had been raising young Lionnette for four years. She had built a charming palace on top of one of the mountains, but it was inaccessible to any human because of the clouds by which it was incessantly surrounded. The enjoyments of life, the amusements and all the solid and frivolous pleasures were assembled there. The palace was marvelous in its grandeur, and yet built of a single opal, so transparent and so beautiful that through its walls one could see a grain of millet at the end of the garden, which was worthy of the magnificent palace, by virtue of its woods, its terraces, its flower-beds and its fountains.

The elegant Cornue had also spared no effort in her adornment when, in taking the prince into the vestibule of her palace, she rendered herself visible to his eyes. She had enveloped her horn with a green velvet sheath that she had sown with diamonds; her slightly graying hair was powdered in white and tied up with an infinity of green twirls, in the middle of which shone a huge diamond; and her silver and flesh-colored coat hugged her figure with so much accuracy that the graces would have disputed as to which of them had put the finishing touches to it.

The prince was surprised by that apparition. She kissed his hand and begged his pardon for having extracted him from his solitude without permission.

"If I can avoid being a king with you, Madame," he told her, in a manner that did not suggest that he had been frightened by the fashion in which he had been brought there, "I shall be quite content here, for the dread of mounting the throne made me desire to find a way of escaping from my realm, and you have given me pleasure by taking me away from it. But I would like," he added, immediately, "To know why you are coiffed so pointedly, and why it is that your coat is such a tender color?"

"One permits a man of your age," the fay said to him, blushing slightly, "to ask such puerile questions. You will be ashamed of them one day; but let us go into the palace, and you will find there the wherewithal to occupy yourself more agreeably."

Then she presented her hand to him, and they went into a drawing room that responded to the beauty of the palace. A hundred black slaves were arranged there in two rows; the prince and the fay passed through the middle. There was still enough daylight to see the rarities that ornamented the beautiful place: the statues, the marbles in relief, the porcelains and the furniture. All of that was praised tastefully by the young prince.

The slaves opened a magnificent gallery full of charts, world maps, geometrical instruments and plans in relief of the most beautiful cities of Asia, Europe and Africa; palaces in which men and women of every nation were dressed in accordance with their customs; and by virtue of the fay's art they were coming and going, each speaking their own language and in accordance with their status. That amused the prince for a long time. He begged the fay not to leave that place as soon as she wished. He had the slaves accompanying him explain what everything was; he had them repeat what they said and was delighted by it.

He recognized the Fortunate Isles; he saw the tutors who were looking for him and were desperate at not being able to find him. That touched his heart with pity. The fay drew him away from that object, in order that he would not see the catastrophe that was about to happen; she amused him with other objects. A vast sea that surrounded the isles on another map offered him a great subject for amusement, Ships filled with passengers were making marvelous maneuvers; there was a naval battle, and then a storm, which dispersed them, and sank several of them, terminating his day.

The fay offered him supper, and then an opera was performed; a ball followed, at which he danced with the fay, and beautiful nymphs from the fay's retinue. Finally, six slaves conducted him to a beautiful apartment, where he went to bed.

The next day, and those which followed, were filled with conversations, sometimes serious and sometimes frivolous; the slaves had been ordered to give him a taste for the sciences while amusing him; he lent himself to that gladly; he was already accustomed to strolling in a second gallery, which was a superb arsenal; he heard talk of armies and war with pleasure; he almost desired to see how he would perform therein, and began to be afraid of having thought otherwise. The slaves formed battalions; he set themselves at their head; he loved to triumph over the opposition; he invented rules; he sought glory everywhere. There was no more question of a dread of reigning; the gallery of maps had shown him the advantages of royalty. He spent three hours there every day; he took lessons in the subtlest politics; the secrets of cabinets were not concealed from him.

A relief map of the entire world filled that gallery, but what artistry there was in that famous work! Not only the kingdoms and their provinces, including the smallest habitations, but all the people who covered the earth each found their employment there; all of them spoke their own language; they could be seen, and heard; the most secret things were unveiled there, the sea and ships, rivers, lakes and the smallest streams, and deserts, even unknown lands, nothing was hidden from the savant Cornue, and she had described them in her plans; there was enough there to amuse someone during the longest life.

The prince was impressed by that miraculous effect of the fay's art; he amused himself there for a long time, only tearing himself away with difficulty, and only consenting to do so when he was assured that the gallery was part of his apartment and that he could visit it whenever he wished. He finally emerged from it in order to savor new pleasures: an opera, a supper followed by a magnificent ball, in which the fays of Cornue's court surpassed themselves in spite of their ugliness and old age—for she did not want anyone to be able to reproach her with being less beautiful than her courtiers, and the designs that she had formed on that young heart did not allow her to neglect anything that might enable her to give birth to them.

His education was confided to six fays, who took him into the gallery of the world every day to spend his three hours there; they explained to him the various interests of the princes; he learned their languages; in the meantime he heard and saw the effect of their politics; wars on sea and land showed him the skill of ministers and generals; he judged it well already, and became accustomed to speaking of everything knowledgeably. His natural beauty developed; he burned with the desire to acquire glory, and was ashamed of having been fearful. The pleasures of royalty also touched him; he began to find that it was pleasant to be the master. The seraglios of the kings of Persia and Constantinople provided relaxation from the serious matters to which he applied himself, but he did not envy that soft and effeminate life; he preferred that of kings who, reigning as absolute masters over their subjects, were certain that they would shed all their blood to conserve their crown.

Gradually, he succeeded in becoming the most accomplished prince there ever was on earth. There was nothing he did not know; the beauty of his mind substituted for his lack of experience; he judged everything with a marvelous accuracy and discernment.

"But where can that world be seen, and those inhabitants that I see in my map?" he sometimes said to Cornue.

"I'll show it to you some day," she replied. "It's not yet time."

That gave him chagrin. He would already have liked to be regarded as something important in the beautiful map of the world; he was annoyed not to be able to see himself there. That caused him to make reflections, but as they only departed from his mind, he did not pause on them overmuch; those of the heart interested him more; he did not know yet what they were.

The fay did not fear that the beauties that he saw would make him feel anything contrary to her ideas; he saw them on such a small scale that, at the most, he could take them for pretty marionettes. Even the tallest figure of a man was no bigger than a finger. What amused him greatly were the Opéra and the Comédie; he went there often; those little figures performed marvelously, and as he had a taste for intelligent things, he listened to all the speeches at the Académie and judged them very well.

Until the age of eighteen, that gallery held the greatest pleasures for him; he knew no others. At that age, he began to desire to know the people whose portraits he saw. The fay, who desired to please him, dared not contradict him too much; she amused him with her promises, but she feared that he might escape her.

"I go hunting in your park," he told her. "I walk there, I always see the same things; it's boring; I'd like to see other things occasionally."

"Oh, truly," said the fay, "you have conserved all the faults of humankind. Wretched human condition! Are they perfectly happy? They don't believe themselves to be; they desire what they do not have, and when they have it, they lose their appetite for it. What have you to wish for here? Do you not reign over us? Are you not the master? Have you to fear treasons, false friends, or bad advice? We all respire to please you; you have everything here; command, and we obey. What king is greater and more fortunate than you?"

The prince shook his head throughout that enumeration of the good fortune that he owed to the fay, and signified that he still wanted more; he did not say so, but his anxiety, his agitation and his ennui appeared involuntarily in all his actions.

Cornue redoubled her adornment; the prince paid no heed to it; he did not even look at her. She was desolate, for the project formed at the time when she had abducted him, the project of being loved passionately, had only been fortified since. The prince's pretty face contributed a great deal to that, while he was at the fortunate age when one pleases without difficulty, and when one loves with the frankness that men conserve for such a short time. Cornue was enraged to see that he had no thought of it.

"You ought to love me, in order to amuse yourself," she said to him one day, when he was very melancholy.

"Love you?" he said, looking at her with very distracted eyes. "Don't I love you?" Then, without reflecting, he added immediately: "I shall never love; I sense it clearly."

"Why?" said the fay. "What prevents you?"

"Nothing," he said. Then he stood up, sent for a rifle, and went hunting for the rest of the day.

The fay, in despair at his indifference, feared losing him if she continued to contradict him any longer. Seeing that he was already growing thinner, and that the color of his complexion was fading, she resolved to let him go out. To that effect she summoned him one morning.

"The time has finally come," she said, "when I can give you the liberty to go out; the vast world, of which I am going to open the paths to you, will become for you a very stormy sea; but after all, you want to expose yourself there, and I shall no longer retain you. All that I will advise you to do is to confide yourself to me in your difficulties, for you must experience some before you become a king; and you would do well to commence by going to see my sister Tigreline and asking her on my behalf for the marvelous necklace, to preserve you from the misfortunes attached to your destiny. Here is my flask; pour a drop of its liquid over the clouds that surround the park. They will open to give you passage; and here is a dog that will guide you in order to find the palace again.

The prince, who had not expected such a favor, caused such transports of gratitude to appear that the fay found herself almost compensated for her trouble by the caresses she received therein. He promised to follow her advice in all points, and departed immediately.

The end of the park was succeeded by a forest so arid and so frightful that Coquerico found that the world was not as beautiful as he had imagined; nevertheless, he went into that vast solitude, solely accompanied by his dog.

As he was crossing a road in order to go into the Forest of Tigers, to which his faithful companion was guiding him, he saw a lion of extraordinary size coming straight toward him. At first he was surprised by such an encounter, having never seen one in Cornue's park, but, having reassured himself slightly, he launched an arrow so accurately into the lion's heart that it fell at his feet. He drew away very rapidly, and was stopped a moment later by frightful roars that struck his ears. He looked to see where they were coming from, and saw in the distance another lion, which was running at top speed, carrying a young child who was sitting on its back. He wanted to run after it, but his dog tugged him so forcefully by his coat that he thought that the fay Cornue must have ordered the dog to look after him, so he abandoned himself to its guidance.

He arrived without any further adventure at Tigreline's abode. As soon as he had explained the reason for his journey, she said to him: "Prince Coquerico, tell my sister that I have disposed of the necklace for which she is asking me; it is doubtless for you that she desires it; however, I desire that it does not come into your hands so soon, no matter what advantage you might obtain from it. But in order to repair the loss of that gift, which I am no longer able to make you, I warn you that if you ever pronounce your name recklessly, and without an absolute necessity, you will lose, perhaps forever, that which is most dear to you. I advise you, therefore, to hide your name, or at least not to pronounce it lightly. Go, Prince, I can do no more for your service."

The prince thanked the fay very much, and, having kissed her hand, he withdrew and returned to Cornue's palace, very satisfied with the little that he had seen. He was received marvelously; he was questioned; he told the story of his adventures; he thought he would never finish narrating them; he found a singular beauty in everything. He was very cheerful all evening; he was praised, and he was caressed.

That did not put an end to his curiosity. He resolved to go out again, and the fay, who saw him in such a good humor, let him do as he wished.

For nearly a year he explored the limits of the beautiful region. He sometimes went on horseback, he frequently dismounted in order to sleep at the foot of a tree during the hottest part of the day. The exercise had rendered him taller and stronger, he was then at his greatest beauty. He was gripped by a desire to ask the fay to render him to his subjects; he was weary of the private life; his soul, as fine as his body, made him desire to see his kingdom again. He learned the way from his map, but dared not asked Cornue as yet; her feared not seeming sufficiently grateful. That caused the return of his earlier melancholy.

Cornue was alarmed by that; she sought to do everything she could imagine in order to amuse him, but nothing worked. He hardly went out any more; he spent entire days in the map gallery, and whenever he saw an army in battle he could not be torn away from it. What was worse, one day he saw the coronation of a young king; that sight nearly finished confusing his brain; the cries of joy, the military instruments and the pomp of that ceremony transported him with anger and pleasure.

What! he said to himself. *My youth is enchained here, and when I could command peoples, make war and peace, and finally enjoy the rights of my birth, they want to hold me captive, like Achilles at the court of Lycomedes? Shall I not have a Ulysses who will come to liberate me?*

He would have taken his reflections further if he had not been informed that the fay was waiting for him, in order to commence on opera that she was having performed.

What, always fêtes? He thought. *Oh well, it's necessary to resolve oneself to it.*

The opera that was being performed was *Armide*.[7] The fay, who had been informed of the prince's bad

---

[7] *Armide* (1686) is an opera by Jean-Baptiste Lully, with a libretto by Philippe Quinault, based on a famous episode in Torquato Tasso's epic poem *Gerusalemma liberata*, in which the knight Rinaldo [Renaud in French] is waylaid during the Crusade by the enchantress Armida [Armide in French], who is commissioned to kill him but falls in love with him instead, and imprisons him in a magical garden, having bewitched him in order to make him forget his duty. The opera is unusual within its genre for its intense focus on and development of the character of Armide, much as the present story is unusual within its own genre for its development of the character of

mood, examined him during the spectacle. She thought that he was amused by it, for she saw that he was very attentive to the play. In fact, he found the fourth and fifth acts marvelous; he talked about them all evening, praising, above all, the imagination of the buckler that renders the hero his glory.

"What!" said the fay. "Armide doesn't interest you at all? Don't you feel sorry for her? So much love merits a better recompense."

"In truth, Madame," the prince replied, "your Armide only got what she deserved. I would like to know whether the heart follows the will. For myself, I think it is independent."

Cornue felt all the harshness of that response, but she made no semblance of it, and turned the conversation in another direction. The prince retired early in order to go hunting the next day.

That was the day on which his hand was pierced by the beautiful Lionnette's arrow.

On returning to the fay's palace, the prince consulted himself as to whether he ought to talk about that adventure; he found himself quite astonished to feel that he desired to keep it secret. A joy that was sweet and yet unknown to him spread through his soul and filled it with so much empire that he was not the master of hiding it. He wondered what that might mean, and could not find the reason for it. Lionnette's name charmed him; he recalled it incessantly; the grace and beauty of the young woman delighted him; he found himself in the palace without having perceived it.

Cornue. Mademoiselle de Lubert might well have seen the 1724 revival of *Armide* at the Paris Opéra.

It was then that he came back to himself somewhat; in the excess of his delight he said a thousand gallant things to the fay. She was surprised by it, but, flattering herself that her charms might have produced that effect, she did not seek to penetrate the cause of such an extraordinary joy. His wound troubled her, but he made the decision to say that one of his own arrows had injured him, and the amorous Cornue, attentive to anything that might interest him, healed it immediately by blowing on it, without enquiring as to how the accident had happened.

He was charming for the rest of the day; Cornue nearly lost her mind; she enabled him to hear music that he found delightful, although he heard it every day, so much is it the property of amour to embellish the objects least susceptible to that perfection; that one made him dream sweetly, and caused him to make discoveries in his heart of which he had had no suspicion before.

He retired quite early and spent the night in the gallery searching for what he had seen during the day; he discovered what he was looking for, and saw the beautiful Lionnette, pensive, in the company of the two old people. He saw her re-curling her beautiful hair under her nightcap; he dared not look at the moment when she was about to get into bed; veritable amour is always respectful. He would not have seen anything anyway, for she extinguished the light and the obscurity would have hidden everything, but he wandered around the cabin all night and only left the gallery when the daylight was bright enough for him to go in search of the beautiful huntress himself.

As he went through the forest paths he went astray; that was why he took such a long time to find the beautiful Lionnette again.

Unfortunately for the fay, her art was then useless to her. As soon as they are subjugated to the passion of amour, fays become impotent, and the art of enchantment cannot protect them from it; when they recover their reason, they recover their power, but until then, they do not have it, either to punish their rivals or even to discover them, unless hazard serves them as it might serve simple mortals.

Three months passed without her being able to imagine what had caused the change in Prince Coquerico; there was no longer any question of ambitious thoughts, the returned rural life now served all his desires. He only dressed as a shepherd; he composed eclogues and madrigals; on the trees in the park he engraved gallant and amorous figures that the fay did not understand; when she asked him for an explanation he smiled and said that it was not for him to instruct such a knowledgeable person. "Ask your heart, Madame," he added. "It will inform you; it is mine that dictated all that to me."

The fay was quite content with that response; she turned it to her advantage; but she could not accord his frequent absences with the things that he said, for he went out at dawn and did not return until after nightfall. She spent the days imagining new adornments and singular fêtes; as she had a vivid imagination she succeeded in the latter, but the former were absolutely futile; her age and her horn defeated all her measures absolutely. It was for that reason that she invented masked balls, which have since had great success.

The prince allowed himself to be seduced by that pleasant error, and, his heart full of the beautiful Lionnette, he said things to the fay that were only addressed to her, and all the merit of which the credulous Cornue attributed to herself.

It was toward the end of the third month of that keen and secret passion that the prince finally decided to ask the fay to be returned to his kingdom. It was not ambition that was guiding his desires, but a finer and more delicate sentiment—which served to hide it—amour itself caused him to desire to remount his throne in order to place Lionnette upon it.

He had no sooner spoken to the fay than she granted his request, flattering herself that it was her that he wanted to have the pleasure of crowning. With what pleasure the fay ordered the preparations for departure.

The prince, as we know, took his leave of the beautiful shepherdess, and he departed with the fay and a numerous retinue for the kingdom of the Fortunate Isles. She was with him in a chariot of rock crystal drawn by twelve celadon unicorns, their harness of gold and rubies shining like the sun. Twelve other chariots just as pompous followed that one, and the prince, as handsome as Amour and magnificently adorned, attracted everyone's gaze.

He had hidden with great care the necklace that the beautiful Lionnette had given him; he was wearing it on his left arm, as a bracelet, and his clothing covered it. He took a charming pleasure in finally appearing before Lionnette's eyes in that pompous apparel, and reading in her gaze the joy that the cares of his amour must have given her, but he could not help feeling a secret anxiety that gave him moments of sadness; he attributed it to the distance that he was from that charming object, and sometimes cursed himself for being so far away from her.

Is what I'm seeking really worth as much as what I'm losing? he asked himself. *Lionnette loved me such as I appeared to her; will she love me more with a crown?*

Oh, Lionnette, I know you to well to do you that wrong; your noble and simple soul only knows the veritable grandeur that elevates us above other men by sentiment.

Finally, he arrived in the Fortunate Isles, and the people, charmed to see their prince again, received him with acclamations of joy. He was crowned, and thanks to the cares of the amorous Cornue, there were magnificent fêtes, in which the prince, out of gratitude, wanted her to share all the honors.

The fêtes came to an end, and the affairs of the beautiful kingdom having been restored to order by the fay and the ministers she chose, she finally wanted to explain her sentiments to the king. She made the proposal to him adroitly that he marry her; she employed the intermediary of the Ministers, in order to reserve that of counsel for herself. That succeeded; he did, indeed, want to make her party to the propositions that had been put to him; but what was her astonishment when the young king, after having told her that he had responded to his people that he had no intention of any such engagement, confessed to her all his tenderness for the beautiful Lionnette and asked her to complete his happiness by giving her to him in order to share his throne.

"Eh! Where have you seen this Lionnette?" said the fay, with astonishment, fury and chagrin equally evident in her facial expression; but she added: "What! Is this the price of my cares, then?"

The prince, surprised by that abrupt retort, and not fearing reproaches, finished piercing the fay's heart by recounting his meeting with Lionnette and depicting his tenderness in colors so vivid that she saw clearly that all the contrary force she could employ would only serve to irritate and strengthen his passion

Then, choosing her course of action cleverly, she said to him: "I am only speaking thus to reproach you for your lack of confidence. Why did you not open your heart to me? I could have served you better, and Lionnette would now be the Queen of the Fortunate Isles; but you have acted like a young man who lacks experience, and I doubt that I can render you as happy today as I could have done then."

"But Madame," said the king, "you can do anything you wish. Give me your chariot and let me go seek the beautiful Lionnette...."

"I want to do more," she said to him, with a forced smile. "I want to go there with you as soon as midnight chimes. Get ready; we shall return before the sun has risen. If it is possible to satisfy your urgency, I only know this means."

The prince embraced the fay's knees with a transport of joy and gratitude, which wounded her more than his unfortunate confidence. She dismissed him under the pretext that she wanted to consult her books, but in fact, it was because she could not constrain herself and because her fury had risen to the most horrible excess. Who could represent it? Everything that an amorous, jealous and scorned woman can sense, a fay senses even more, and the most vivid description would be too feeble to approach the horrors that this one felt tearing her soul. She had promised to accompany the prince, but that design served for the vengeance she was meditating.

She believed that to be all the more certain because the prince had dropped the necklace that he had on his arm, and had gone out without perceiving that loss. She picked it up and, thanking the fate that had served her so fortunately, she did not delay a vengeance whose movements would have been futile for her without the precious necklace. She had the doors of her apartment closed in order that her absence would go unperceived, and sent word to the prince that it was necessary for her to consult her books without being disturbed, but that she would be visible at midnight.

She mounted a winged dragon and arrived diligently in the cavern, where everything was already buried in the most profound slumber. The dragon sneezed; that was like a clap of thunder that almost caused the cavern to collapse. She accomplished, as we have already seen, her deadly projects, and found herself back in the Fortunate Isles as eleven o'clock chimed.

She could hardly contain her joy; she found an occupation in order to wait for the king, but soon the idea of knowing that he was in love, and doubtless beloved, returned all her anger; she was transported by it when he entered her room with an urgency that served in some measure to increase it further.

She only thought of calming down, or, rather, of dissimulating her anger; her fury was so excessive that her horn was ablaze. The amorous and overly credulous Coquerico, believing that it was a favor she was doing him in order to guide him in the obscurity of the night, thanked her a thousand times for that precaution. They both mounted a chariot drawn by three screech-owls, which departed at top speed, and landed in the forest near the grotto where Lionnette had been brought up.

The prince only knew it because Lionnette had described it to him. Everything is precious in amour; the smallest circumstances become interesting matters. It had pleased him to ask her for a description of the place where she lived; he had retained it with more exactitude that she had depicted it. He could not be mistaken, all the more as he recognized her bow and quiver, which were in the cabinet in which she had told him that she slept.

His dolor was extreme at not finding her there. He called to her, going into and out of the grotto thousands of times. He begged the fay to take the light of her horn into the most obscure places, and noticed some of the little pictures that she had painted. "Oh! This is her work," he cried. "I want to conserve them all my life."

The fay was so irritated by his transports that a flame emerged from her horn, which consumed everything in the grotto in an instant. The prince would have had difficulty escaping from the conflagration, but she pulled him out of the grotto, and, privately triumphant at the absence of her rival, she advised the prince to search elsewhere.

"Perhaps," she said, "her parents have married her, or perhaps," she continued, darting a mocking glance at him, "the dolor of your loss has caused her to die."

"I don't know what has happened," said the prince, in a tone that marked the agitation of his soul, already utterly distressed at not having found his mistress, "but I would believe in her death rather than her infidelity, and if it is true that she is no more, I shall soon follow her."

"That is a furious obstinacy of amour!" cried the fay; but, reflecting that, in the circumstances, it was better not to irritate the king, she calmed herself. "What I am saying," she told him, "is to show you the interest I take in you. I am ashamed that your tenderness has settled on a person of such base extraction, and I cannot praise highly enough the destiny that accords with my sentiment; it has removed that shepherdess from you in order to help your heart recover from its error."

"I do not know whether destiny wanted to aid you to make me impatient," the king replied, rather hotly,

"But I know full well that it has succeeded. As for Lionnette, whether she is a shepherdess or a queen, it does not matter to me; I would repair the fault of her birth, if it were possible that someone like her had an obscure birth, but it is impossible that she was born as appearance suggest. In any case, any princess born with a soul as elevated would be fortunate,"

Then the king seeing that it was futile for him to continue searching in that place, climbed back into the chariot with the fay and they resumed the route to the Fortunate Isles, where they arrived as the sun was rising without having proffered a single word, both being pre-occupied, one with her fury and the other with his des-pair.

On his return, the king shut himself in his palace and no longer wanted to think about anything except how he could find Lionnette. He thought that it was nec-essary to go see Tigreline; having taken that resolution he went to Cornue's apartment in order to make her par-ty to his project.

"I cannot imagine," he said to her, "why you are not helping me in this matter; is your power limited? And is Tigreline's more extensive than yours? For I believe," he added, immediately, "that you are sufficiently interested in my happiness to employ all your power therein if it were possible for you to do so. I cannot doubt that with-out ingratitude; I have had sufficient proof of it to be sure of it, and I do not feel capable of forgetting it."

Cornue blushed at that question, which she had not foreseen, and knew the full extent of her woe in conse-quence of the king's speech.

"It is a consequence of the very attachment that I have for you," she told him, "that you ought to under-stand that I do not want serve you in a passion that would tarnish your glory, and if you were as grateful as you say you are for the cares I have taken to render you happy and conserve your life, you would suppress a passion that can only serve to doom you. What idea do you expect your people, and the whole world, to have of a king with such scant mastery of himself that he runs after a vile shepherdess to give her a crown that he could share with the foremost princesses in the world, no matter which—and perhaps a fay would not have disdained to receive it from you."

Those final words, which escaped her involuntarily, opened the king's eyes, and, looking at the fay in surprise, he was convinced of the verity of what he thought when he saw her confused and carefully avoiding meeting his gaze. It took him some time to be able to respond, because of the excess of his astonishment, but, not wanting to shock the fay at a moment when he had so much need of her, but not wanting either to give her a hope that he felt incapable of sustaining, he finally said to her:

"The knowledge that you have of the human heart, Madame, ought to have informed you that a king is no more dispensed from the laws of nature than anyone else. A passion as pure and vivid as the one I have for Lionnette is not of a character to be easily extinguishable. If all your combined powers could have rendered me insensible to it I would not be feeling the unhappiness that I am experiencing today, but the good fortune of which you speak. The choice of a great princess or a fay who might have deigned to receive my prayers and my crown; that good fortune, as I said, does not touch me.

"Is it necessary that, in order to be happy, I must sacrifice myself eternally to the whim of my people? My choice is my own; I would like to render them happy; I would even feel pleasure in desiring it and being able to accomplish it, but what does it matter to them who I give the for a queen? I only sense the value of my grandeur because I can elevate the person that I love; that delicate pleasure enables me to support the weight of it; without that, what can all the others do? And is it necessary, because I am their master, that I deprive myself of the sole happiness that I can savor? No, Madame; in giving them Lionnette I count on rendering them as happy as myself. If they refuse to subscribe to that, I shall be able to make them repent of their temerity, and whoever opposes it will know that, for being sensible, I shall not forget that I am the king."

"Finish, ingrate, taking my life away from me," said the fay. "You know the violence of my tenderness, and you are only pretending not to see it in order better to overwhelm me with all your rigor; it is me alone who will expose myself to the baseness of your sentiments; dare to punish me for it, that is all that your crime lacks. But how will you do it? You are in my power, and the necklace that I have, which you dropped in my room yesterday, will avenge me for your ingratitude."

With those words she got up and, touching the king with her wand as he advanced in order to take back his mistress's pledge of amour, she transformed him into a cock. Then, opening one of the windows, she precipitated him into the courtyard of the palace.

Afterwards, having assembled the council, she told them that, the king having absented himself for an important affair and she being unable to stay any longer in the kingdom, she was establishing the council as regent. That matter having been concluded, she mounted her chariot and disappeared from their sight.

The king was bewildered by his fall, but his wings sustained him involuntarily, and when he had recovered his intelligence somewhat, he leapt on to a balustrade of white and pink marble, which bordered a magnificent pond in the middle of the courtyard, in order to see his appearance. He was surprised by it, although it must be admitted that he was the most beautiful cock in the world. His body looked as if it were made of emerald, his wings were a bright roseate hue; on his head he had a crown of brilliant diamonds which cast a dazzling light; the plumes of his tail were green and roseate, his feet also roseate, with talons blacker than ebony, and a beak made of a single ruby.

Let us leave the unfortunate king reflecting on the cruelty of that metamorphosis and return to Lionnette, whom we left even more unfortunate than him.

That unfortunate princess, after having been among the tigers of the fay Tigreline for six months, deploring her sad destiny, was finally extracted from it by the fay herself, who, touched by her condition, came to look for her and took her into her palace with her two unfortunate companions. There, after having caressed them and taken them to comfortable lodgings, she said to the princess: "My dear Lionnette, you have made a long enough penance for the imprudence that escaped you of giving away your necklace, without adding further remonstrations to the misfortune that you have in being unable to change form until after you have recovered it. So, my dear child, I shall not scold you; on the contrary, I shall do everything I can to soften your punishment, and I will give you proof of it by rendering your good conductors their ordinary appearance, in order that they can take pleasure in conversing with you and consoling you."

Poor Lionnette prostrated herself at the feet of the fay, and by doing so she demonstrated simultaneously her joy and the dolor of not being able to reply. Tigreline touched the lion and the lioness with her wand, and they recovered human form instantly. After having embraced the fay's knees they gave Lionnette a thousand caresses, which she did her best to return.

After that touching scene, during which even Tigreline had been unable to hold back her tears, she said to the old man and his wife: "The days of your metamorphosis will not be counted in your years; nor will the ones that Lionnette will spend during hers. Live to serve her and console her, until the time when the rigor of destiny has run its course. I do not want her to be imprisoned; she can come and go in my gardens and my forest; as for you, you will stay in my palace and take care of her. Let us wait for a happier time for the conclusion for which I dare not hope, and let us at least, by means of our courage, make fate blush at its injustice."

After those words the fay fell silent, and embraced Lionnette with all her heart.

The latter's heart was so swollen that she shed a torrent of tears, uttering groans that moved the fay, and the good people even more. She spent her days in the forest, hunting game that the fay had put there; the tigers respected her, and always saluted her when she passed by. She reposed in the heat of the day in the most remote and densest parts; there, reflecting on her destiny, she was less afflicted by her condition than by the absence or loss of Prince Coquerico. She sighed tenderly at the memory of him, and her greatest pain was in being separated from him. She engraved amorous figures of hearts and arrows on the trees with her claws, and wept for her misfortune and that of her lover. At night she returned to her lodgings, and the fay, who showed her a great deal of amity. The old man and his wife amused her with the stories that they told her.

One day, when she was in the fay's abode with her conductors, she seized a sheet of paper and a pen, and wrote on it that she begged the fay to tell her who she was. She presented it to her; Tigreline, because she was very clever, was able to read what the lioness had written; no one but a fay could have deciphered it. She sighed, and raised her eyes to the heavens; then, looking at Lionnette tenderly, she said to her:

"I will satisfy you, my dear Lionnette. The misfortunes that one experiences often serve as lessons to persons of your rank. I wish to Heaven that those with which it overwhelmed you at the beginning of your life were the measure of the torments that it prepared for your virtue. But do not weary of sustaining them with submission and with courage.

"You were born a princess, my dear child; you were not deceived when you were told that. You are the daughter of the King of the Golden Isle. The queen, your mother, died in giving you life, and the king, your father, resolved not to marry again in order to conserve his crown for you. You were scarcely four years old when a fugitive queen expelled from another realm came to implore the aid of your father the king, in order to remount the throne from which her rebellious subjects had cast her down because of the ardent desire she had to reign, at the expense of her only son, whom she kept far away from her, in the dread that he would reign in his turn.

"That ambitious princess, seeing that the king, your father, promised her his aid, but too slowly for her impatience, turned her eyes in another direction. It was not important to her where she reigned, provided that she did, so she resolved to marry the king, your father. Knowing, however, that he no longer wanted to have children, in order to give you the crown, and that as long as you were alive he would not remarry, she came to consult me.

"She did not conceal from me the sanguinary designs that she had on your person, and I knew that if I were mistress of the necklace that she wore, I would be able to save your life with it. I therefore listened to her tranquilly, in spite of the horror that her projects gave me for her. 'Queen,' I said to her, 'you will not be able to achieve anything unless I have your necklace; give it to me, and be sure of the success of your enterprises.'

"'A fay who presided over my birth,' she told me, 'ordered me always to wear it. She did not say any more. but since it did not prevent me from being deposed from the throne where my birth had placed me, I shall quit it without regret and put it in your hands, far more certain of my happiness with you than I was with the pretended charm that it contains to render fortune.'

"'Go,' I said to her, 'return to the Golden Isle and wait in repose for the effect of my power; and above all, make no attempt on the life of the young princess. I shall be better able than you to make use of that cruel means.'

"She did, in fact, return to the island, and after a time, she married the king, your father. On the night that followed that day, I transported you, with the king and the queen, into the cavern where the old man found you, and I changed both of them into lions, the king because I feared his weakness and her to punish her for her wickedness, for I took away the power to do you harm and constrained her to care for you. As for the king, I had no need to give him sentiments of humanity; he conserved them in spite of the natural ferocity attached to his form."

At those words, poor Lionnette interrupted the fay with her roaring. Tigreline smiled, and caressed the lioness.

"Reassure yourself, my dear daughter," she said. "You are mourning a good father and you regret him; your heart, susceptible to sentiments of grief, will perhaps also be susceptible to the joy of knowing that I saved his life. He is presently living in a place to which I transported him after he was wounded, and he desires to see you again as much as you can desire it yourself."

Lionnette, who was sitting on a large cushion at the fay's feet, licked her hand gently in order to mark her keen gratitude; and her eyes shone with such a great joy that the fay, charmed to see her sensible, kissed her tenderly.

"As for the lioness, your stepmother, she really did die, not of the regret of having lost the lion but of the rage of seeing her projects aborted by his death, which she believed to be veritable, and the tears that you shed for her recompensed her too well for the obligatory care that she had taken of you."

The fay was at that point in her story when a cock of singular beauty flew in through the window, and perched on her shoulder. That astonished the entire company; the fay, who was spinning, dropped her spindle, but when that first shock had passed she extended her fist to the cock, which hopped on to it, and, flapping its wings as a sign of rejoicing, sang *coquerico* two or three times. At the first, the lioness started running and fled at top speed. Her tutors followed her.

In the meantime, Tigreline examined the cock, and, seeing that it was marvelously beautiful, suspected the mystery hidden beneath that adventure.

"Prince," she said, "I believe that I know you, and unless I am much mistaken, you have just told me your name."

The prince—for it was him—lowered his beak all the way to his feet in order to make a profound reverence to the fay.

"O Heaven!" she cried. "Can there be such an enchainment of misfortunes! The barbarian who has reduced you to this disastrous estate has left you the faculty of pronouncing a name that constitutes your misfortune; it has just made your princess flee, and perhaps it is the last time in your life that you will have seen her."

The cock, surprised by those words, looked at the fay in astonishment. He had not seen anyone in the room except a lion and two old people; he did not understand what Tigreline meant. She read his thought, because he could not express it.

"She was here, I assure you," she said, "but I forgive you for not having recognized her. If my sister, the barbaric Cornue, has been able to make you into a cock, has she not been able to change the princess into a lion?"

The cock nearly fainted at that cruel news.

"O destiny, pitiless destiny," continued the fay, "how blind your decrees are! Why do you punish the innocent, and why do you let the guilty live?"

Her reflections would have absorbed her if her eyes had not fallen upon the poor cock, who had fallen over, ready to die. She took him in her arms, and, making him respire a marvelous liquid, she brought him round; but he sighed bitterly at being forced to see the light again.

"Don't be afflicted, my dear prince," the fay said to him, "all my art will be employed to help you, but in order to render it invincible, it is necessary for your cleverness to second me. I can only render you perfectly happy if I have the necklace of which Cornue is in possession, and only you can acquire it for me. Repose, dear prince; my books, which I shall consult tonight, will give me the enlightenment of which we shall make usage as soon as tomorrow."

The king could not express his gratitude sufficiently; he kissed the fay with his beak and caressed her with his foot; in sum, he did his best to express his sensibility.

After giving him something to eat and drink, of which he made scant usage, Tigreline perched him on one of the shutters of her cabinet, and after having saluted him, she retired to her chamber in order to set to work on what she had promised to do.

While that was happening, poor Lionnette, vanquished by a fear of which she had not been the mistress, fleeing with all her might, had already plunged deep into the Forest of Tigers, in spite of the efforts they made to retain her; for they all loved her, and several of them were even in love with her; but she had overcome every obstacle and knew no other guide than fear, believing that the cock was still on her heels. She covered a hundred leagues in quick succession and only paused when her strength was exhausted.

Her poor guardians called to her and searched for her in vain; they came back at daybreak very afflicted, found the fay and informed her of Lionnette's flight.

The fay, who knew that if Lionnette had emerged from the limits of the forest, see no longer had any power over her, and that Cornue would have it entirely, allowed destiny to take its course, and no longer thought about anything but being of service to King Coquerico. She went into the cabinet where he had spent the night in order to tell him what he had to do. He flapped his wings when she arrived and flew to the ground in order to kiss the hem of her robe. The fay took him in her hand and placed him on a small table, which she placed in front of the armchair in which she sat down.

"Great King," she said to him, "the destiny that has pursued you since your birth orders me to tell you that you will only resume your ordinary form on two very harsh conditions. It is necessary that you be fortunate enough to recover from Cornue the necklace that Lionnette gave you; if you cannot obtain it, you can only become a man again by marrying Cornue. If Lionnette, whom the malevolence of my sister is bound to render witness to that ceremony, can resist the dolor that it will inevitably cause her, I glimpse that you might eventually be happy, but if she cannot support with courage the terrible sight of that hymen, I cannot answer for anything."

At those words the cock lowered his head and shed tears, by which the fay was moved.

"Sensibility that departs from the heart," said the fay, "is forgivable, and even desirable in a king. Your dolor, given that principle, is very excusable, but it is necessary not to abandon yourself to it excessively. Let us leave plaints and cries to vulgar souls, Sire, and, without trying to be stronger than humanity requires, let us resist the blows of destiny courageously. If you have only withdrawn from yourself that which has proven your virtue, and know it to be unshakable, you will be content. That is the foremost of all concerns, and it is rare that we request it from the gods, because we do not know its cost. Here is a bottle, which I am giving you; try to pour a drop of the liquid it contains over Cornue; it

156

will make her drowsy and you will be able to bring your designs to a conclusion."

The cock, who was in no hurry to depart, looked at the fay as if to request further clarifications; she divined what he wanted to say, and she told him Lionnette's story in a few words. He thanked her as tenderly as was possible for him; in fact, it had come to mind more than once that the fay, in talking about her, had called her Princess. He was delighted to learn that the beautiful young woman was so nobly born, but it did not augment his tenderness, which could no longer increase.

It was not the same for the indignation he had against Cornue; that took on new force at every moment, especially when he fay, at the end of her story, told him that the unfortunate princess had fled at his song by virtue of the antipathy that lions have for the crow of the cock, which the malevolence of the fay had surely augmented further; that she had started running in the fright that it had caused her, and that Cornue might have her in her power, but that, having emerged from the Forest of Tigers, it was no longer possible for her to enter it again until she had resumed her original form.

King Coquerico then felt the impatience of making his journey; he marked it as best he could, and Tigreline, having understood the implication, after having embraced him and attached the bottle under his right wing, opened the window. He departed, firmly resolved to let himself be devoured by lions rather than sing to frighten them.

What can the passions not do in souls that have never made any effort to vanquish them? The implacable Cornue, torn by turns—or, rather, simultaneously—by the most violent amour and the most frightful jealousy, spent her days in the opal palace meditating some deadly vengeance against her rival and her lover. What more did she want? Were they not unfortunate enough? They could not recognize one another and fled one another as soon as they were able to come close. Nothing more barbaric is perhaps imaginable.

Poor Lionnette, vanquished by lassitude and overcome by fatigue and fear, fell down on a beautiful green lawn, which served her as a bed for the moment. As previously mentioned, she had covered a hundred leagues in a single rush, and with incredible diligence, for she had emerged from the fay's abode in the evening and found herself at daybreak in that new country, so true is it that fear gives one wings.

She looked around, and saw nothing but that lawn, through which ran a little silvery stream, which refreshed the grass and ornamented it with little wild flowers. She slept profoundly there after having drunk the beautiful water in question, which had the property, while slaking her thirst, of refreshing her and taking away her hunger. She slept for fifteen hours in succession.

When she awoke, she felt quite well, and crossed the lawn, at the end of which she perceived a small palace of verdure, the architecture of which appeared as simple as it was marvelous. She went into it through a beautiful portico of foliage; she saw cabinets, chambers and galleries, all of green palisades, and what charmed her was hat in the middle of all the chambers or cabinets there were large clumps of flowers of all kinds, which saluted her amicably and all of which said as she approached them: "Good day, beautiful Lionnette."

That marvel surprised her; she stopped at a tuberose plant that had greeted her even more graciously than the others. "Beautiful flowers," she said to them, "by what fortunate chance have you given me the power of speech, which all the science and amity of the generous Tigreline could not render me? Is it you that has that power? I desire to know in order signify to all my gratitude to you."

"Only the stream that slaked your thirst, beautiful Lionnette," said one of the tuberoses, "has that glory; we can do nothing, and it is when we are irrigated by its water that we have the faculty of hearing, seeing and expressing ourselves. We are the flowers of the garden of the fay Cornue; for some time she has been very sad; she comes to converse with us, but we do not have the power to soothe her; perhaps that gift is reserved for you. It's necessary to try; she will come here in two days, since she came yesterday. Her palace is a long way from here; wait here, and we will do our best to amuse you while awaiting her return."

The tuberose fell silent then, being not very talkative by nature; but she yielded out of politeness to the desire that Lionnette had to ask her a few questions.

"I would like to know, obliging tuberose," Lionnette said, "whether Cornue, of whom you speak, and to whom you belong, "is a benevolent fay; and then I would like to know how you know my name and how you knew me right away."

"A rose-bush, who is the oracle of this place," said the tuberose, "at the last sacrifice that our mistress made to it, predicted that a great princess in the form of a lioness, would come to this place one day, and that she would find the end of her disgrace here. At that the fay burst forth into immoderate laughter; she redoubled the incense and the honey-bees, which are the only victims immolated here. That answers both your questions at the same time, for you will easily infer from the fay's joy her good intentions toward you."

The good Lionnette found enough plausibility in the conjectures of the tuberose; she thanked her with all her heart, and asked her to tell her where the rose-bush was, in order that she might consult it, in order to know what she ought to do.

The tuberose told her, and she soon arrived there; it was not far from the cabinet of the tuberoses. It only represented a temple because the palisades formed a vault, which preserved the rose-bush from the ardor of the sun; a little balustrade of jasmine and pomegranates surrounded that beautiful plant, which was covered with such a great quantity of roses that its splendor was dazzling; the lioness closed her eyes more than once.

She approached the balustrade tremulously, and, having prostrated herself respectfully, she said: "Divinity of this beautiful place, deign to receive my homage, and tell me what you ordain of my destiny."

At those words, the rose-bush seemed to feel a great agitation; its leaves and its flowers trembled and paled. Then a voice, punctured by sobs, emerged from its branches, and Lionnette heard these words:

Know your blind and dire destiny;
It is in this beautiful country
That an unfortunate Princess
Will see the end of her woes.

The princess was frightened by the marks of dolor that the rose-bush was showing, but if its first words had overwhelmed her, the last ones had rendered her a little courage.

"Alas," she said, "I fear nothing more than living for a long time; if I can finish my unfortunate life here, I will bless the fate that led me here, but, sage and generous rose-bush, may I not, before terminating my days, know whether the one to whom I desired to consecrate them is still alive, or, at least, whether he is happy, wherever he might be? That is my only curiosity; I shall have no other regret of life if I learn that his destiny is fixed, one way or another."

The rose-bush agitated forcefully again and replied:

This is the last time
I shall answer your desire
Your lover will only lose life
If you oppose his choice.

"Oh. sage divinity," cried Lionnette, "I shall ask you nothing more; if he lives I am happy. May I suffer all the rigor of the fays! They will appear trivial to me if he is exempt from them and if I can see him happy. Why would I constrain him? Alas, the choice to which I might oppose myself, whatever it is, can never offend me; what does he owe me, and what can I offer him that is worthy of what he merits? The unfortunate Lionnette, unable to render him happy, ought not to oppose that he might be; it is at least permissible for me to desire to be the cause of it."

After those words she returned to the cabinet of the tuberoses, where she spent the night talking about her shepherd, whose amours she recounted to her faithful friend, who told her in return in a little more detail what she knew about the fay Cornue and her companions, the flowers.

"As for the rose-bush oracle," she said, "all that we know is that he is not of the rose race. He was here when we came here, and I believe that the fay transplanted us here in order to embellish his dwelling. He speaks without being watered and hardly takes any pleasure in our conversations. He is naturally sad, as you have remarked yourself. He has a perfect knowledge of the past, the present and the future. The fay spends the days when she comes here talking to him; she rarely does us that honor, and I believe that it is because of the annoying things she learns from him that she does not want to amuse herself with us. A pomegranate flower who is a good friend of mine has often related their conversation to me. The rose-bush conceals who he is, and the fay cannot discover it. All that is known is that he has not been a rose-bush all his life."

She was at that point when a carnation, a buttercup and a few other flowers came in, and, after having greeted the lioness politely, they told the tuberose that Cornue had bought her visit forward by a day, that she was expected the following day, and that she was going to make a pompous sacrifice to the rose-bush. They did not know the reason for that great ceremony, but it had to be an important matter. The flowers discussed that event at length without being able to determine anything certain; then they talked about good weather and rain, a conversation in which they excelled, and which would have amused Lionnette if her mind had not been elsewhere, but she said little and listened even less,

At sunset all the flowers retired to their own abodes, and after having made a light meal of herbs on the lawn and drunk the water of the marvelous stream, Lionnette went to sleep at the foot of her faithful friend the tuberose.

The first rays of the sun having struck her eyelids, she woke up. All the flowers were already in motion. Lionnette got up went to the dwelling of the rose-bush. She lay down in a corner of its little temple, and saw all the flowers arrive and arrange themselves artistically in order to honor the fay, who was expected before long. The whole temple was shining with the beautiful colors of those flower species; some formed arbors, others garlands, wreaths and girandoles. In sum, thousands of different ornaments mingled so marvelously that the sight was dazzling. The sweetness of their perfume was admirable, and what extracted Lionnette from her reflections was that, after that arrangement, when they were alerted that the fay was approaching, they formed a concert so melodious that the most melancholy individuals would have forgotten their dolor and yielded to the mild delight that the music bore into the soul. The tuberose, in particular, recited perfectly.

That charmed Lionnette effectively; she listened to the marvelous concert with pleasure and was admiring the gallant choice of words that composed the hymn that they were singing when she saw the redoubtable Cornue enter, brilliant with precious stones but more frightful than anything one can say. At that sight she was seized by a horror the cause of which she could not divine, and she reproached herself for it.

Might it be, she said to herself, *that I am still attached to the feeble prejudices to which my sex is susceptible? Does a little more beauty or a face disgraced by nature decide the qualities that a soul can have. What sentiment would my face inspire if poor Lionnette were judged by it? Judge yourself before judging others, and don't hide it from yourself that if ugliness gives you an aversion for someone, you must inspire a frightful horror.*

While Lionnette was striving to vanquish the sentiment of hatred to which the fay's presence had given birth in her soul, the latter, to the sound of songs of joy with which the temple of the rose-bush was resounding, advanced toward the balustrade, and perceived the lioness, who, sitting in the corner to which she had retired, bowed profoundly when the fay directed her eyes at her, where an excessive joy shone at that adventure.

"Oracle, always true in your words," she cried, "You promised me that I would one day find what I sought with so much application, and which you were doubtless reserving as a recompense for the honors I have rendered you." To the fays who were following her she said: "Go and enchain that cruel beast, and tether it to my chariot. Then let us immolate our victims."

Four fays threw a chain over Lionnette, who allowed herself to be dragged outside the temple, in spite of the dolor marked by the flowers, who were adorned as they are when the dawn pours its gentle dew over them. They all loved Lionnette; but their tears did not soften the inflexible and jealous heart of Cornue in the least.

The rose-bush darted a flame from its stem that devoured the offering of honey-bees that the fays had just placed on a little golden altar that they had approached to it; its roses became the color of amaranth.

Cornue was alarmed by that change. "What prodigy is this?" she exclaimed. "Divinity of this place, are you protecting my rival, or has the joy of having delivered her to me produced this mysterious change?"

The roe-bush shivered at those words, and a loud and frightening voice responded to the fay thus:

Immolate to my just wrath
The first cock that you see;
Do not be bold enough
To dare save it from death.

After those words the rose-bush closed its flowers and its leaves, and by that action seemed to be dismissing the fay, who went out rather discontented and climbed back on to her chariot, to which Lionnette had been tethered, with four other lions, which were beautiful. She held the reins of those animals, which was walking slowly over the lawn along the stream, whose gentle murmur was augmenting her reverie, when one of the fays who were following in another chariot shouted that she could see a cock that was drowning. Cornue stopped her own and ordered that the unfortunate beast should be brought to her, thinking that it would serve to reconcile her with the oracular rose-bush.

A few lightly-dressed fays threw themselves into the water, swam and caught the poor cock, which had already lost consciousness. It was brought to Cornue, who was not surprised by its beauty, because she had recognized the unfortunate King Coquerico.

"O Heaven!" she cried. "Is it thus, barbaric oracle, that you intend to make yourself understood? She suspended the prince by his feet, and made him render the water he had drunk. He opened his eyes, already obscured by the approach of death. Then she hastened to touch him with her wand. "Resume your ordinary form," she said to him, "and save me thereby from the horror of taking away a life on which mine depends."

At those words, the king, safe and sound, appeared more brilliant than the sun, his royal mantle on his shoulders and his crown of diamonds circling his head very gracefully.

What became of Lionnette at that sight? Her lover was before her! Her royal lover, more beautiful than the daylight, her dear lover! It would have robbed her of speech if she had not already resolved not to speak to the fay until she had determined what interest she had in maltreating her so badly. She therefore kept quiet, but attached her gaze so tenderly to the king that if he had not been occupied with the encounter he had just made he would easily have recognized the unfortunate princess

"What do you want with me now, Madame?" he said to Cornue. "Is it to try to render my misfortunes more sensible that you have returned the form that you took away from me so unjustly, or are you finally repenting the harm you have done me?"

"Ingrate, and ever more ingrate," said the fay, offering him her hand so that he could help her descend from the chariot. "Come and justify yourself, and no longer accuse me."

With those words she marched over the lawn to the edge of the stream. Leaving her chariot and her companions some way behind her she sat the king down next to her and spoke to hum thus:

"I am not telling you anything in saying to you that I have loved you since your childhood; the care that I have taken of you has convinced you sufficiently of that, if the memory remains to you; for I do not expect gratitude for such feeble benefits. I shall only pause lightly on what happened then, in which I recognized in your heart nothing but a cruel ingratitude that my sentiments for you disguised under the name of indifference, perhaps founded on the aversion that you had for my scant beauty; I thought for some time that, by means of benefits, I could overcome that coldness. Beauty, I said, is a feeble advantage; a reasonable man can only be touched by it initially; a limitless power, a fay who descends so far as to want to please a mortal, is always beautiful enough.

"I recognized only too soon the abuse of my confidence, and I saw with horror that I had a rival. What I did them to avenge myself, what woman would not have done? Far from wanting to make use of my power, I only employed my reason. I took Lionnette away from you, but I did not kill her. What an excess of weakness, since I could have done! You ought to recognize amour for you in that sentiment. Your outrages and your disobliging coldness caused me to yield to my despair; I deprived you of your form and distanced myself from you. What more could you do against me than the cruelty I exercised against myself? All your hatred could not punish me so sensibly. In what horror have my days gone by since that frightful separation!

"I accused myself of cruelty, and carefully refrained from recalling your injustice, and when, being more tranquil, I depicted it such as it was, I reproached myself for having given rise to it by too much vivacity. In sum, ever present in my memory, and believing you to be incessantly irritated against me, I could not savor any repose. Some of the fays who were with me in the opal palace told me that I ought to consult the rose-bush oracle regarding my destiny. That oracle, without anyone knowing the reason, came to establish itself here, or at least was found, on the eloquent lawn, the one that you see here, and which takes its name from the stream that surrounds it, because it has the faculty of giving speech to everything its water irrigates.

"Persecuted by my enemies, I finally came to see that new oracle; at first I found some relief from my pains; I took pleasure in embellishing its abode. My power gave birth there to flowers of every species; I raised a little temple of verdure and, irrigating all the flowers with the water of the stream of eloquence, I rendered them capable of keeping the rose-bush company and being able to relieve its tedium. The things that I learned concerning my destiny gave me gratitude for and confidence in the oracle; I came to converse with it often, and tried to figure out who it might be. It is not one of the gods who take pleasure in making themselves manifest to humans, as at Delphi; it is a man changed into a rose-bush and protected by a power that is unknown to me, and who hides with care. I offered it all of mine in exchange for the recompense that it promised me, but it has always refused.

"Finally, having predicted what has happened to me today in the beginning, it demanded of me in sacrifice the first cock that I saw. Judge whether everything fortunate that I can expect of its promises ought to be put in comparison with your life; that is what is being asked of me. Can I feel, can I know, a happiness that is detached from it? Let the oracle harass me and overwhelm me, if it can, with the cruelest woes; I shall not seek to avoid them by the sacrifice of your life. Call me again, if you wish, inhuman and barbaric; I shall suffer it, provided that I see you; for I am resolved to suffer everything that your hatred can make me feel of the most frightful, rather than consent to immolate you to the bizarre whim of the rose-bush."

Cornue having ceased speaking, the king, having expressed his gratitude, continued thus:

"What can I do for you, Madame? My heart is no longer mine. It is not with you that I want to dissimulate; apart from the fact that my character is incompatible with that sort of perfidy, you know too much of what I have thought for me to want to abuse your credulity; and I owe you too much gratitude for having saved my life to want to deceive you. But why have you saved it, that life, which can never render you happy? It would have been better to follow what your oracle prescribed; sure that you would always be opposed to my happiness, I would have received death from your hand with pleasure, since I could never offer you anything but my gratitude; you would deliver me from the horror of appearing ingrate to you, and that of living far from the object of my tenderness."

The king softened in pronouncing these words, and the fay was moved by them. They maintained silence for some time.

"Whatever the deceptive oracle promised you," said the prince, finally, "if you can render yourself happy by ending my life, why defer the sacrifice? The generosity that you have had in conserving me excites a stir of jealousy in my heart. Take me to the temple; it will not be you who immolates me; at least amour will acquit me toward you, since amour is disposing of my life, and opposing the pleasure I would have had in leaving you its mistress."

"Let us not talk any more about sacrifice," said the fay, getting to her feet. "Your life is precious enough to me to conserve it at the expense of anything that might happen. Come into my palace; we will see tomorrow what we have to do."

Then she walked to her chariot, which she mounted with the prince, and the lions ran so swiftly that they were in the opal palace in an instant.

It was then that Lionnette abandoned herself to the most bitter dolor, when she saw the fay descend from her chariot with the prince, and ordered that the lions be put in a grotto, where a thousand other animals as cruel served to pull her carriages. "Oh gods," she cried, "to what are you reducing me?" She allowed herself to be led away, and, choosing an obscure corner to which to retire, she lay down on a little straw and spent the night bemoaning her destiny.

A few days passed without anyone troubling her sad repose; at the end of that time two young fays came to fetch four lions, a few tigers and two bears to serve for the diversion of a hunt that the fay was giving the king. As the princess did not know for what those animals were destined, she did not speak to the fays, but how terrible was her situation! Her lover, whom, she could have no doubt, was in the palace, and who could not know her, the harshness of the fay, and the horror of spending her life in that strange solitude, all gave her an aversion for life, which could only cede to the amour that she conserved for the king, which had regained new strength at the sight of him.

But what does it matter to me whether I still love him? she cried. *Doubtless he no longer loves me, and to render my torture crueler, my heart depicts him more lovable than I have ever seen him before. Let us die, and let him remain forever unaware of the extent to which he has rendered me unfortunate. Without that amour, without him, what regret can I have for life?*

It could not enter her head that that the king was in love with Cornue; she lost herself in everything that she was trying to arrange for her sojourn in the opal palace; she greatly regretted the timidity that she had had in fleeing Tigreline's palace in response to the song of the cock. In bringing together the few ideas she was able to have in that regard, she believed that the cock that had flown in through the window might well have been the same one whose form Cornue had changed on the eloquent lawn.

What a contrariety in my destiny, she thought. *It's necessary that my heart is only sensible to an object that makes me flee at every moment; foreseeing the end, waiting for death is one torture more. Coquerico, the ingrate Coquerico, has forgotten me, why seek to doubt it any longer? Come on, let us expire at the foot of the rose-bush, and flee forever a place that only serves to sharpen and redouble my dolor.*

Fortunately, the fays had not closed the door of the grotto; the deplorable princess went out. She found herself in Cornue's forest, and heard a loud noise of horns and dogs. She went into a dense part of the wood that seemed to her to be propitious for hiding. She wanted to let the hunt pass by. She had plunged under the branches when she heard a voice too dear for her to be able to mistake it. That voice was speaking to someone she soon recognized as being the fay Cornue.

"Yes, Madame, I confess that I have an invincible repugnance for hunting lions, since the unfortunate Lionnette has taken that form. I don't know what has become of her; you want to leave me ignorant of that; you even oppose the things that I might do in order to find out; you want me to die. Well, why should you oppose it, when your oracle demands it? Let me go to con-

171

sult it, or I will make use of my sword to deliver myself from a life that is insupportable to me because of our tyranny."

"How can you expect me," said the fay, "to let you go to that oracle, which demands your death? For it has no desire to have a cock in sacrifice rather than anther bird; it's you that the barbarian is demanding—and you think I would be able to resolve myself to that? I love you, and you hate me, that is my entire crime toward you, and if I returned Lionnette to you, you would forget even the feeble gratitude that you owe me."

"Me, forget it—never!" replied the king, hotly. "Me, forget that I would owe you the happiness of my life! Don't believe it. Return her to her ordinary form and I swear that I will grant you everything that can depend on me. You will reign forever over my will; my amity would be boundless. In sum, if my heart cannot be yours, at last there would be little difference, and even you cannot doubt it."

"Well," said the fay, "I will trust your oaths, and render to your impatience. Tomorrow we will go to the temple of the rose-bush; I will expose myself to its anger; I will try to appease it, and there, we shall see whether your words are inviolable."

With those words, the king and the fay drew away, and the princess, delighted to find her lover as faithful as she had thought him inconstant, directed her steps toward the rose-bush, and arrived there well into the night. All the flowers were asleep; she did not wake them; she went to lie down at the foot of the tuberose; she did not go to sleep.

The beautiful night, as it was then, filled her soul, already prepared to receive the pleasant impressions of a pure and unmixed joy; the lovable Coquerico, faithful

172

and amorous, was depicted in her imagination so worthy of being loved that she did not regret at all what she had suffered for him; it did not even enter into her thought that he was a king; she disdained everything that was only an advantage of fate. He was worthy to please her; that was the only thing that she considered.

Cornue's reproaches had revealed her jealously to her, so, in the blink of an eye, she understood why the fay had treated her so badly, and how the most fortunate amour is subject to opposition. She was afflicted by what the prince would have to suffer if he resisted the fay's amour. She already consented to sacrifice her lover to her rival if it would save his life, which the oracle said that he would lose if she opposed his choice.

Exceedingly dolorous reflections on that situation succeeded those that had occupied her so tenderly at first; she resolved to go and find the oracle without waiting any longer. In fact, she rose to her feet quietly and went into the temple as the first light of dawn appeared.

King Coquerico was not in such a mild situation. The horror that Cornue had inspired in him by her new barbarity, of wanting to make his mistress perish by his own hand, under the pretext of giving him the diversion of a lion hunt, had revolted his soul; his patience was at an end, and he had only pretended to consent to her desires in order to have the time to avenge himself more fully by taking away from her the necklace that was in her possession.

Fortunately, the fay had not seen the little bottle that he had under his wing on the day when she returned his form to him, so he still had it, and promised himself to make use of it. He retired early that evening, under the pretext of being fatigued, and the fay asked him to adorn himself the following day with the ornaments that she had ordered to be put in his room, in order to appear more worthy in the eyes of the rose-bush.

He was no sooner in his room than, thinking about what Cornue had said to him, and what he had promised, he fell into an excessive dolor at the idea that, if he did not anticipate the cleverness of the fay, he would only extract from that jealous enemy the pleasure of seeing Lionnette again, and that she would doubtless demand that he marry her.

That cruel thought armed his ardor for vengeance, all the more so because, having cast a glance over a large basket of filigree, pearls and garnets, which was on a table, he did not doubt that those were the presents with which she had said that she wanted him to adorn himself. He lifted up the white taffeta embroidered with gold that covered the gallant basket, and saw with an astonishment mingled with fury, royal garments like those that the kings of the Fortunate Isles wore on their wedding day; but as they were the works of fays, their magnificence was indescribable.

A moment later, thinking that he might appeared thus adorned to the eyes of the princess, he could not forbid himself a little complaisance in thinking that perhaps there would be need of that to please her. Believing that the fay was asleep, however, he resolved to follow his project, and, throwing all his adornments into the basket, he went out, in order to go to a hidden stairway that opened in Cornue's bedroom.

He arrived beside her bed without any obstacle; the curtains were open and retained by two amours of nacre and pearls, which were holding crystal girandoles full of candles to illuminate the room. When she had difficulty sleeping the amours sang, or read the latest news from a gazette, or new tales that were written about the fays;

that evening they must have read for as long as necessary, for she was snoring heartily.

She had not foreseen the undue visit of the king, for she had never been as ugly as she was in her bed; she was devoid of rouge and beauty spots; her livid and unhealthy skin gave the impression of a person already dead rather than that of an amorous fay; her horn completed rendering her hideous. She had the fatal necklace around her neck; her cleavage and her semi-naked arms would have disgusted the least delicate and most enterprising of men.

The king was, therefore, not retained by her charms; but, the sight of her having reawakened in him the desire to liberate himself from such an odious object, he took out his bottle.

As he tried to shake it over the fay, all the amours cried: "Who goes there?"

The fay opened her eyes, and the king stood there, more surprised and more afflicted than one can say.

"What do you want with me, prince?" she said to him, sitting up. "What design brings you to my room without having informed me?"

She could have asked him a thousand similar questions if she had had the inclination, for the king, more frightened by her ugliness than her menacing tone that she gave to her words, let her speak and made no response.

"What do you want, then?" she said, again. "Explain your designs to me."

"I am sorry, Madame, to have interrupted your repose," the king said, finally, "But, not knowing what your project is, before engaging myself to keep my word to you, I want to know what you demand of me."

"Would there not have been time tomorrow morning," said the fay, "to pose that fine difficulty to me. Was it necessary to wake me up to say such a futile thing to me? Go to bed, Sire. And tomorrow we will be in a fit state, you to propose and me to resolve."

The king was, in fact, unable to see any other means of getting out of the embarrassment, and was about to return to his room, when the fay called him back. The beauty of the young prince, augmented by the agitation of his soul, which had given his eyes and his complexion more vivacity than usual, his hair in disorder, falling over his shoulders with a negligent grace, the sound of his voice, and perhaps even the silence of the night, which gives ideas a force that the day sometimes effaces, awoke Cornue's desire.

"Come closer then?" she said. "Where are you going? Are you not going to beg pardon for your imprudence? Or do you think that you have not committed any?"

Annoyed by that new obstacle raised to the desire he had to withdraw, he prince said "Madame, don't make me commit a greater fault by troubling your repose any longer. It ought to be precious to me, and all that I owe you of respect...."

"No, no," said the fay. "Come closer; I no longer want to sleep, and I want absolutely to know what brought you here; have no fear of having offended me, but fear hiding your sentiments from me; I want a sincere confession of them." Looking at him with eyes in which she was trying to put a very tender languor, but in which he could only see extinct pupils, she went on: "I want you to entertain me in order to punish you for having woken me up,"

At that disagreeable proposition, the king nearly lost patience, but, being in the power of that terrible person, he suppressed his first impulse and sat down, as if out of respect, some distance from the fay's bed. "Since you order it, Madame," he said, "I will obey you. I came, thinking that you were not yet asleep, to ask you to restore the princess, at this moment, to her ordinary form, and to declare to you that without that, I cannot go with you to the temple of the rose-bush."

"In truth," said the fay, rather piqued by that beginning, "that's a fine subject to raise such alarms. Couldn't it wait until tomorrow?"

"No, Madame," said the king, "And I'm annoyed not to have seen you put more urgency into it yesterday, without putting me in the necessity of waiting another day."

"Well," said the fay, "what will you do for me afterwards"

"I've told you, Madame. The most tender amity, and everything more that a sensitive heart can give...."

"Of amity?" said the fay. "No, no, King Coquerico. It's not at that price that I dispense my graces; I need more than that."

"What do you want me to say?"

"Isn't it worth the trouble, either, of waiting until tomorrow for me to inform you? I can't demand amour from you, I agree; you're incapable of feeling it for me, you've made me understand; but I'll forgive you on condition that tomorrow, you give me a formal pledge of your faith."

The king, fully prepared as he was for that eventuality by Tigreline, could not hear that speech tranquilly and see himself so close to renouncing forever the princess he loved without feeling a cruel dolor."

"If my heart were free," he said, finally, in a tone of voice changed by the excess of the violence he was exerting not to explode, "I could offer you both, but Madame, I have disposed of my heart by virtue of a power above mine, and I cannot give you a hand whose possession would render you too unhappy, since at every instant, involuntarily, I would make you sense that, my heart being separated from it, I would be unworthy of the honor that you had done me. The gratitude that I owe you forces me to refuse absolutely, even at the peril of my life."

"We will see about that tomorrow," said Cornue finally. "Go and fortify or change your noble resolutions; but remember that if you resist mine, it is not your life that will answer to me for it. Perhaps I shall be able to find, in spite of you, the sensitive place of a heart that you assure me is so indifferent."

The king, beside himself with anger and dolor, went out and returned to his apartment, where he abandoned himself to the cruelest despair. Twenty times he wanted to pierce his heart with his sword and make a sacrifice of his life to the princess, but, remembering that he might perhaps be able to avenge her better, or at least save her from the fay's fury, he suspended that frightful project and resolved to go to the temple of the roe-bush.

As soon as daylight appeared, the fay's palace resounded with the noise of instruments and wedding songs; she sent to ask whether he was ready, and gave the order that he was already to be served as her husband. A pompous carriage was in the courtyard of the palace; all the fays of the region, and even of the world, had been invited to the ceremony; they were arriving from all directions. Tigreline only let it be known that she would be present at the temple. Finally, the prince appeared; his pale and distraught face marked, however, that he was the victim of the sacrifice, the one that was about to be offered. Even so, he was more beautiful than the day. Cornue was dressed as a queen; all the art in the world had been employed in her adornment.

She climbed into her carriage with the king, and all the fays followed, in accordance with their rank, borne on eagles, dragons, tigers or leopards. Twelve young and beautiful fays of Cornue's court led twelve lionesses on leashes, to which the king attached his eyes, throughout the journey, trying to discern whether the unfortunate Lionnette was among them. They progressed to the sound of trumpets and drums, and they arrived at the lawn of eloquence.

The flowers were already at the limits, and had formed two palisades six feet high, between which the brilliant cortege passed to the sound of their acclamations and songs of joy. The temple was full of them. The most beautiful had formed two thrones of exquisite taste, and the sight was surprising, so well arranged were they.

The unfortunate Lionnette was already in the temple, and the pleasure of seeing Tigreline arrive there, who had recognized her immediately, had suspended slightly dolor that she had in being a witness to the happiness of her cruel rival.

"I shall die, Madame," she said to the fay, "but at least tell the king after my death that my tenderness was equal to his and that I forgive him for a sin that fate caused him to commit. I do not criticize his inconstancy."

She wept so bitterly on finishing those words, and her soul was pressed by such a sharp dolor, that she did not see the king and the fay enter.

Cornue approached the rose-bush first. "I have come," she said, "to disengage my word. Your orders, divinity of this place, demanded of me the sacrifice of a cock; I have understood your oracle fully; here is the one you demanded, and I believe that I understand the meaning in demanding of him, at the foot of your altar, a faith that he is so reluctant to give me; that sacrifice is for him much greater than that of his life."

The rose-bush lowered its leaves and its flowers, as if to approve the fay's words.

Then Cornue turned toward the king, who had remained slightly behind her. "Approach, Sire," she said to him. "Come and fulfill the will of destiny."

At that moment, he was much more occupied with what he could see than what was being said to him; he had perceived Tigreline, and had no doubt that the lioness that was beside her was his divine princess; he gazed at her tenderly and dolorously, not daring to approach for fear of displeasing Tigreline, who had made him a severe gesture to forbid it.

Cornue, surprised by his silence, turned toward him, and saw him in that pleasant occupation; then, placing on the altar the crown that she was holding in her hand, in order for the king to place it on her head, she approached him.

"What are you doing, then?" she said. "Is this a time for dreaming?"

"I am waiting for you to respond, Madame," said the king, without being greatly moved. "For you to render the princess of the Golden Isle the form that you have so unjustly stolen from her; afterwards, I will do what my gratitude demands, and I shall not deceive you."

Cornue, seeing that it was not a time to recoil, all the more so as she could see Tigreline present, her superior in power, and because the day she had chosen for the ceremony was precisely the one on which fays are subject to death. She had carefully refrained from telling the king that, for fear that he might profit from the twenty-four hours to avenge himself for the cruelties that she had exercised upon him, but had not wanted to delay her happiness. Seeing that it was impossible to deceive the king again, she turned to Tigreline, who led the lioness to the altar.

"My sister," she said to her, detaching the necklace and giving it to the fay, "I return the princess to you, and you can make use of your power to enable her to resume her form; but spare her the chagrin of seeing her lover's hands crown me and depart with her, since she cannot be his."

Tigreline had not wasted a moment; rather than respond to Cornue, that good fay had touched Lionnette with her wand, and the princess was already more beautiful and more lovable than ever; by virtue of the cares of the fay she was dressed magnificently and even more elegantly; she was wearing a costume of silver cloth covered with garlands of flax-gray immortelles; her beautiful blonde hair, sprinkled with diamonds and flax-gray flowers, like her garment, fell in curls over her shoulders and rendered hr more beautiful than the day.

The king was beside himself; he advanced toward her and put one knee on the ground.

"Will you suffer, beautiful princess," he said, "that the faith I gave you should be stolen, and that the unjust fay who has rendered us so unhappy will enjoy tranquilly a crown that can only be yours?"

Princess Lionnette, while her lover was talking to her, kept her eyes upon him tenderly, and by the tears that were flowing slowly over her cheeks she made visible all the effort that she was making in order to yield. Finally, she said: "I cannot oppose destiny; yes, my dear prince, it is necessary for you to submit to it; I render you your oaths; live happily without me, if it is possible for you; and since it is necessary that I lose you, I shall quit this life without regret, and find myself happy, in dying, to have been able without crime to tell you once again that I love you."

"Yes, you shall die!" cried the furious Cornue. "That's enough of insulting me, and you shall also take away the pleasure that you have not counted among those that you enjoy at this fatal moment."

At those words, the king got up from the knees of the princess, who was not afraid to see her rival advancing toward with a dagger in her hand. The king stopped the fay with one hand and, drawing his sword with the other, said: "It's me who will immolate myself," he cried, "and you cannot attempt the life of my princess without mine answering for it."

"O gods! Stop!" cried the fay and Lionnette simultaneously.

Tigreline then advanced toward Cornue. She had not said anything thus far; she had allowed all those to act and speak who had had the most urgency. She raised her wand and touched Cornue. "Receive today," she said to her, "the price of your sins, and be witness in your turn to the happiness of these two lovers."

At those words, Cornue remained immobile, but her eyes lit up with a fury so terrible that, finding no expression, her horn caught fire and she foamed with rage.

"And you, sage rose-bush," said Tigreline, "finally resume your form and enjoy the pleasure of embracing your lovely daughter."

She had not finished speaking when the rose-bush, having shaken momentarily, appeared under his veritable form. He was a man of about fifty, nobly made and magnificently dressed; he had a long royal mantle and a crown of gold and gems on his head. Lionnette resembled him so perfectly that no one in the assembly had any doubt that she was his daughter.

The beautiful princess threw herself into his arms, with a haste so natural that the whole assembly was moved. The good king received her with transports of joy that would have been further extended if that prince had not perceived the young king of the Fortunate Isles at his feet, who was embracing his knees; he quit his daughter momentarily in order to lift up the handsome Coquerico.

"I give you my daughter," he said to him, embracing him, "receive her, and live as happily as I have seen you close to the contrary. I will join my crown to that present; I do not count on it adding to your happiness, given the contradiction it has brought to the repose of my life, but such as it is, I give it to my daughter in order to present it to you."

At that moment, the prince wanted to take off his crown.

"No, Sire," cried the young king. "You shall not cease to reign; the charming and tender Lionnette fulfills all my wishes, and my crown is at her feet; suffer that we live with you, and that nothing will ever separate us again.

Tigreline applauded that mark of generosity on King Coquerico's part and, taking Lionnette by the hand, presented her to him. He received her with transports of amour that are easier to imagine than to describe. Then he took off his crown and, putting one knee on the ground, he presented it to Lionnette, who received it in giving him her faith.

Wedding songs resounded in the temple; they were only interrupted by Cornue, who uttered a piercing scream and expired, being in her fatal day. That did not appear extraordinary; only the king and the princess seemed touched by the excess of that despair. Tigreline had her taken away, and the ceremony was concluded.

King Coquerico then turned to his father-in-law, and asked him whether he desired to come and witness the coronation of Queen Lionnette, ot whether he wanted to stay in that place for a few days.

"And I," said Lionnette, "have a favor to ask of the kind Tigreline and my dear husband, if I dare to speak at this moment."

"My dear princess," replied the king, tenderly, "what do you have to fear?"

"I would like, then," said the princess, "that, rid of the cares of our royalty, we could always live together here, and that, content with my happiness, I could occupy myself with nothing but the pleasure of enjoying it. It is here that I have recovered what I have that is most dear; what does the rest of the world matter, if I live with these two persons, and if you, Madame," she added, addressing the fay, "deign to come to see us here, and will return my two faithful guardians to me?"

"I consent to that," said the two kings, simultaneously.

"Yes, my daughter," said the fay, in her turn, "I approve of that nobility of sentiment, and you shall live here as a queen, but without sensing any inconvenience in it; and both of you will enjoy the gift of enchantment, which I shall give you."

Then, touching the palisade walls, she transformed them into a palace of emerald so brilliant and so magnificent that nothing had ever been seen so beautiful and so perfect. The flowers became living and speaking people, having as the sole mark of their metamorphosis a flower of their name on the head. The meadow became a magnificent garden; on one side, a vast forest appeared, on one edge of which the fay erected a little palace of rose and white marble; and on the other, one of rock crystal, in which she had the intention of putting the beautiful map of the world that had been the delight of the king's youth. The princess was delighted by it.

"For me," said the king, "it is an inestimable present; it will incessantly retrace for me the pleasure I had in exploring it, in order to find my dear princess there."

"And it will be dear to me," she said, "since it told you that I was occupied with you."

The fay was charmed to see them so happy, by virtue of an amour so rare in our present century, and even in the one in which they were living then. "Always love one another thus, my children," she said, embracing them. "I cannot give you anything preferable to that wealth; it is unique, and the only veritable one."

She also showed them that each palace had its separate gardens, waterfalls, fountains and charming flower beds. On the other side of the garden was a broad and full river, on which there were a thousand superb gondolas, silver and flax-gray; the river led to a manor house entirely made of flowers, the marvelous variety of which formed an admirable view, and which stood on a mountain, the terraced gardens of which descended all the way to the river, and which served the country house as a lawn.

"I give you all this," said Tigreline. "Live here, my children, for millions of years; your subjects will love you, and will not betray you. If you want any more, a stroke of the wand"—she gave hers to Lionnette—"will change all the flowers into speaking and reasoning people, and they will become flowers again at your whim."

The king and Lionnette threw themselves at the fay's knees and thanked her tenderly; she lifted them up and embraced them again.

"Give a thrust of your wand," she said to the princess," in order that your guardians have the pleasure of being recalled by you."

The beautiful Lionnette acquitted that first proof of her power urgently; the good people appeared instantly. She ran to embrace them; they dared not receive her caresses at first, but the beautiful queen pressed them so tenderly that they returned her embraces with a tenderness that drew tears from the entire assembly.

The queen, seeing them so exhausted and decrepit, turned her beautiful moist eyes to the fay, who understood that she was suffering.

"I like to see you so sensitive, Madame," said Tigreline. "Use your power; you could not employ it better than for what you presently desire."

"Well," said the queen, "I wish that they become again the age that I am, and that they always live with me." She had not finished speaking when the old man and his wife appeared, he was a man of twenty and she a woman of eighteen. They prostrated themselves at the fay's feet and kissed the hands of the queen, who, delighted to see them so young and so amiable, embraced the fay in order to thank her for that favor.

The good king then addressed his daughter, who was already turning her eyes toward him tenderly. "Don't wish the same thing for me, my dear daughter. I don't want to experience a new youth. I see you happy; that is the only thing that is able to touch me; I could not experience another joy so sensible; leave it to the gods to dispose of my days."

"It is for me," said the fay, "to render them happy. You shall live, Sire, and you will only cease to live when you hate life enough to want to lose it. Adieu; I shall leave you. I shall come back incessantly to see you but my affairs oblige me to separate from you."

The queen escorted the fay back to her chariot; the two kings aided her to climb into it. After that, they returned to their palace, where, charmed to be together, they spent days spun in gold and silk, happier than if they had never been unhappy. They lived for millions of years, and the king and the queen gave the world benevolent fays and genii, which are presently occupied in making the happiness of the world.

PRINCE FROZEN AND PRINCESS SPAR-KLING

In the realm of Scythia, under the coldest of all climates, a prince once reigned who was as insensitive in his temperament as the ice of his homeland. He had become king early in life, and, in consequence, delivered himself to all the pleasures that age and the flattering advice of courtiers had inspired in him. He was handsome and marvelous, and no mortal or celestial creature had ever combined so many graces and talents, but his heart had never been able to take pleasure in tenderness; he was astonished that anyone could be attached to something, and his coldness went as far as finding it extraordinary that people should try to please him. He was called Frozen.

The beauties of his court were in despair; ten or twelve princesses of the blood. more beautiful than the day, had already died of chagrin at his indifference. His only occupation was hunting white bears, and he spent his life doing that. He was already twenty-three years old when his subjects assembled to beg him to think about marrying. He nearly fainted with surprise when it was proposed to him, so much distaste had he for a knot that would attach him to a woman. He promised that he would think about it, but at the same time he promised himself firmly that he would not think about it soon.

However, his principal ministers secretly sent messengers to all courts to seek portraits of the most beautiful princesses, and had five or six dozen made of him, in order to charm those who saw them. They ordered, above all, that it was necessary to find a princess whose soul was a little less cold than that of the prince, in order not to risk losing the fruit of an alliance which had already cost them so much difficulty.

Not far from that country reigned a queen who had only one daughter, who was not only beautiful but was so susceptible to tenderness that the queen guarded her carefully, in order that she did not fall into the inconvenience of loving someone who was not suitable. It was in vain; the princess had a vivid imagination, and merely on seeing a portrait she could lose the will to eat, drink and even sleep, over the person it represented; her women were occupied day and night in consoling the chagrins that her chimerical tenderness caused her.

It was even worse when the portrait of Prince Frozen arrived at the court. The queen wanted it to be hidden from Sparkling—that was the name of the princess—but the nurse, who had no other resource to cure her of a mad infatuation that she had just conceived for a statue representing Adonis, ran to take it to her. Now she was mad about the prince. The queen had a little more complaisance for her extravagance at that moment, and resolved to grant the hand of the princess as quickly as possible, more in order to be rid of her than to see her established.

She was proposed; she waited in mortal impatience for the response.

As it was a desirable and very convenient alliance, Prince Frozen's council assembled, and finally extracted his consent. Sparkling's head almost spun. The ceremony was held in the queen's abode. She wanted to leave beforehand, but after all, it was necessary that everything be prepared to conduct her in a dignified manner. She departed with the nurse, several ladies of the court and, above all, the portrait of the prince, of which she did not want to lose sight.

The queen instructed the nurse secretly not to quit the princess, fearing that Prince Frozen's ambassador, who was escorting her, and who was young and handsome, might make her daughter forget the portrait. The nurse promised all her cares, and the entire company set forth.

Frozen, very embarrassed by the word that he had given and already frightened of the constraint to which he was about to submit himself, resolved, in order not to hear any mention of the fêtes that would be held on the occasion of the marriage, to go and spend a few days in a manor house he had had built in the middle of a forest for a hunting rendezvous, and await the arrival of the princess there, without being obliged to go to meet her.

He set forth, accompanied by a single squire, and gave orders that she was to be received if she arrived, and above all, that no one should come to inform him—because, he added, he wanted to surprise her. It was thought that the portrait of the princess had made some impression on his heart, and no one made any objection to that step, so much gallantry was found therein, in the belief that he was departing incognito in that manner in order to see her. The celebrations were redoubled, and in spite of the rigor of the winter, people had never been so greatly amused.

The prince arrived at his country house, and spent his days running on a sleigh along a frozen river that bordered the forest. At other times, armed with a short spear, he went to search for bears in their caverns and combated them perilously, but with marvelous skill.

One day, when he was searching the depths of one of those caverns for a bear that had taken refuge there, he heard a voice, which said to him: "Advance, Prince Frozen, and if you do not fear the danger of loving the most beautiful thing that there is in nature, and simultaneously the most insensitive, you can come all the way here."

In spite of the obscurity of the cavern, the prince advanced rather a long way; but as he could not see anything, and no longer heard the voice, he shouted and asked where it was necessary to go.

"Advance without dread," replied the voice, which seemed very far ahead of him, "and come without delay."

He continued to advance, and it seemed to him that he was descending a narrow and winding path. Finally, after having descended for about three hours, he glimpsed a little daylight; he asked whether it was necessary to continue. No one replied to him any longer, which surprised him. However, he continued on his way and entered a vast grotto, the vault and walls of which were covered in a crystal so pure and so beautiful that he was dazzled by it.

In the middle of the grotto was a large and deep basin, from which a jet of water rose all the way to the vault, as beautiful as the crystal coating the walls; it was bordered by a marble as white as snow. Thousands of candles in crystal chandeliers illuminated that beautiful place, and ledges of white marble formed sofas and very comfortable armchairs around the walls. He sat down on one of those seats, and as he did not see anyone, nor was he able to hear the voice and longer, he made the decision, being very weary, to go to sleep. He was lulled into a profound slumber by the sound of the water falling back into the basin.

Meanwhile, Sparkling was arriving in long daily stages; the cold did not stop her; her impatience and her desire to see her husband sustained her. Finally, she was due to arrive the next day. Surprised that the prince had not yet come to meet her, she had asked the ambassador more than once why that was; he, knowing the prince's temperament, had tried to warn her about what she had to fear therefrom, but he had not been able to convince her yet, so distant was she from believing that anyone could be born indifferent.

The nurse had always obliged the princess to wear a veil during the journey, in order to hide the people who were with her from her sight; she had not even permitted the ambassador to see her with her face uncovered; but as they were due to arrive the following day, the princess wanted, in spite of anything anyone could say to her, to have supper in public and show that she was worthy of a little more concern than she thought that people were showing her. She adorned herself, in spite of everything that could be done to prevent her, and did not appear at all bad. The acclamations she received on seeing her consoled her a little for the attentions that the king was refusing.

As queens in Scythia make their entrance on horse-back, the princess wanted to mount up at the gate to the city. The nurse applauded herself for her cares, which had succeeded so well; but that was because the amorous princess had only been occupied with the portrait during the journey, having not even thought that there were other men in the world than the one she had placed in her fantasy.

The horse that was brought to her by the prime minister was so beautiful and so richly harnessed that the princess was surprised by it, but she could not imagine why the king did not appear. She was keenly piqued by that, which caused her to mount the beautiful horse without thinking of responding to the elegant compliment that the man presenting it to her paid her, and, spurring it with sufficient grace and force, she entered at a fast gallop.

Urged on by the princess, the horse traversed the city, passing through like an arrow; the cries of the rest of the cavalcade redoubled her ardor, and enabled her to outdistance the best of the cavaliers who were trying to keep up with her; she held firm and was not frightened, while her mount carried her over mountains and valleys.

Toward the end of the day, the horse launched itself to a cavern, where it collapsed, throwing the princess to the ground some distance away.

She heard someone sighing nearby, and recovered her senses somewhat. She began to be frightened; she wanted to get out of the cavern, but an invisible hand retained her, and she heard someone say: "Why are you running away, Princess Sparkling? My amour for you has caused me to attempt everything in order to achieve your conquest and to try to please you."

"Who are you?" cried the princess, half-dead with fear.

"I am an unfortunate prince if you flee me," the voice replied, "but at the peak of happiness if you would care to give me your faith."

The princess was somewhat nonplussed by that proposal, but, becoming accustomed to the prodigies of the cavern and making the reflection that Frozen, charming as he might be, had not taken a step to merit her, she finally replied: "I have already pledged my faith to a king, who has not set much store by it, and if it turns out to be possible to take it back, if only to avenge myself, I will promise to give it to you."

"But will you promise me not to love him any longer?" said the voice.

"I'm entirely ready to do that," said the princess, "but I can't promise to be the mistress of it if I see him."

"Well," said the voice, "throw away his dangerous portrait and trust in my guidance. I love you too much to constrain you; if you don't love me I'll respect your choice and return you to the exceedingly fortunate Frozen."

At those words, the princess threw the portrait of the prince against the wall, without reflecting about what might happen to it, and from a corner of the cavern a little ray of light appeared, which allowed her to see a magnificent carriage drawn by six white eagles, which lifted her up in a trice above the clouds.

After having flown for a long time, the eagles finally landed in the marvelous gardens of a palace that was even more marvelous. There was nothing but flower beds, arbors, bowling greens, woods of tall trees, roes and jasmines, waterfalls, fountains and canals, which provided a delightful freshness when the sun was at its zenith. She went via a path through the wood into a cabinet that formed the corner of the building. Although transparent, the walls were prodigiously thick, and seemed to be of the nature of rubies; they were, in fact, constructed of them.

She went through immense apartments, each more beautiful and richly furnished than the last, but no mortal appeared there. She stayed there until dusk without seeing or hearing anything that might inform her as to where she was. Hunger and solitude began to torment her. Having thrown herself on to a sofa and closed her eyes in order to try to sleep and to reflect on the deadly consequences that her reckless intrepidity might have, she was surprised to hear a miraculous concert.

Opening her eyes, she saw with astonishment the palace illuminated, as if for a fête, and a magnificent meal served close by, with only two places set. She stood up precipitately; then a very comfortable armchair full of cushions approached her. She was about to sit down when the doors of the drawing room that she was in opened precipitately.

All that the imagination can present of the most perfect and the most agreeable can only approach distantly the object that appeared to Sparkling's eyes; nothing was as beautiful, nor as worthy of amour. That celestial creature was a prince of about eighteen or twenty years of age. A gauze garment the color of fire and gold, knotted by a diamond belt, dressed him gallantly, and was fastened by precious stones with abundant grace. His white-powdered and curly hair fell with a simple and natural elegance all the way to his waist. A crown of diamonds mingled with emerald leaves completed his adornment. He approached the princess rapidly, who dared not breathe, so much was she gripped by rapture. He put one knee on the floor and kissed the hand that she extended in order to lift him up.

"I owe you everything, Madame," he said, with a grace that finished convincing her that it was futile to look for a fault in him. "You have rendered me life by being kind enough to love me, or at least allowing me to hope that you might; it is by virtue of an amour without limits and beyond measure that I ought to recognize that service, and I am even more disposed to that by the sight of you than by my gratitude. Yes, beautiful Sparkling, I will always love you, but in order to complete my happiness, it is necessary no longer to be infidel to me, and you will make me the happiest person in the world."

The princes would have let him talk for an hour, so ecstatic was she, but for that final sentence, which appeared to her to be a trifle equivocal.

"Dare I ask you, Sire," she said, finally, "why you are reproaching me for having been infidel to you? Have I ever seen you before? Have I promised you...."

"Oh, Madame!" said the prince, "let me efface that cruel moment from my memory; I ought to forget it in this one, it's true, but can one defend oneself from such an unfortunate memory, when one is not yet assured of the happiness that one desires enough to fear that it might escape us? Afterwards, if you order it, I will remind you of that which has passed from memory. Permit me to offer you, in my palace, everything that might please you; I shall be fortunate if I can succeed in that!"

Then the armchair with cushions drew nearer, and the princess went to table. She begged the prince to sit down too, which he did not want to do, out of gallantry, wanting to serve her himself; but there was no need, the dishes rose up and came to place themselves of their own accord; the bottles and cups came at their orders, and the concert went on throughout the time they were at table.

During the supper the prince and the princess did nothing but look at one another, almost not eating. In order to gaze at him, the princess adopted the pretext of trying to recognize him; in fact, there were moments when she believed that she did, but it was fruitlessly that she tried to recall where she might have seen him. As for him, he said fine and touching things to her, which per-

196

suaded her that if she had seen him, she would have loved him in preference to everything.

Finally, the meal having finished, he gave her his hand in order to pass into a magnificent drawing rom. She sat down on a sofa, and the prince on a golden cushion at her knees, whatever she could say to him.

He commenced the story of his adventures, which she awaited with the utmost impatience, very glad to have the pretext to listen to him for a little longer, for she was beginning to fear allowing too much to be presumed for a first evening if she engaged in conversation.

"I am the Prince of the Sylphs, Madame," he told her, and my power is equal to that of the fays; however, it can be limited when we are unfortunate enough to love one of them; in that case, she has complete power over us and we only recover our own when, by chance, being transformed, a mortal is able to fall in love with us; but it is necessary that she love us with the most exact fidelity, for it she fails in that, even in the slightest, the fay resumes her power and punishes us with the same rigor, and even more rudely, since she combines it with the punishment of the person who has betrayed us.

"We do not grow old; we are always equally lovable and amorous. We inhabit the immense space that separates the firmament, we traverse the seas, we descend into the utmost depths without dread, all the way to the center of the earth; in sum, nothing is impossible for us, except for discovering a faithful mistress, even at the price of the immortality that we offer her, and that we extend to her. In the thousand years that I have lived, I have not been able to find one who dared to accept it."

"What, Sire!" the princess interjected, "you live for a thousand years and you appear to be twenty forever?"

"Yes, Madame," he replied, "and if you are faithful to me, you will always be as beautiful and appear as young as you are today."

"Go on," she said "I'm dying to know how I was able to risk losing that good fortune."

The amorous sylph sensed all the delicacy of that response, and, kissing her hand with transport, he picked up the thread of his discourse.

"I had the honor of telling you, Madame, that I am the Prince of Sylphs. While traveling one day the vast empire submissive to my power, I descended into a delightful garden, and you can judge that, since it was this one. I allowed my eagles to rest, and, seeking coolness, I advanced into a grove of myrtles and pomegranates which is in the corner of the wood of roses. I found on a bed of grass the person that I would declare to be the most beautiful in the world if I had not seen you. She was asleep; her negligent attitude allowed me to glimpse beauties that her modesty would have hidden from me if she had been awake.

"I admired for a long time, with transports of amour, that ravishing model of perfection, but in the end, the setting sun let one of its rays pass through the branches, and when it struck the eyes of the fay—for she was one—she opened them. What charms they added to her beauty! I remained motionless, not knowing whether the sun was illuminating me or whether the divine light emanating from her eyes was the one that was shining in the grove.

"Fortunately, I was invisible—we also have that power, when it pleases us—so I was able to follow her without being perceived; but the violence of my amour would not permit me to remain silent for long. What can I add, Madame? I spoke, I was heard; my tenderness was answered. Why were you not born? I would never have loved anyone but you. In sum, I pleased a charming fay for two hundred years, but what time does not come to an end?

"One day, when I was with her in a gallery of this palace, looking at the portraits of the beauties that were praised in the new century, she presented me with yours. I could not see it without a certain emotion, which was noticed by the jealous fay; I tried in vain to hide the impression that you were beginning to make in my heart; she was not duped, its movements had been too natural to be mistaken, and the habit of being loved had given her the conviction that she always would be, so she perceived that change in me sooner than I did.

"I used the pretext of several affairs in my realm in order to go away, and in order to see you without her being able to be offended by it or suspecting it. I succeeded several times, but finally, she found me out, and her fury was extreme. After having heaped me with the cruelest reproaches, which only irritated my tenderness for you and destroyed without remorse what I had felt for her, I quit her and flew to your palace.

"One evening, having already entered your chamber in order to reveal my amour to you, I felt someone seize me by the hair and, having transported me into the gardens, the implacable fay left me on a pedestal and changed me into a statue…."

"What!" said the princess. "It was you who were Adonis? Oh, I can't doubt it. Yes, I recognize you."

But let us leave Sparkling to learn the story of the prince of the Sylphs and return to Prince Frozen, whom we left so profoundly asleep in the crystal grotto. He was woken up by a rather loud noise, caused by the voices of several women who were laughing and chatting together.

He opened his eyes and saw a marvelous individual bathing in the beautiful basin of clear and silvery water, surrounded by several ladies who would have seemed to be the most beautiful creatures in the world if the one who was in the bath had left him the time to admire them. A kind of veil of white gauze covered her; she was sitting on the edge of the basin, and one of her nymphs was occupied in braiding her beautiful blonde hair while the others brought her flowers, precious stones, rouge and beauty spots.

The prince dared not move, and did not even think of it, so amazed was he to see such rare beauty. Fearing that it was a dream, he opened his eyes as wide as he could. As for the lady in the bath and those of her retinue, they were agitating and talking as if he were not present; they did not perceive either him or his ecstasy; they were talking about the pleasure one has in bathing, the concerns of one's toilette and everything that might depend on it. The beautiful person who was being coiffed smiled graciously at the praise her nymphs were giving her; she only spoke to tell them to finish her adornment promptly; she seemed hardly touched by the effect that her charms produced on their eyes as they were augmented.

Finally, after being dressed in a robe of white taffeta, knotted with garlands of flowers matching her coiffure, she stood up, and her figure then appeared in all its majesty. The prince nearly uttered a cry of admiration, but his voice was retained by the surprise caused to him by the event that followed. That miraculous person, having cast her eyes on the king with surprise, plunged into the basin; all the ladies fled, and everything disappeared from his sight, even the grotto and the candles, for he found himself on the edge of the cavern where he had pursued his bear.

The day being about to end, he remounted his horse and went back to the manor house, so occupied with what he had seen, or thought he had seen, that when he arrived there he went to bed without waiting any supper and without speaking to the young squire whom he had brought with him. It was not in order to sleep that Frozen went to bed; if he had wanted to it would have been impossible for him. The unparalleled beauty of the nymph of the grotto did not allow him a moment of repose.

Who is that beauty? he thought. *No, she cannot be a mortal, judging by the emotions I feel; she must be a goddess, for who else could inspire me with them, having seen without emotion the most beautiful women in the world attempting to enable me to know amour? I resisted them without any effort, but this one, merely by the sight of her, has set my soul ablaze with an unknown fire. Oh, wretch! Is Amour, then, avenging himself by means of an image that cannot have any reality? It was doubtless a dream, for only imagination could have forged such a marvel. Oh, Sparkling! Avenge yourself, you and all those I have scorned; come and see me languish and consume myself for the most beautiful, but the cruelest, of all chimeras.*

The poor prince was in despair. Finally, after having tortured his imagination, he got up, lit a candle, and in order to distract himself, took from his pocket the portrait of Sparkling that had been sent to him. What a difference he found there! How insipid her face was, compared with the one that was engraved in his memory, or, rather, his heart! What were the faded blue eyes of Sparkling by comparison with the beautiful dark, bright and modest eyes that he had seen raised upon him in all their majesty? What vivacity there was in the incarnadine of the latter's cheeks and lips, compared with the pallor of the former!

He found an insupportable insipidity in the portrait. That was not the fault of the person it represented, but that of the person it did not represent, for Sparkling was, in truth, beautiful, but even though that was the case, how could she approach the celestial beauty that the king of Scythia had been allowed to see?

"It is very cruel to find such little resource in a portrait in which one searches for so much," he cried, "and it is very unfortunate to be a prince in the situation I am in! For how can I love the princess who has been sent to me, when my heart can scarcely suffice for the one I desire?"

He was quite astonished to find himself talking about his heart, having always regarded with scorn anyone who had taken the liberty of assuring him that he had one and that he would realize it one day. Unable to sleep, he summoned his squire, who was a young man with a good deal of intelligence, and confided to him everything he had seen and everything that as agitating him.

The surprised confidant could not prevent himself from showing his joy at seeing him sensible, but as a skillful politician, he extended himself more on the sympathy he had for the difficulties that sensibility was bound to cause him. "For after all, Sire," he said, "you have given your word to Princess Sparkling, and that of kings is inviolable."

"Hence my despair!" cried the prince. "How can I love an object that has so much opposition to the one that enchants me? If I were still in my ordinary situation,

I would not offend her in appearing insensitive, but to-day, she might attribute my coldness to my distaste, and I could not deny it, for it would be only too certain."

"But also, Sire," said young Nix—that was the confidant's name—"why fill your mind with an object that might be chimerical, in order to leave a princess about whom everything you are told is marvelous? For a man less preoccupied, those charms might appear worthy of admiration; her presence, you see, might develop in you amorous sentiments that you don't suspect. It's said that she is very eager to please you, and you have been told that she's incapable of causing difficulty. Throughout your story, have you ever said that the other even deigned to perceive that you were present? When you thought that she perceived you, did she not flee? Expel the idea of her from your mind and fill it with that of Sparkling."

"Unfortunate condition of princes!" the king interjected. "People torment me to abandon my indifference, but they don't want me to follow the penchant that extracts me from it; either return it to me or let me love the only object that my heart has been able to choose! There is no option henceforth but amour or the cruelest aversion."

Nix allowed the first impulse to pass; the soul of the young king was too agitated for him to oppose the torrent that was dragging it away. He commiserated with him, he consoled him, and finally succeeded in getting him to agree that, having given his ambassadors the authority to marry him, he must, at least, not go back to the cavern, and ought to allow time to destroy an idea that a single instant had engraved so profoundly.

He passed very sad days. Nix did not abandon him, and followed him into the wood or along the river when he went out. In the meantime, the ministers of his council came to inform him of the accident that had befallen the queen on the day of the cavalcade. They had delayed for a few days, believing that they might find her, but having discovered her horse dead in the cavern where it had thrown her and no trace of the princess, they believed that she had been devoured by bears and came to give that opinion to the king.

That news caused him a surge of joy so sensible that, although he lamented such an unfortunate death, he left his subjects in no doubt of the profound aversion that he continued to have for women in general. He ordered, however, that new searches should be made, and that someone should come from time to time to inform him in his retreat, where he said that he still wanted to remain for a few days, as to what had been discovered regarding the life or death of the unfortunate Sparkling.

That solitude did not have the approval of his confidant; he foresaw that isolation would only augment the dolor and amour of the king, whereas the occupations and amusements of the court were more appropriate to cure a passion that could only be chimerical. No longer having to fear the engagement that had caused him to flee, he resolved to talk to him about returning, and to try to extract him from ideas that the woods and the idleness of life could only maintain. At the first word he tried to pronounce, however, the king anticipated him and shut his mouth, communicating to him the project that he had of returning to the cavern, since he could now give his heart to the beautiful person who had appeared to him without any scruple.

Nix found him inflexible; he had resolved to finish a life that could only be importunate without her; thus, he could go and inform the nobles of the realm that if he had not returned in a year, they could choose a king at their whim, and govern on his behalf in the meantime.

Surprised by a project so disadvantageous to his master, Nix represented its inconveniences to him with a great deal of intelligence and mildness, but he gained nothing, except that the king wrote to his council himself to communicate his will, and permitted Nix to go with him and not to abandon him.

In fact, after several days of delay, obtained with difficulty, in order to wait for confirmation of the loss of the princess, he gave the letter to his prime minister to read to the assembled council, and departed the following morning with Nix to go to the cavern.

He had brought what was needed for illumination, in order to penetrate into the subterrain if he did not find the same facilities as he had the first time. Having left their horses to graze, he put on a magnificent coat, which he had brought by design, and penetrated into the cavern by the light of a hooded lantern that Nix carried ahead of him.

They searched for the subterrain with care, but did not discover any trace of it. What confusion, and what despair for the prince! Nix dared not look at him, fearing that he would read his eyes the conviction he had that the adventure had only been a dream. The prince, beside himself with fury, did not speak, but he did not weary of searching; he did not want to leave the cavern, in order that Nix would not believe that he doubted having been able to recognize it. In fact, he could not have made a mistake; there were others, but that one could not be other than remarkable once it had been seen.

After a scrupulous examination of all the nooks and crannies of its concavities, he sat down on the ground and, crossing his arms over his stomach, he inclined his head and sank into the most bitter reflections. Nix dared not interrupt him, but finally, seeing the king's tears flow, he said: "Sire, we cannot doubt that enchantment enters into this; the beauty that appeared to you only wanted to surprise you, and doubtless she doesn't want anyone to find her."

"Oh, my dear Nix," cried the prince, relieved to be put at his ease regarding the adventure, "I can see that the cruel person, whatever she might be, is taking pleasure in rendering me unhappy, and I cannot complain to her about the few woes that she is making me suffer but I shall not quit this cavern until I can have some news of her. My cries and my plaints might perhaps penetrate as far as her, or, at least, my death will convince her that I would have been able to love her as much if I had known, before seeing her, the amour that I fled and that she alone has made me feel."

Frightened by that resolution on his master's part, Nix dared not combat it forcefully at first, for fear of redoubling a chagrin that, in his opinion, had a hint of mental deregulation about it. He gave him reasons so good and so sensible, however, that he persuaded the prince, toward the end of the day, to take a little nourishment and to speak with a little more common sense about the lack of foundation there was to be made between past and present events.

After having eaten a little and reasoned a great deal, far into the night, the prince, overcome by drowsiness and chagrin, went to sleep, while Nix kept watch in order to defend him against the bears, The later collected wood and straw and made a big fire at the entrance to the cavern in order to keep the cruel beasts away.

The light of the fire illuminated the interior sufficiently to allow Nix to perceive a large snake, the dazzling scales of which seemed to be covered in diamonds and which, slithering along the walls, was heading toward Frozen. He ran back into the cavern in order to wake him, and, taking him in his arms, he tried to carry him outside. That movement caused him to open his eyes, and, Nix having warned him of the danger they were in, the prince unburdened his squire's arms and drew his sword against the snake, which, instead of defending itself against then, crawled toward his feet and came to lick them.

That action surprise him, and, gazing at the frightful beast, he saw words on its back written in diamond letters on its skin, which resembled red morocco leather covered in diamond scales:

To find her, to know her
Requires an amour without equal;
Whoever wants to be her master
Must undergo a fatal ordeal,
Which he might perhaps run
With more benefit than woe.

"Oh, divine serpent!" cried the prince, after having read those words. "You have saved my life, and I already sense more pleasure than I have felt pain. Yes. My amour will be immortal, and perhaps it will not be for your immortal mistress; but where shall I look for her? And how am I expected to find her, if she always hides from my eyes?"

At those words the snake raised its head and stared at him fixedly. Then it emerged from the cavern and, after having crawled with extreme speed, it disappeared from their sight.

Full of hope, in spite of the little that he ought to have had, the prince embraced Nix and begged him to help him find the unknown divinity. Nix swore him an inviolable fidelity, and, having aided him to mount a horse and then mounting up himself, he asked which way he intended to go.

"Alas, I don't know," said the amorous prince; "but since I'm permitted to search, doubtless she won't let me go astray; let's follow the route of her faithful interpreter and leave Amour the care of doing the rest."

With that he pushed his horse in the direction in which the snake had disappeared, and Nix followed him.

While he undertakes that journey, let us return to Princess Sparkling; we left her in the admiration and joy of recognizing in the Prince of Sylphs the charming statue of Adonis that had inspired such tender sentiments in her. Naturally, she let them appear, and the sylph, penetrated by his happiness, became a thousand times more amiable and more amorous; they said such touching things to one another that he would have forgotten to relate the rest of the adventure, and she to ask for it, if she had not felt slightly ashamed of appearing so sensitive and begged him to continue; for the princess was very sage, although born very affectionate, and would not have wanted, for anything in the world, to violate the laws of the most severe honesty and the most exact decorum.

"What remains for me to tell you, Madame," he said, "is so agreeable that it is with an infinite pleasure that I shall retrace it for your eyes, since it is the fortunate epoch of my happiness. In spite of my transformation, I retained the usage of my eyes and of sentiment. I saw you in your gardens, but, beautiful princess, will you permit me to render an account of the favorable interpretation that I gave to the expressions of your face?"

"Yes, Sire," said the princess, blushing. "You may recall the circumstances that I helped to develop, in case any of them were still hidden from you."

"Well, Madame," the Sylph went on, "I believe I saw that you were struck by my figure inanimate as it was; I saw in your beautiful eyes a kind of complaisance in gazing at me, which made me forgot my misfortune for that moment; but I sensed it very vividly the following day, when you approached me with one of your women and said to her: 'I would like the husband that Heaven destines for me to resemble that lovely statue, for I sense that it would be impossible for me to love him if he were otherwise.'

"Your confidante wanted to turn you away from that idea, but you constrained her to be quiet, and a few days later, you came alone to lean on my pedestal and say things so tender to Adonis that I was almost jealous of myself. In those happy moments, nothing could console me for not being able to respond to your tenderness; I hoped, however, that if it were sincere, I would have the pleasure of resuming my ordinary form and compensating you for the silence I was keeping, by the confession of a passion that seemed able to make the happiness of your life. Destiny and my jealous fay, however, set out to prevent that; you were brought the portrait of Prince Frozen…."

"Oh, Sire," said the princess, "pass rapidly over that distraction; I am ashamed of having been able to agree to it; I shall never console myself for having been able to believe that I could forget you for him, and for having tried to occupy myself with that."

"You are quite justified, Madame," said the prince, "and I am only mentioning that moment in order to compare it to my happiness. Yes, I felt a jealous rage in seeing you admire his portrait. Should I tell you this? Yes, I can today, since I enjoy the most perfect happiness; I thought you similar to other women, and I detested the fay, who had left me sufficient sentiment to know that fault in you. Finally, I no longer saw you except preoccupied with Frozen, and, your marriage being rumored, if I had been able to die, I would now be dead of dolor.

"You departed, and that was the culmination of my woes. The fay, who still loved me, took pity on my torment; the day after your departure she came to seize me by the hair and lifted me up in order to take me to her palace. 'I am avenged,' she said. 'I don't want anything more. Go, Miriel, go and see your rival happy with his mistress, and don't think that I'll recall you; I'm quitting this region forever, and I give you this palace and its gardens, which I ornamented to please you, since I can do no more with them; I abandon them to you, and would like you to enjoy them, in order at least to conserve the memory of my benefits and not that of my wrath.' She disappeared at the same time.

"I flew to you; it was me who, beside myself with amour and dolor, pressed your horse and made it carry you beyond the city.

"Those are my crimes, justified by their cause; order my fate and punish me, beautiful princess, if I offend you by loving you too much."

The princess responded tenderly and modestly to Prince Miriel.

As it was late and he thought that she might be fatigued, he conducted her to an apartment destined for her; it was paneled with mother-of-pearl and gold thread, and all the ornaments of the room were matching. The bed and the furniture were silver gauze patterned with gold branches. Twelve young women more beautiful than daylight received the princess at the door of her apartment, and undressed her as soon as the prince had taken his leave of her.

She went to bed and slept, if not tranquilly, at least very agreeably, for she continually saw the handsome Miriel. She was, however, troubled by the memory of Frozen, who was retraced in her thought as she slept.

When daylight had brightened the room, she woke up and heard the sound of a harmonious concert, to which a thousand nightingales responded. She rang; the sylphides came in and attended to her toilette, during which she adorned herself with so much taste that she took pleasure in looking at herself more than once. Then the prince sent to ask whether she was visible, and whether she would permit him to visit her. It was no longer an uninhabited palace; the prince had transported his court there in an instant, in order to make it that of the princess he adored.

She replied obligingly that it was a little late to re-member that, and that she would only pardon that forget-fulness on seeing him. He came running, transported, and spent the day at Sparkling's feet. She finally permit-ted him to hope that she would give him her hand and her faith if she could be disengaged from what she had promised to Prince Frozen via the ambassadors. That scruple, very well founded, desolated Miriel, since it delayed his happiness; in spite of the princess's tender-ness, however, she wanted to retain the most exact deco-rum.

"What can you be looking for in that regard?" her lover sometimes asked her. "Don't you believe that Frozen is convinced that he will never see you again? Perhaps new ties engage him."

"If I were quite sure of that," said the princess, "I wouldn't delay your happiness, but it would be necessary to prove it to me. Being so powerful, can you not inform me of what is happening at his court?"

"I can," said Miriel, "but I thought our amour would be sufficient for you to give yourself to me, and it is still necessary that I battle in your heart a rival that you assure me that you do not love. In fact, if you loved me perfectly, beautiful princess, would you not make it a merit to sacrifice a vain decorum to me? You haven't promised Prince Frozen to love him; your faith was pledged for you, you haven't given it to him; you aren't taking anything away from him and you're refusing me everything; that's granting him more than me, maintaining a fidelity to him for which you haven't even been asked."

An amiable lover is easily persuaded. After having calmed the jealous Miriel's anger with further assurances of her tenderness, the princess promised to give him her faith the following day, if she could at least be assured that Frozen was no longer thinking about her.

The prince, delighted to have finally extracted that tender promise, had one of his light subjects depart for Scythia, carefully instructed as to what he had to do, and that same evening, the ruby palace resounded with sweet wedding songs; the gardens were illuminated in a new manner, the sylphs and sylphides, in elegant and magnificent costumes, came to congratulate the prince and the princess, who received their homage on a splendid throne. After that ceremony there was a concert, a ball, a comedy, an opera and a marvelous supper.

The sylph, intoxicated with pleasure by the flattering hope that he had conceived, was walking with the princess in the gardens, and was expressing his passion to her by means of transports that only amour is capable of inspiring when one of the princess's women came to ask whether she might have a word with her. She drew away from Miriel, imploring him to leave her alone for a moment.

He loved her too much to contradict her; her slightest whim was law. He went into another pathway in order to leave her in liberty, and the princess, who wanted to surprise the sylph with a gallantry that she had imagined, and with which she had charged the maid, advanced far enough into the depths of the wood where they were to ask her whether it was time to take Miriel into the arbor that she had had prepared.

"Yes, Madame," said the confidante, "and I've come to inform you."

"Well," said the princess, "I'll go there first; I want to be there to receive him; find him and bring him, telling him that I'm waiting for him."

The confidante departed, and the princess, continuing her route in order to reach the arbor, went past another that seemed poorly lit, and, hearing voices, she stopped for a moment.

One of the voices that as speaking very quietly, said: "That it's Sparkling, I can't believe, Sire. How could she have gone such a long time without informing the queen, her mother, or you, of such a bizarre adventure?"

"I can't understand it," replied another voice, "unless a secret inclination that she had conceived before wanting to marry me...."

By those words, the princess could not mistake the king of Scythia. She hastened her steps, very troubled by what she had discovered, and arrived in the arbor at the moment when Miriel had just entered it. He ran toward her and looked at her with eyes filled with amour; he thanked her warmly for the attention she had had in augmenting the pleasures of that day by something that marked her tenderness. Sparkling tried to constrain herself in order not to afflict her lover; she resumed her cheerfulness, sat down on grass strewn with flowers and made him sit down next to her.

The fête commenced with a concert of flutes and oboes; then several sylphs and sylphides danced a ballet, in which they represented the advantages of constancy, and a sylphide, under that fine name, came to present a crown of myrtles to Miriel, singing words whose meaning was that, having wanted to give that crown to mortals, she had not been able to find one more capable of meriting it than Miriel. A firework display followed; a thousand brilliant rockets intersected and formed the sylph's name.

"What!" he said, tenderly. "Shall I not see yours?"

At those words a little amour at the height of the blazing palace launched an arrow that traversed a diamond heart, which fell at his feet; he picked it up; around it was engraved: *you render her faithful*. The fête finished thus.

The prince, delighted by that last proof of Sparkling's tenderness, marked his gratitude for it, and, giving her his hand, he conducted her back to the palace, which was still illuminated.

As they went through the vestibule that gave entrance to the drawing room where the apartments were distributed, two men, one of whom seemed perfectly well-made, turned toward the one who was accompanying him and said, quite loudly: "It's her."

Miriel, very occupied with his conquest and surrounded by a crowd of courtiers, heard nothing, and did not even notice the two strangers. Sparkling was not so distracted; what she had heard in the arbor had struck her with the idea, and that second adventure moved her so forcefully that, having turned her head to look at the person who had spoken, she recognized Frozen, and fainted in the arms of the sylph, who, fortunately, sustained her.

She was carried to her apartment and put to bed without recovering consciousness.

Miriel was desperate. The court was in mortal anxiety. Finally, by dint of cares, she opened her eyes. He made his joy burst forth in a thousand transports. He asked her the cause of such a cruel accident. The princess, not wanting to let him know, in the dread that his vengeance might fall upon Prince Frozen, after thanking him for his cares, pretended that she was subject to the vapors. She begged him not to worry about an illness that would have no consequences.

As he feared fatiguing her, he dared not press her further, and went out in order to let her rest. When she was alone, she recalled the peril in which she believed the king of Scythia was engaged for her.

He's searching for me, she thought. *He might have believed that he was disputing me with a prince equal in power; he doesn't know the risk he's running, and I dare not trust anyone to inform him of my destiny. Why hide my embarrassment from Miriel? Why not dare to tell him that I've seen his rival? His generous soul wouldn't listen to his anger in a circumstance in which he offends more than he is offended. But if I confess it to him tomorrow, he'll have reason to believe that I was afraid that'd discover it. The mystery that I've made of it this evening might give him a jealousy that my good faith might not be able to destroy; even less so for being well-founded. By doing that, I'd be risking the life of a prince whose amour has doubtless caused his imprudence. It's better to act, continuing as I've begun and not emerging from my apartment until I'm married; then I'll dissipate the suspicions of my husband, if he can have any regarding my retreat, and I'll leave fate to act with regard to Frozen.*

After forming those resolutions, the princess went to sleep, and was only woken up by Miriel, who came in search of news of her. In order to begin to execute what she had projected, she said that she was a little fatigued, and that she desired to rest in her bed for a few days and not see many people. As she was anxious, she seemed unwell, so the prince of sylphs was taken in. Sylphs as well as humans are blinded by amour.

All rejoicing ceased in the palace, and the court was modeled on its prince; nothing was seen but a general sadness spread over all faces. Miriel did not quit Sparkling's bedside. She dared not ask for news of the court of Scythia, fearing that he might find out that Frozen was in his own. They were both sad for different reasons, for Miriel had learned that he prince in question was traveling, in search of a person with whom he was in love, but his art did not go as far as discovering who that person was, and he believed, with sufficient plausibility, that it was Sparkling.

One evening, when she seemed more depressed than usual by her anxiety regarding Miriel's profound silence regarding what she had charged him with finding out, he broke it, and asked her whether her illness had taken away all curiosity about news of Scythia.

"Alas, Sire," she said, "I thought that your silence told me that I ought not to expect a response favorable to our desires, and I thought that you had decided to hide it from me."

"He is searching for you, Madame," he said, with a profound sigh, "and I believe he is in despair at your flight."

"Eh? How do you know that he is in despair, Sire?" said the princess.

"I presume it, Madame," said Miriel. "Can one lose you and remain tranquil?"

"Alas," said the princess, "I don't know how to accord what you say with what I've experienced, for that prince even refused me the politeness of coming to meet me; it appears singular to me that he has only taken it into his head to love me having lost me."

"Men are capricious," said the sylph. "A possession of which they're sure flatters them less than one that escapes them, and I wouldn't be astonished that he was piqued to see you snatched away from him, even if he did not experience the sentiment that you inspire. Vanity, more than amour, produces that effect, and I would be glad to be sure that that is not the motive that is causing him to act."

The princess made little response to that, and fell back into her reverie. The sylph was privately obliged for that, and let her know, by means of touching words, how penetrated he was by it, but he was far from understanding it.

The amour that Frozen appeared to have conceived for her, which exposed him to such a eminent danger, was beginning to touch her; she thought with pleasure that he had repented of his indifference, and Miriel, utterly amiable and amorous as he was, was depicted in her soul in less sensible colors than that indifferent man who, according to her ideas, knew via her the price of amour. She was allowing herself to drift in those reflections, although she criticized herself for being too ingrate, without thinking that the prince, totally occupied with her, was by her bedside, waiting for her to speak, when he uttered a dolorous cry that suddenly extracted her from her reverie.

"What's the matter, Sire?" she asked.

"O Heaven!" he cried, launching a gaze at her in which amour and anger were equally depicted. "See to what you've exposed me!"

Then, as he showed her his hand, she perceived that it was the most beautiful white and pink marble one could see.

"Just gods!" she cried, "Is what I see possible?" As she finished those words she fainted, and when she recovered her senses two hours later, she found herself alone in the beautiful palace. The gardens no longer presented anything but frightful precipices, rocks denuded of all verdure and so steep that one could not hope to cross them, and profound seas. A silence reigned that redoubled the horror of those sad places; only owls and large toads had permission to trouble it.

Sparkling was seized by a terror that nearly caused her to die, but the extreme dolor that she felt at the fault she had committed caused her to shed so many tears that she found a slight relief. And she remembered with a dolorous dread what the sylph had said to her, that if she were unfaithful, she would be punished like him, and perhaps even more rigorously. However, not seeing any visible evidence of punishment, she stood up on her bed and dragged herself to the cabinet from which the sea was visible. That sight suited her sadness more.

On entering it she was surprised to find two large full-length portraits, one of the implacable sylph and the other of the charming king of Scythia; she could not understand why those two objects, as fatal to her as one another, were found together in order to increase her torment. She turned her eyes away from that of Frozen and gazed at that of the sylph; she remained buried in a reverie so profound, and her misfortunes were retraced so vividly in her memory, that she did not perceive that night had already fallen before she had thought of leaving the cabinet. It was illuminated as soon as she formed the wish; she was surprised by that attention, and when she desired to eat a table appeared; but, when she tried wishing to get out of the palace, it was not granted; her power was limited to the needs of life alone.

She did not make great usage of the delicacy of her supper; the despair of not being able to get away from that place redoubled her dolor and caused her to take in aversion the care that as being taken of her. Then, looking at the portrait of Frozen, she seemed, by virtue of the pleasure she strove to find in it and that which she did, in fact, obtain, to be avenging herself for the harshness of the person who was retaining her there against her will. But as she looked at it, the features faded, and only recovered their vivacity when she was no longer looking at it.

She amused herself for a long time into the night watching the play of Miriel's power and jealousy; then she returned to her bedroom, where, overwhelmed by dolor and fatigue, she lay down on her bed and went to sleep.

She was woken up by a loud noise, with seemed to be near her room. She opened her curtain and in a mirror that was extended from the top to the bottom of her alcove she saw the young king of Scythia on his knees, next to a woman who was lying on a cot covered in pink taffeta embroidered with silver and secured with strings of pearls. The woman in question was negligently dressed and seemed to be profoundly asleep; her only coiffure was a large quantity of beautiful wavy ash-blonde hair, bound confusedly over her head by a pink ribbon from which curls were escaping and falling gracefully over her cleavage, which was sufficiently exposed to allow her beauty to be seen. A corset garnished with the most beautiful lace and knotted with pink ribbons was tight enough to display the neatness of her waist; the rest of her body was hidden by a white satin quilt garnished with magnificent lace, as were the pillows of the bed.

Frozen seemed to be waiting in ecstasy for the moment when that incredible beauty would wake up, and his eyes were attached to her face, allowing the penetration of the full extent of his rapture.

"What!" cried Sparkling, in her first transport. "Frozen has abandoned me and is already becoming unfaithful!"

At her voice, Frozen turned his head as one does when one hears a sound that deflects the attention away from something, but it returned immediately to the field of its first object. Sparkling got up and, approaching the mirror she cried: "You've forgotten me, ingrate, and I quit for you the most amorous and most amiable of lovers!"

As she spoke and drew nearer to the mirror, the objects therein moved away; she soon lost sight of them. It is then that it would be necessary to write very well in order to depict her despair, rage and jealousy. She had naturally vivid passions, but, excited by objects so sensible, they were stirred with so much violence that it is difficult to imagine how she did not die right away. Doubtless Amour, in order to punish her for her inconstancy, was reserving crueler tortures for her. But alas, what use are threats and even torments against a penchant that nothing can repress and that our reflections cannot vanquish?

The princess, in the excess of her fury, no longer seeing anything in the mirror, went into the cabinet in order to exact on the portrait of the prince the vengeance that she believed she owed to his infidelity, but that of the sylph, which offered itself first to her eyes because of the disposition of the cabinet, in which they were placed next to one another, retained her anger momentarily in order to give way to what she thought at that moment.

That object, inanimate though it was, reminded her of all that she had lost by yielding to such an unfortunate passion. One never reproaches oneself for one's faults as bitterly as when one feels the penalty of them.

"Oh, Miriel!" she cried, "Was I, then, culpable enough to be punished so rigorously? Yes, undoubtedly I am, for having abandoned your heart in order to give mine to the most ingrate of all men. Enjoy, Miriel, enjoy my torment; it is such that I believe that it surpasses my offense, and the jealousy that I feel could expiate the most frightful crimes. Yes. I love the ingrate and infidel Frozen; I can no longer hide it; I do not even seek to defend myself, and I sense that I love him a hundred times more since I believe that he no longer loves me."

At those words, the princess was interrupted by a cry that made the cabinet resound; that cry came from the portrait, which, in an instant, became the statue of Adonis that she had seen in her mother's garden, and at the same moment, she felt her legs becoming numb, and she became a statue of black marble herself, and found herself placed in a niche in the cabinet, opposite the portrait of Frozen and the statue. For the sake of her torture, she did not lose sentiment, but, more enclosed within herself, with the aid of the plaint that was refused her, she experienced more sensible torments.

I left the king of Scythia traveling with his squire in pursuit of the snake the color of fire, the trail of which they were following. You will already have suspected that the snake led them to the ruby palace, and that it really was him, astonished to find Sparkling, for whom he was not searching, who was talking to Nix in the arbor, and, out of curiosity, followed her into the vestibule of the palace where she fainted when she recognized him.

That sight having troubled him, fearful of seeing her again and being obliged to marry her, in spite of Nix's advice, he went out during the tumult of that event and went back into the gardens. There, searching for a route through the wood in order to escape from that palace, so fatal to his amorous ideas, he found himself, after many detours, near a lively fountain, which fell back into a magnificent basin, and being tired for having walked so far, he sat down on the rim in order to rest.

His zealous confidant was about to ask him what he intended to do when a sweet harmony was heard in the depths of the water, and the prince made a gesture with his hand to bid him to be quiet and listen. That symphony seemed to be drawing nearer.

By the light of the lamps and chandeliers that were still illuminating the garden, they saw six tritons and as many sirens, which emerged from the depths of the water and arranged themselves on the rim, forming a kind of round. The tritons, with their marine conches and the sirens with their voices, and very harmonious lyres of a sort, executed beautiful pieces from the operas of Lully. During that delightful concert, a coral chariot drawn by two dolphins rose up in the middle of the basin. After the act of the shades from *Proserpine*,[8] which the musicians had just finished, two sirens took the prince by the arms, and two tritons did the same with his confidant, put them on the chariot and dived into the basin, with the chariot and the entire orchestra.

Frozen, as intrepid as he was amorous, allowed himself to be conducted by that strange carriage without showing the slightest fear; on the contrary, he allowed a joy so vivid to burst forth that Nix was obliged to conform to his master's humor. They did not take long to descend to the bottom of the basin, although it was extremely deep; what surprised them was that Nix made the remark that they were not getting wet, which the prince, entirely occupied with his object, had neglected to perceive.

The chariot stopped at the door of a palace, which was worthy of the attention of a man curious about marvelous things; it was entirely built of white, red and black coral; the doors were made of rock crystal garnished with gold, and they opened to give entrance into a vast peristyle sustained by columns of artistically min-

---

[8] As in the previous story, the presence of Jean-Baptiste Lully's music here is blithely anachronistic. *Proserpine* (1680), like *Armide*, had a libretto by Philippe Quinault.

gled corals of different colors; the walls, around which curled branches of marine gladioli and roses, formed by emeralds and yellow, pink and violet diamonds, matching the colors of the corals they ornamented.

In spite of the prince's preoccupation, he was dazzled by the splendor of that magnificent architecture. The sirens and the tritons who had conducted him as far as the door of the palace left him in the hands of twelve nymphs clad in silver and roseate gauze, who greeted him and invited him to come with them to an apartment that was destined for them. He went in, surprised and amazed by the youth and beauty of those beautiful individuals.

He traversed an immensity of chambers, galleries and halls; finally, he arrived in a large cabinet that overlooked the garden, all the trees of which were the beautiful coral that had served to build the superb palace. The flower beds were strewn with the most beautiful precious stones which formed flowers of very species there; the variety emanated such a brilliance that obliged him to close his eyes from time to time.

The nymphs that were guiding him took him into an avenue of coral in order to bring him to a small pavilion of rock crystal, all the foundations of which were gold; the pavilion was at the end of the avenue; the nymphs left him there after making profound reverences. He went in; the furniture responded to the elegance of the pavilion; silver and roseate gauze covered the beds and the armchairs; he judged that it was the favorite color scheme of the goddess who lived there, and was even more convinced of that by an elegant coat that he found on a table, of the same adornment. He thought that it was destined for him, and he put it on with the aid of Nix, who was still following him. Large diamond clasps fastened it; a kind of silver helmet or morion, with a multitude of rose-colored plumes, heightened by a diamond brooch, served as his coiffure, and for the first time in his life, he allowed himself, without impatience, to be bathed, powdered and primped, and felt a kind of pleasure in seeing himself in a mirror.

When his toilette was finished the nymphs served him an elegant meal, and while it lasted they formed a concert that delighted him. After the meal a caleche harnessed to two pink gazelles with white and violet spots came to collect him and take him for a ride in the park, where he discovered a thousand beauties that he had not been able to perceive before. Nix and the nymphs followed him on gazelles of all colors, but none were as beautiful as his. Eventually, he returned to the crystal pavilion, which was superbly illuminated, and the nymphs withdrew until the time for his supper.

The prince sat down on a sofa and seemed plunged in a greater reverie than the one that had borne him during the excursion; Nix asked him respectfully what he was thinking about.

"How can you not know?" cried the prince. "Everything that I am shown here is admirable, but I cannot feel the pleasure of it if I do not see my divinity here. What can I say, my dear Nix? Everything is tedious, everything displeases me so much that if they continue not showing her to me, I shall shut myself away in the pavilion and perhaps die there of dolor."

In fact, he let himself become dejected to the point that he did not want supper and sent away the nymphs who tried to divert him with concerts and games that they devised in order to amuse him. He spent a fortnight shut away, refusing obstinately to come out except to walk alone in the most remote part of the coral wood.

He dared not try to find a means of getting out of that enchanted palace, believing that it was the dwelling of the beauty that had rendered him so amorous, but he could not imagine how he could find her, as she had seemed to make him understand by way of her snake. Furthermore, how could he prove that his was an amour without equal, since he did not have to resist any other passion, seeing no one but the nymphs, at whom he scarcely glanced? All that embarrassed him and augmented his sadness.

One night, when he was wandering in the paths of the wood and had descended into a rather deep bowling green, where there as a spring that irrigated the charming place, he thought he heard a noise behind the rock from which the seething water emerged. Full of contradictory ideas that were driving him to despair he initially paid little attention to what he heard, but finally the moon came to pierce with its silvery rays the place from which the noise was coming; he looked in that direction and perceived a woman behind the rock, whose garments were so bright that he was almost dazzled by them.

He went up precipitately to the place where he saw her and came to throw himself on his knees before her before she had time to defend herself. A large veil of white gauze dotted with silver stars covered her from her head to her feet; he did not doubt that it was his unknown lady; the beauty and majesty of her figure aided him in that belief.

"Why are you taking pleasure in driving me to despair, Madame?" he said to her. "Is it not enough to have made me suffer since that time I saw you, without adding the torment of making me wait for a happiness that my constancy and my amour dare to request as the price of their perseverance? That price is to see you, so deign to tell me, I implore you, whether you approve of my flame?"

Frozen fell silent after pronouncing those few words with vivacity.

"What, Prince!" replied the veiled woman, finally. "You count for nothing in my regard the time that you have spent in loving me without seeing me, and you want me to be grateful to you for having taken the trouble to look for me and for remaining by my order in the most beautiful place in the world, in the midst of a thousand pleasures?"

"Pleasures, me?" he cried. "Happy, me, where you are not? How unjust you are! Can I enjoy a moment of repose where I do not see you? And have I asked to be grateful to me? No, Madame, I only want to declare my tenderness to you and to die before your eyes to convince you of it; I know that you are insensible; I dare not even flatter myself that I might touch your heart, but I want you to have the glory of having softened mine, and that you do me the favor of believing that it is your work."

"I am neither unjust nor insensible, Prince," the lady replied, "but I have always believed that men are fickle and perfidious. My heart, made to feel a veritable tenderness, believed that I had found what I sensed; I had a cruel experience, and that is what renders me more difficult in the second choice; I wanted to tell you that, in order for you to judge whether you are capable of compensating me for what I have lost, and for that which perhaps I still regret."

The prince did not make any reflection on the novelty of that confidence; he had so much amour that he took the excess of confidence to be an excess of tenderness.

"How happy I would be," he said to her, embracing her knees with a transport that did not displease the unknown woman, "if I could hope to replace in your heart the man who did not know its value! If the most vivid, the most tender and the most veritable amour can only repay your amiable sincerity, I swear to feel it for you always, and never to ask you for any other proof that that of believing myself to be fortunate on that point alone."

"But you have a liking for my sister," said the lady, "and I don't know whether I ought to trust your protestations."

"Me, Madame?" he replied, as astonished by that question. "How could I have? I've never seen her."

"I've been told," she interrupted, "and moreover, I know that you're searching for her here, for how could you be searching for me, whom you don't know?"

"Heaven!" cried the prince, getting up promptly from the lady's knees. "Then you're not the adorable person I saw bathing in the Scythian grotto?"

"No, ingrate," said the lady. "I'm the fay Leoparde."

At those words the prince took two steps back, so alarmed was he by that terrible adventure. The fay lifted her veil at that moment, and showed a face that would have been beautiful had it not been inflamed by anger, which rendered it a little too harsh.

"You don't love me, from what I can see," she said to him, "and I suspected as much, but in order to punish you for having so lightly devoted yourself to the idea of persuading me of the contrary, I'll enable you see my sister; that insensible object will avenge me sufficiently for your scorn, and we'll see whether you or I will be the most wretched."

Far from being frightened by that threat, the prince wanted to embrace the fay's knees in order to thank her for that punishment. She did not give him time; she disappeared, and he found himself in the crystal pavilion, in an apartment underneath his own, which he had neglected to visit, so incapable was he of taking pleasure in seeing the magnificence of a place in which he did not believe the person for whom he was searching which so much care could be; the charming individual was in her bed, sleeping so peacefully that it was easy to see that her soul was not experiencing the agitation that she had caused her lover. He knelt down beside that divine object, whom he recognized with delight as the beautiful person he had seen in the grotto.

It was at that moment that the jealous Sparkling perceived him in the mirror in her alcove. It is not extraordinary that he was not disturbed by the dolorous cries she uttered at that sight; he heard them, in fact, but how could he tear himself away for an instant from what occupied all his imagination?

"How beautiful she is!" he cried, "and how sweetly Leoparde is punishing me!"

The fay woke up at that exclamation and looked at him with astonished eyes, but in which indifference was painted.

"What renders you so daring as to come and trouble my sleep? And by means of what power have you reached my palace?"

The king, more touched than alarmed by the fay's anger, bowed profoundly before her. "Amour," Madame," he said to her, "guided me himself; his power is unlimited, and when one knows him through you, nothing is impossible."

"Amour?" she said. "Do you know, audacious stranger, the peril to which anyone who pronounces that word in my presence is exposed?"

"I know, Madame," said he prince, "the woes to which your cold indifference exposes me; I know no others, and all those you want to inflict upon me will be favors, since it will be by your order that I suffer them."

Without responding, the fay looked at him disdainfully, and, picking up a little golden wand that was near her bed she struck the parquet with it. It opened near the prince, and a large black cat emerged from it, which had pink horns and wings.

"Take this mortal to the gallery of lovers," the fay said to it, "and come back afterwards so that I can tell you what punishment is reserved for him."

The black cat struck the ground in front of it three times with its horns, apparently to mark its obedience and respect, and made a sign with its paw to the prince to follow it.

He was so troubled by amour and regret for having offended the beautiful fay that, without saying a word to justify himself, he followed the large cat, which, after taking him via a staircase into the garden, conducted him along an avenue of four rows of black coral and into a gallery at the end, which the prince had never noticed; there he found an immense number of small tables with human heads. The prince was surprised by the marvel, and even more so when the tables greeted him. The large cat left him there, and locked the door.

He sat down on a sofa that was between two of the tables, which asked him whether he was in love with the fay Limpide.

"For a long time, Sires," replied Frozen. "I've loved her for some three months, and I sense that I shall love her all my life.

"Fortunate," said the tables, "if you are the man reserved by destiny to touch her and to conclude our enchantment!"

As those words finished, all the tables sighed and fell silent.

Overwhelmed by dolor, the king did not ask them any questions, and maintained a profound silence.

After an hour, the black cat came in; the sight of it caused the prince to shiver.

"What power acts for you here?" it said. "My mistress, the fay Limpide, cannot exact her vengeance on your person. She orders you to flee her palace and her presence, and to forget her forever."

"Let her rather order my death!" cried the prince. "I could at least obey her; but that order I cannot carry out. Go on," he said to the cat, which was standing there, astonished to see him sitting on the soda, "Go on, barbaric minister of an excessively beautiful and excessively rigorous mistress; take my head, if you wish, for I cannot obey her." As he finished speaking, he turned his head away, and the large cat, which was not prepared for that reply, or perhaps had no order for that eventuality, went out, very surprised at that new audacity.

The day passed without the cat returning. Toward the middle of the night, when he had dozed off, he felt someone take his hand gently. He woke up, and asked whether the pitiless Limpide finally wanted to accept the sacrifice of his life.

"No, barbarian that you are," replied a low voice, which did not want to wake the human tables "Limpide, perhaps, does not want your death, but would you like that of the excessively tender Leoparde? She is burning for you with the most ardent amour, as you can imagine, since, forgetting what she owes to her glory, she has come to free you from the peril that is menacing you, without any other recompense than saving your life.

"Eh! What use is it to me, Madame," said the king, "since I displease the lovable Limpide, and my heart, filled with an amour that nothing can shake, is insensible to the generosity you are showing me? Cease to move my gratitude, it is a sentiment too feeble to offer you, and it is all that I can give you."

"No matter," said the fay. "I want to help you, and since my destiny only leads me to find ingrates, I want at least to render them happy, even at the expense of my own satisfaction. No, prince," she went on, "no, don't believe that my sister is insensible to your amour; listen to me, and judge whether I love you by what I have come to tell you. Although we are fays, we are born subject to the laws of destiny; my sister was born threatened by the misfortune of losing her gift of enchantment if she surrendered her heart to amour, and furthermore, of seeing her lover in the tomb a year after she had confessed her tenderness. When she reached the age of reason and began to make her power felt, she knew the force of that prediction; she resolved not to love all her life, and to punish rigorously those who dared to turn her away from that sage resolution.

"Her vengeance, exercised on a multitude of princes and heroes, attracted to her the title of insensible, which she did not merit, for she was pained by punishing hearts that only offended her by loving her too much; it is not that she did not find some of them lovable, but none had succeeded in making her feel what they expressed. She fled the gaze of men, and it was only by chance that they saw her. Weary of the rigors that she exercised and the incense that was lavished on her uselessly, she resolved to go to Scythia and fix her abode there, imagining that, the climate being colder than anywhere else, she would have less difficulty in saving herself from amour among an icy people and that she would at least punish more rarely.

"She established her dwelling in a grotto that had only ever had bears for guests until then. By the effect of her power she hollowed out an agreeable dwelling, and whenever she desired to return to the palace where we are she dived with the nymphs of her retinue into the basin in the middle of the subterrain and came to spend a few days with us; she only stayed here long enough to settle a few business matters with our fay companions; the rest of the year she did not emerge from her subterrain.

"A powerful enchanter who had established himself as our king, against our will and in spite of our power, fell in love with Limpide at one of the assemblies to which she had been summoned. Her power could not extend to metamorphosing him into a table, as she had one with all her lovers, but her rigor and her scorn for him avenged her as cruelly. He followed her everywhere, and rendered himself invisible solely for the pleasure of seeing her, which she could not prevent; he rendered her desperate by his sights and plaints. Finally, weary of a constancy that only served to render him unhappy, and no longer seeking to please her, he resolved to torment her by showing her an object that could render her sensible; his choice fell on you, Sire, and he succeeded only too well.

"You were summoned by the enchanter into the cavern, where you thought you were pursuing a bear; it was him, who had taken that form in order to attract you. You saw the admirable and overly fortunate Limpide; the effect that she had on your soul would have justified her beauty, if she had not been accustomed to miracles; she only saw you at the instant when she was dressed, but you can well imagine that her sagacity and modesty, if you had not been rendered invisible by the cares of the enchanter, would have hidden from you the disorder she was in during her bath.

"She was struck by the sight of you, but in order to flee the danger of it she hastened to return to our palace; she stayed here for much longer than usual. Her secret anxiety, the disturbance that reigned in her mind, and her eyes, often bathed in tears that she strive to hide from us, were the first symptoms of a passion that became only too veritable.

"In spite of the frightful jealousy that he conceived, the enchanter took pleasure in seeing her torment. What efforts she made to vanquish her penchant! But the enchanter, instead of weakening it, sought to determine it, and, finding himself unhappy by virtue of her scorn, he wanted her to be tormented by her own tenderness. A strange effect of passion that enables one find pleasure in things that ought only to cause pain! His own were frightful and cruel.

"My sister languished, and her beauty only became more touching in consequence. She had acquired an aversion for the subterrain and destroyed it. This beautiful palace served as her retreat; she believed it to be a sure refuge against amour; but the more she sought the remedy for it, the more it was augmented. The ingrate that I was lamenting at that time was a kind of relief for her. 'Perhaps,' she said, 'I shall lament the same inconstancy in the king of Scythia, if I listened to my weakness, or I would mourn his death'—for veritable passion, in fact, always brings fatal things to mind.

"The pitiless enchanter, deceived by his jealousy, hastened to complete her misfortune; it was him who, in the form of a flame-colored serpent, determined you to follow her. We had retired, as you see, to this palace; I had abandoned the ruby palace to my infidel lover; he was about to crown my rival there. A fit of jealousy seized me at that fatal moment; I transported myself to that deadly palace where everyone only respired pleasures. Invisibly, I passed into the princess's dressing room, and with a stroke of my wand I had your portrait and that of my lover placed there in the wood paneling; I desired that yours appeared with all the pleasing features to which it might be susceptible, in order that I could avenge myself on my lover by giving amour to my rival. I paid less attention to the perfection of that of my inconstant.

"I was obeyed, but what a cost to my heart! I found that the vengeance would be too cruel for me if it effected what I had promised myself a moment before. Miriel—that is my lover's name—no longer appeared to me to be culpable, and I sensed that if I had loved him, it was because I had not known him."

At that moment the fay stopped; a somber lamp that illuminated the middle of the gallery made her fear that her shame might appear to the king's eyes. As for him, he was transported, and so penetrated by everything he heard that he did not have the strength to reassure her, or to say cruel things about his indifference for her, after all that she had done to be obliging to him. He therefore kept a profound silence, and would never have broken it if she had not resumed speaking.

"Limpide," she said, "in asking me for advice about her situation, had named you, and I had promised to work to cure her, by keeping you away from the places she might inhabit, She had sighed at being constrained to flee you, but she consented to it rather than serve to doom you, as destiny ordered. I therefore saw your portrait by the effort of my art; having returned to myself somewhat, I thought that I might well have been too flattered by it. I turned my eyes away from it and wished that it had not appeared so in the eyes of my rival.

"How I excused my sister! But how I envied her! For we knew that you were searching for her; the jealous enchanter had not left us unaware of that. As my art is equal to his, I resolved, in serving my sister, to satisfy my taste. I came back to this palace and I enchanted Limpide in the crystal pavilion, in order to be able to draw you here without wounding her eyes. The enchanter, in concert with me, enabled you to descend into this palace, but he could not wake her from the sleep into which I had delivered her; I took care of your adornment and ordered that you be amused, until the moment when I dared to show myself to your eyes; your sadness, your scorn for everything that I did to please you, taught me too visibly what I had to dread.

"The rest you know, and I was convinced of your indifference; then, only listening to my chagrin, I permitted my sister to wake up at your approach; forgive me, but I found pleasure in rendering her as unhappy as me, for a different reason. My fury also reawakened against my former lover; he was the cause of all my misfortunes, and furthermore, his inconstant mistress had recovered her liking for you and forgot her tenderness in order to acquire one without measure. I avenged myself on both of them; I shall not tell you how; you will learn one day.

"In sum, Limpide's awakening was nearly the epoch of your doom. In order to save the shame of her defeat, she wanted to deliver you to the black cat to change you into a table, but when you had departed with it in order to come here to await your sentence, I appeared before her and tried to soften her anger. I allowed her to believe that the enchanter alone had opened the roads to her palace to you, and I saw that she took pleasure in knowing that you were guilty of one crime less.

"I offered to take responsibility for her vengeance. 'No, Leoparde,' she said to me, 'I want to punish him myself and make him hate me, is order to try to detach myself from him.' I had to press her hard to leave that care to me; except for telling her the interest I had in it myself, I tried everything to soften her projects, but she did not want to listen to me. Only one means remains for you to avoid it; if you want to subscribe to it, I am the mistress of rendering you as fortunate as you would be unfortunate; think, prince, and pronounce, in a word, the sentence of your life, or perhaps your death."

"If it is only necessary to die, Madame," said the prince, "I subscribe to her vengeance; I am already culpable enough to feel determined to refuse your generous help. Abandon an ingrate to his sad destiny, and allow him to expiate by a just death the crime of daring to tell you that he can only live for Limpide."

Instead of becoming angry with the prince, Leoparde seemed touched by that resolution; she expressed her dolor with such tender regret that anyone but the king would have been penetrated by it.

"At least," she said, don't refuse to take this bracelet." She removed it from her arm and gave it to the prince, who, out of respect, dared to accept it.

237

"Blow on it in your greatest peril, and don't remember, if you wish, that it is me who is offering you this help; it's enough for me to render you happy, I don't ask for anything more."

With those words, without waiting for a response, she disappeared, and the prince remained amazed by what he had just seen and heard. Soon, however, the impulses of generosity to which his soul had yielded while Leoparde was speaking gave way to the impetuousness if his amour; it had been increased by the certainty of being loved; frightful as the fate might be that menaced him, it became mild by virtue of the pleasure that it offered of proving that amour at the peril of his life. He was in haste to abandon it for such a fine cause, and no fortunate lover had ever desired to conserve life as much as he wanted to lose it.

He remained imprisoned in the gallery of lovers for a week without hearing mention of anything. Those days seemed to him to be years. Only the idea of being loved sustained him against absence. The tables had tried to ward off his ennui with marvelous stories of the adventures they had had, but nothing extracted him from his reverie; he only emerged from it for the despair of being imprisoned.

Finally, no longer able to resist the torment that was overwhelming him, and ready to end a life that had become odious to him, he remembered Leoparde's bracelet. *What have I to do to get myself out of the peril in which I shall be engaged?* he thought. *If it is by Limpide's order, I ought to run it, and that bracelet will be no use to me; the only thing I have to dread is dying far from her, and I sense that if my sword does not take away my life, my despair and my amour will take it away before long. That is the only peril I have to fear here, and the only moment when Leoparde's present can help me.*

Then, without consulting the tables, which manifested an extreme dolor at his resolution, he detached the bracelet from his arm and blew on it. At the same moment he found himself transported to the ruby palace, where he had seen Sparkling and the jealous Miriel. But what appeared to him more extraordinary was that the tender and powerful amour that he had felt with so much violence a moment before had given way to the keenest urgency for Leoparde, for whom he searched in that palace as he had searched for Limpide; and the beautiful fay only left in his heart a pleasant and feeble memory, like something of which one retains a pleasant memory, but with which only amuses when one is not occupied more seriously.

In spite of the vivid and impetuous passion that he felt for Leoparde, he was astonished, as he went through the gardens of the palace to search for her, that it was possible that he had almost forgotten Limpide; but that reflection touched him too lightly to stop him, all the more so when, in an arbor that he was passing, he perceived Leoparde in the midst of a dozen nymphs, who were picking flowers with which they were making a garland. He stopped, transported, at the entrance to the arbor, and the fay got up and came toward him. He threw himself at her knees and received the garland that she gave him with an amour full of gratitude.

What did he not say? He had never been so eloquent, but it seemed to him that it was not sufficient to express all the tenderness that the sight of the fay and the repentance for having taken such a long time to love her could inspire.

Charmed by her lover's transports, Leoparde found in forgiving him a pleasure that recompensed her for the pain she had felt in feeling that she was hated by him; she made his swear an eternal amour. She took him to the palace, and his days were marked by as many fêtes, which, all different as they were, could not outweigh the pleasure that he felt in expressing to the fay the passion with which he was burning and that to which he was sensible.

That happiness had already lasted a year—he thought it was only a day—when Leoparde was obliged to go to an assembly of fays. What regrets preceded that sad day! The dread of losing her made him sense more keenly the charm of seeing her. In the end, though, it was necessary to separate. He led her to the fountain by which one descended into the coral palace.

What farewells! What oaths to love one another forever! What tears shed! The fountain was troubled by them. However, a nacre chariot having appeared, the fay climbed into it, leaving the prince in despair.

She had taken care to enchant Nix in the subterranean palace, in order that his reflections would not aid the king to make his own regarding his inconstancy. He was alone in the ruby palace with Leoparde's nymphs, who had orders only to talk to him about her and her tenderness; they came to look for the prince at the fountain and took him back to the palace. He did not want to listen to the consolations that they tried to give him; he shut himself in his cabinet, and composed elegies on absence, which, if they were not extremely poetic, were at least full of a sentiment that was worth as much as the art that has been put into them since. He read them to the nymphs, who were moved by them, so natural and touching did they find them.

He often walked around the fountain and counted the days that separated him from his beautiful fay. If those he had spent with her had seemed too short, these seemed mortally languid. "What! Still the sun!" he cried, sometimes. The nights, long as they were, appeared to him more supportable; it seems that their obscurity softens the pains of lovers. Leoparde's absence was to last forty days; thirty of them had already passed; the ten that remained seemed to the prince to be interminable, and he believed that he would not have the strength to await their end. He walked around, going from one place to another; he looked at all the clocks; the hours never went fast enough for his liking, flowing with a mortal slowness.

In order to pass the time he decided to go from one end of palace to the other, in order to see its curiosities. He had seen them hundreds of times, but does one notice them when one's mind is so occupied? He had not paid any attention to them. He began with the fay's cabinet; the two statues one of Adonis in white and roseate marble, the other in black marble of the fickle Sparkling, struck his eyes.

The Adonis was so perfect in its genre that he was touched by a stir of jealousy on seeing it in the cabinet. Sparkling seemed beautiful enough, but he would only have paid it slight attention if, on approaching it in order to examine the drapery that covered it, which was singular, Leoparde's bracelet, which he still had, had not touched it, causing it to sigh. He stepped back, astonished by that marvel.

"Oh, Prince Frozen!" cried the statue. "Unfortunate prince, to what have you exposed yourself?"

Accustomed as he was to marvels, this one surprised him. He looked at the statue attentively; it seemed to him that he recognized its features, but so confusedly that he could not remember where he had seen them.

"What interest do you have in me, Madame?" he said. "And what risk am I running here that ought to be lamented?"

The statue made no reply, but it sighed bitterly, and shed a few tears.

"What a prodigy!" cried the prince. "Perhaps the Adonis can tell me more."

He unfastened his bracelet and put it in the arm of that statue, which, immediately changing its form, became the admirably handsome Miriel. He gazed at the prince with a majestic smile.

"Don't be astonished, Prince Frozen," he said to him, "if I appear thus to your eyes; the charm enclosed in that picture is the cause; and to recompense you for the important service you have just rendered me, I will oblige Limpide to forgive you. The offense that you have committed against her was involuntary, and if you had not blown on Leoparde's bracelet you would never have been unfaithful."

At those words the prince thought that he was waking up from a dream.

"Me, unfaithful to Limpide!" he cried. "Me, in love with Leoparde! Oh, Heaven! Could that ever be?"

"Yes, Sire," said Miriel, "and the excess of your dolor proves that you have never consented to it; but know that, your inconstancy having been made known to Limpide by the black cat, who came to tell her, she abandoned herself to her dolor and confessed aloud that she loved you enough to want to die of dolor at your change. That confession gave power over her to the enchanter; and, wanting to avenge himself for her rigor toward him and the love she had for you, he redoubled the charm of the bracelet to attach you to Leoparde, and, enchaining the beautiful and unfortunate Limpide, he locked her in a dungeon from which you alone can extract her—but I cannot hide from you that it is at the peril of your life."

"Oh, what would I not give to expiate my fault?" cried the prince. "Judge, Sire, he went on, whether I would spare it in order to save Limpide from my rival's fury. Only add to the favor that you are doing me in instructing me of my fate that of telling me what route I ought to follow and what I can do for the deliverance of that adorable fay."

"I will give you the means," said the sylph. Then, as he struck the parquet with a golden wand that he had in his hand, a magnificent chariot emerged therefrom, drawn by four winged unicorns whiter than snow.

"They will take you where you need to go, Prince," said the sylph. "Go as soon as possible to snatch Limpide from your rival; your courage is your only defense; I can do nothing more. Go, and don't delay."

The king had scarcely heard those last words than he had already mounted the chariot, from which he bowed profoundly to Miriel, and set forth.

The sylph savored in long draughts the pleasure of his vengeance; sovereign of the palace, the fay was about to be submissive to him. It is rather unjust to punish an inconstancy that one has merited, but men generally want others to be more faithful to them than they are themselves. The sylph had the fault of humankind; sylph though he was, self-esteem is always the same; he was jealous that a mortal could enter into competition with him, and the mortal in question had been able to please the only two persons that he loved; vengeance was regarded by him as a effect of justice, and far from repenting of it, he applauded it. But let us leave him to inform the amorous Leoparde of her lover's departure, and let us see what becomes of the king of Scythia.

His unicorns bore him away rapidly, and after traveling millions of leagues lightly they entered a vast forest and stopped near a tower of black and gold Chinese lacquer, so high and smooth that it was impossible to hope to climb it. He descended from the chariot and made a tour of it without perceiving the smallest window or opening, and judged that it must be the fay's prison.

"Beautiful Limpide," he cried, "your lover has come to your rescue; deign to receive him, and that his blood, shed before your eyes, will wash away the insult he has done you."

At those words, which he pronounced while shedding torrents of tears, a large black sack fell at his feet from the top of the tower, which he would have taken for a sack of charcoal if his state of mind had permitted him to judge present events with a cool head. The sack was very mobile, and rolled round him to the point of inconveniencing him and preventing him from approaching the tower. That irritated him; in the end, he drew his word and struck the sack several times.

"Alas, I am dead!" a voice shouted, dolorously.

What became of the king when he recognized it as that of his beloved fay!

He threw himself on the ground next to the sack and tried to open it; he could not do it. He was in torment; he agitated; he embraced the unfortunate sack. He was not unaware that fays are subject to death for one day a year; he did not doubt that this was a vengeance on the part of his rival. He uttered dolorous screams and accused himself of being the cause and the instrument of the death of the person he loved most in all the world.

Finally, unable to resist the despair that possessed him, he got up, took his sword and pierced his heart with it; he fell on the sack and inundated it with his blood. Then the sack stirred, and the enchanter emerged from it, who, seeing the king about to expire, put him in the sack and went back into the tower by means of a door that the prince had not perceived.

The beautiful and unfortunate Limpide was chained up within it, in one of the chambers, which was entirely paneled in black and red lacquer, and would have been the most beautiful prison in the world if it is possible that a prison can be beautiful.

"What have you come to add to my woes?" cried the admirable fay, on seeing the enchanter come in.

"They are not complete," he said, looking at her with a bitter smile, "But at present I am content, and you are free, since I no longer have anything to fear."

With those words he threw the sack at her feet, touched her with his wand in order to make her chains fall away, and, striking the middle of the floor, he raised a magnificent tomb of white and gold porcelain, and then disappeared.

All that was done in such a short time that the fay did not have the ability to reflect on his action or his words; the tomb alone was the first thing that struck her gaze.

"Oh, cruel individual!" she cried. "It's the death of my lover that you're announcing to me, then, and that fatal tomb contains his precious ashes."

A long groan that emerged from the sack put a stop to the unfortunate Limpide's laments; she turned round and saw the bloody sack, which was making efforts to open. She ran to it, very troubled, but what became of her when, on opening it, she saw the unfortunate king of Scythia expiring, bathed in his blood!

Can one describe, can one ever have the vanity of believing that one could express, what that tender person said and thought? That is above human effort, for who-ever has not experienced it. She only conserved enough strength to utter dolorous cries, which she only inter-rupted in order to embrace the cold and bloody body of the prince.

Even the enchanter would have been moved by that frightful spectacle, and would have been horrified by his cruelty, but he had gone away and had flown to the ruby palace to celebrate triumphantly with Leoparde such a cruel vengeance.

Very far from applauding it, however, in spite of the dolor that fay had felt at his flight, at the news of his death she heaped the enchanter with a thousand re-proaches, and asked Miriel, who was present, to punish him.

"I consent to that!" cried the redoubtable sylph, "and I shall not lose a single moment."

Then, struck by his foot, the earth opened and the porcelain tomb rose up, in which the unfortunate king of Scythia could be seen, lying dead, and his beautiful fay, who was clutching him in her embrace and was scarcely any different from her lover; her tears, which were flow-ing, were the only difference. The table-princes sur-rounded the mausoleum, and were consternated.

Miriel approached the tomb and touched the prince with his golden wand. "See the day again Frozen," he said to him, "and finally enjoy the prize of your constan-cy."

Then the prince awoke as if from a profound sleep; the tomb was transformed into a triumphal arch, under which there was a throne, where he found himself seated beside his beautiful fay. He descended from it promptly in order to embrace the sylph's knees.

"You do not owe me anything," the sylph said to him, lifting him up. "It is necessary to cede to me, before thanking me, the pretentions you had to Sparkling."

"Can I not make you a veritable sacrifice?" replied the king. "That one cannot acquit my gratitude, for I have no rights over that princess."

"Suffer, then," said the sylph, "that I give her shortly to the enchanter for a wife; she will punish him enough for the harm he has done you, in order not to demand a greater punishment."

Then he turned round and struck the statue of Sparkling with his wand; it became the princess herself. "Be united in order to avenge us," said the sylph, making the enchanter approach; "but to complete your woes, after having seen King Frozen and Limpide happy in spite of you," he added, addressing the enchanter, "have no power over your wife until her hundredth infidelity; bear the public shame of it, by the augmentation every time of one eye more than you have now.

"As for you, beautiful Limpide," he said to the fay, "you have recovered your power, but the decree of destiny, in uniting you with the king of Sycthia, deprives you of your immortality. However, by renouncing your amour, you can still pretend o it. Consult your heart; there is still time to decide."

Frozen wanted to speak, but the generous fay did not give him time; she preferred to lose her life, since her husband could not be immortal.

Everything tender and generous that could be said on that fortunate occasion without insipidity was exhausted. The sylph finally ceded to the insistences of the fay; he was not able to render her immortality, but he could grant them numerous years filled with happiness; he used that power with generosity.

She was immediately crowned queen of Scythia, and at that moment returned their natural form to the tables. They had loved her so much that they were not jealous of her happiness; they were all kings and princes, and had not grown older during their enchantment. They honored her wedding celebrations with their presence, and made her know that veritable amour is only happy by virtue of the happiness of the object of the amour.

As for the king of Scythia, who sensed more than any other that noble fashion of loving, in the midst of the pleasures of his glorious wedding, he experienced the cruelest bitterness in thinking that, in order to render him happy, the beautiful fay had renounced the privilege of immortality. Such is the fate of kings; the source of pleasures often gives birth to the cause of the woes inseparable from humanity; his life was only a mixture of pleasure and dolor.

He finally departed with the queen, his wife, and was received in his kingdom with acclamations so flattering that they could only be sincere. Nix had been transported there. Their posterity was innumerable; Gustave-Adolphus and Charles XII, Kings of Sweden, descended from them, those kingdoms being united in those days.

As for the enchanter and Princess Sparkling, they lived as unhappily as once can be when one hates a great deal. The enchanter saw only too clearly the extent to which the princess entered into the project of vengeance that had been prescribed for her; he awaited with impatience the hundredth eye that would return his power and to avenge himself for her infidelities, but unfortunately, she died after the ninety-ninth, perhaps of the excess of the chagrin, which she imagined to be so imminent, of the time when she would cease to please; at any rate, she died..

As for Miriel, he quit the earth, and went to seek among the sylphides the wherewithal to console the woes that mortals has caused him, and the sad Leoparde, prey to remorse and jealousy, no longer occupied herself with anything but persecuting amour in all the objects that were presented to her eyes, in order, at least, to try to render them as unhappy as she was herself. Some have said that she married the enchanter after Sparkling's death, but those authors are so unreliable that one cannot found any belief on the authority their chronicles.

PRINCESS CAMION

There was once a king and a queen who had only one son; he was their unique hope. In the fourteen years since he had been born, the queen had never had the slightest suspicion of pregnancy. The prince was marvelously handsome; he learned everything that was wanted of him. The king and the queen loved him madly, and their subjects had put all their tenderness into him; for he was affable to everyone, and yet knew how to make the distinction of the people who approached him. His name was Zirphil.

As he was an only son, the king and queen resolved to marry him as soon as possible, in order to see princes born who could sustain their crown if Zirphil, unfortunately, were to be taken away from them. A search was therefore made on foot and on horseback for a princess worthy of the dauphin, but none was found who was suitable.

Finally, after a great investigation, someone came to tell the queen that a veiled woman wanted to speak to Her Majesty in private, about an important matter. The queen went swiftly to her throne in order to give her an audience.

The lady approached without removing her white crepes, which fell all the way to the ground. When she was at the foot of the throne she said: "I am astonished, Queen, that you thought about marrying your son without consulting me; I am the fay Marmotte, and my name has made enough noise to have reached you."

"Oh, Madame," said the queen, descending promptly from the throne in order to go and embrace the fay, "you will easily forgive me for my fault when you know that I have only listened as if to a tale to all the marvels that I have been told about you; but now that you have done me the favor of coming to my palace, I no longer doubt your power, and I beg you to be kind enough to honor me with your advice."

"It does not go thus with the fays," said Marmotte. "Such an excuse might satisfy a common one, but I am mortally offended, and to commence your punishment, I order you to have your Zirphil marry the person that I am bringing you."

With those words she rummaged in her pouch and took out a little toothpick case; she opened it and took out a little enamel doll, so pretty and so well made that the queen, in spite of her dolor, could not help admiring it.

"This is my goddaughter," the fay continued, "and I have always destined her for Zirphil."

The queen was in tears; she implored Marmotte in the most touching terms not to expose her to the ridicule of her people, who would mock her if she announced that marriage to them.

"What is there to mock, Madame?" said the fay. "Oh, we shall see whether anyone will mock my goddaughter, and whether our son will not adore her. I want to tell you that she has merit; she is small, it's true, but she has more intelligence that your entire realm put together; when you hear her, you'll be surprised, for she speaks, I can assure you. Go on, little Princess Cami-

251

on,"[9] she said to the doll, "Speak to your mother-in-law a little, and show her what you can do."

Then the pretty Camion jumped on to the queen's tippet and paid her a little compliment so tender and so reasonable that the queen suspended her tears in order to kiss Princess Camion with all her heart.

"Here, Queen," the fay said to her. "Take my case and put your daughter-in-law back into it; I want your son to become accustomed to her before marrying her; I believe that won't be long delayed, your obedience might soothe my anger; but if you go against my orders, you, your husband, your son and your kingdom will feel the effect of my wrath. And above all, put her back in her case this evening, for it's important that she doesn't stay up late."

With those words she lifted her veil, and the queen fainted in fear when she perceived a veritable living marmot, black, hairy and as large as a human. Her women came to her aid, and when she had recovered from her faint she could no longer see anything except the case that Marmotte had left her.

She was put to bed and the king was informed of the accident; he arrived, very frightened. The queen sent everyone away, and, with a torrent of tears, related her adventure to the king, who did not believe it until he saw the doll, which the queen took out of its case.

"Just Heaven!" he cried, after having meditated a little, "can it be that kings are exposed to such great mis-

---

[9] *Camion* is nowadays the French term for a truck or wagon carrying goods; at the time when the story was written, however, its far more common referent was a small pin used by dressmakers, and that is the resemblance that the name is supposed to evoke.

fortunes? Oh, we are only above other men in order to feel more dolorously the pains and misfortunes attached to life."

"And to give greater examples of firmness, Sire," said the doll, in a tiny, soft and clear voice.

"My dear Camion," said the queen, "you speak like an oracle."

Finally, after an hour of conversation between the three individuals, it was concluded that they would not divulge the marriage as yet, and would wait for Zirphil, who was away for three days, hunting, to decide whether to follow the fay's orders, of which the queen took charge of informing him.

In the meantime, the queen, and even the king, shut themselves away in order to converse with little Camion. She had a very well-ornamented mind, she spoke well, and with a singular turn that was very pleasing; however, although she was very animated, her eyes had a fixity that was unpleasant, and the queen was only shocked by that because she had begun to love Camion, and feared that the prince might acquire an aversion to her.

More than a month had already passed after Marmotte had appeared, and the queen had not yet shown him his intended bride. One day, however, he came into her apartment when she was still in bed.

"Madame," he said to her, "the most surprising thing in the world has happened to me some time ago while I was hunting; I wanted to continue to hide it from you, but it has become so extraordinary that it's absolutely necessary that I tell you.

"I was following a wild boar very ardently into the depths of the forest, without noticing that I was alone, when I saw it hurtle into a hole in the ground. My horse having gone after it, I fell for half an hour, but found myself at the bottom without having been wounded. There, instead of the wild boar, which, I confess, I dreaded seeing again, I found an exceedingly ugly woman, who invited me to dismount from the horse and follow her. I did not hesitate, and gave her my hand. She opened a little door that had previously been hidden from my sight, and I went with her into a green marble hall, where there was a golden vat covered with a curtain of very rich fabric. She lifted it up, and I saw in that vat a beauty so marvelous that I nearly fell backwards.

"'Prince Zirphil,' said the lady who was bathing there, 'the fay Marmotte has enchanted me here, and it is by means of your help alone that I can be liberated.'

"'Speak, Madame,' I said. 'What is it necessary to do to recue you?'

"'It is necessary,' she said, "to marry me directly, or to flay me alive."

"I was as surprised by the first proposal as I was frightened by the second. She read my embarrassment in my eyes, and continued speaking: 'Don't imagine,' she said, 'that I'm making fun of you or that I'm proposing to you something that you might repent. No, Zirphil, be reassured; I am an unfortunate princess, to whom the fay has taken an aversion; she has made me half woman and half whale, for not having wanted to marry her nephew, King Merlan,[10] who is frightful, and even more wicked,

---

[10] *Merlan* is the French term for a whiting. The word is used in the story both as a proper name, when I have left it untranslated, and as a trivial noun, when I have translated it, as with Marmotte/marmot and other words employed in the same dual fashion. I have, however, always translated *baleine* as whale, because it is not really used as a proper name with reference to the princess in the vat.

and she has condemned me to the estate that I am in until a prince named Zirphil has fulfilled one of the conditions that I have just proposed to you. In order to achieve that end, I had my maid of honor take the form of a wild boar, and she is the one who lured you here. I even have to tell you that you will not get out until you have fulfilled my desire in one way or the other. I am not the mistress of that, and Citronette, whom you see here with me, will tell you that it cannot be otherwise.'

"Can you imagine, Madame," said the prince to the queen, who was listening attentively, "the state in which that last speech put me? Although the face of the whale princess pleased me infinitely, and her graces and misfortunes rendered her extremely touching, the whale part gave me a frightful horror; however, when I thought that it was necessary to flay her alive, I was in despair. 'But Madame,' I said, finally—for my silence had become as stupid as it was insulting,' is there not a third means?'

"I had not finished speaking when the whale princess and her maidservant made cries and lamentations to pierce the vault of the hall. 'Ingrate! Cruel man! Tiger! Everything there is of the most savage and inhuman!' she said to me. 'You want me, then, to be condemned to the torture of seeing you expire? For if you do not resolve to grant me what I request, you will perish, the fay has assured me, and I will be a whale all my life.'

"Her reproaches pierced my heart; she raised her beautiful arms out of the water, and joined her charming hands in order to beg me to chose promptly. Citronette was at my knees, which she was embracing, screaming as if to render me deaf.

"'But how can I marry you?' I said. 'What sort of ceremony is necessary for that?'

"'Flay me,' she said to me, tenderly, 'and don't marry me; I love you as much as that.'

"'Flay her,' said the other, still screeching, 'and don't be embarrassed by anything.'

"I was in a perplexity that I cannot describe, and while I thought about what I ought to do, their cries and tears redoubled, and I no longer knew what would happen. Finally, after a thousand combats, I raised my eyes to the beautiful whale princess again, and I confess that I found her inexpressibly charming. I threw myself to my knees next to the vat and took her beautiful hand. 'No, Princess,' I said to her, 'I will not flay you; I would rather marry you.'

"At those words, joy spread over the face of the princess, but a modest joy, for she blushed, and, lowered her beautiful eyes. 'I shall never forget the service that you are rendering me,' she said. 'I am so penetrated with gratitude that you can expect anything from me after that generous resolution.'

"'Don't waste time!' cried the insupportable Citronette, 'Tel him quickly what he has to do.'

"'It is sufficient,' said the whale princess, 'for you to give me your ring and that you receive mine. Here is my hand, receive it as a pledge of my faith.'

"I had no sooner made that exchange and kissed the beautiful hand that she presented to me than I found myself back on my horse in the middle of the forest. Having called my men, they came to me and I returned here, without being able to say a word, so astonished was I. Since then, every night, I have been transported, without knowing how, into the beautiful green hall, where I spend the night next to an invisible person; she speaks to me, and tells me that it is not yet time for me to know her."

"Oh, my son!" cried the queen. "It is really possible, then, that you are married."

"But Madame," said the prince, "although I love my wife infinitely, I would have sacrificed that tenderness if I had been able to get out of it without doing that."

At those words, a little voice emerged from the queen's pouch, which said: "Prince Zirphil, it was necessary to flay her; but your pity might perhaps be fatal to you."

The prince, surprised by that voice, remained quite nonplussed. The queen tried in vain to hide the cause of that adventure from him; he promptly rummaged in that pouch, which was on the armchair next to the bed and took out the case, which the queen took from his hand and which she opened. Immediately, Princess Camion emerged, and the astonished prince knelt down next to the queen's bed in order to consider her at closer range.

"I swear to you, Madame," he cried, "that this is the miniature of my dear whale. Is it, then, a gallantry that you are making me, and did you want to frighten me by letting me believe any longer that you did not approve of my marriage?"

"No, my son," said the queen, "my chagrin is veritable, and you have exposed us to the cruelest misfortunes by marring that whale, because, in sum, you were promised to Princess Camion, whom you see in my hands."

Then she told him everything that had happened with the fay Marmotte, and the prince let her say everything she wanted without interrupting her, so surprised was he that she and his father had lent themselves to an affair that seemed so ridiculous.

"God forbid, Madame," he said, finally, when the queen had finished, "that I would ever oppose Your

Majesty's designs and go against my father the king, even if he had ordered me to do things as impossible as these seem; but even if I had wanted to, even if I had fallen in love with this pretty princess how would your subjects ever have…?"

"Time is a grandmaster, Prince Zirphil," said Campion, "but it's over; you can no longer marry me, and my godmother appears to me to be a person who will not suffer it easily when some breaks their word to her. Tiny as I am, I feel as much as another the annoyance of this adventure, but as it was not entirely your fault, except that you were a little too stupid, perhaps I can persuade the fay to reduce her vengeance."

After those words, Camion fell silent, for she was exhausted by having said so much.

"My darling," said the queen, "I beg you to rest, for fear of doing yourself harm, in order that you will be in a fit state to speak to the fay when she comes to desolate us. You are our consolation, and if we are punished, mine will be mild if Marmotte does not take you away from us."

Little Camion felt her tiny heart moved by the queen's words, but being completely out of breath, she could only kiss the queen's hand, over which she shed a few tiny tears.

Zirphil was touched by that situation, and asked Camion for her own hand, in order to kiss it in his turn. She gave it to him with a great deal of grace and dignity, and then she went back into her case.

After that tender scene, the queen got up in order to go and tell the king what had happened and to take reasonable measures against the anger of the fay.

The following night, in spite of the guard having been doubled in his apartment, the prince was removed as midnight chimed, and found himself, as usual, next to his invisible companion; but instead of hearing the pleasant and touching things that she was accustomed to say, he heard her weeping, and the person drew away from him.

"What have I done?" he said, finally, after tiring himself out running after her. "What have I done for you to treat me so badly? You're weeping, my dear whale, when you ought to be consoling me for what I have to dread for my tenderness!"

"I know everything," said the whale princess, in a voice punctuated by sobs. "I know everything cruel that can happen to me, but, ingrate, it is of you that I have the most to complain."

"O Heaven!" cried Zirphil. "For what have you to reproach me?"

"The amour that Camion has for you," said the voice, "and the tenderness with which you kissed her hand."

"Tenderness!" said the prince, hotly. "My dear whale, do you know mine so little that you accuse it so lightly? Furthermore, if Camion could have amour for me, which is impossible, since she only saw me for a moment, how could you fear it, after the love I have for you, after the proofs that I have given you? It is you that I ought to accuse of injustice, for if I looked at her with some attention, it was only because her face represents yours, and, deprived of the pleasure of seeing you, everything that resembles you pleases me extremely. Don't hide any longer, my dear princess, and I will never look at another woman."

The invisible woman seemed consoled by those words and drew nearer to the prince. "Forgive me," she said, "that little fit of jealousy; I have enough reasons to fear that I might be separated from you to have been afflicted by something that seemed to commence announcing that misfortune to me."

"But may I not know why it is not permitted for you to show yourself?" said the prince. "For, if I have delivered you from the tyranny of Marmotte, how it is possible that you are still submissive to it?"

"Alas," said the invisible princess, "if you had chosen to flay me, we would have been much more fortunate; but you had so much horror for that proposal that I did not dare to proffer it again"

"By what hazard," the prince interjected, "is Camion informed of that adventure, for she said something very similar to me?"

Scarcely had he finished pronouncing those words that the whale princess uttered a frightful scream and leapt out of the bed. The surprised prince got out precipitately. What was his fear, though, when he perceived the hideous Marmotte in the middle of the room, holding the beautiful whale princess—who was no longer either a whale or invisible—by the hair. He wanted to draw his sword, but the whale princess, in tears, begged him to moderate his anger, because it would serve no purpose against the power of the fay. The horrible Marmotte ground her teeth, and a violet flame emerged therefrom, which singed the hairs of his beard.

"Prince Zirphil," she said to him, "a fay who is protecting you against me prevents me from exterminating you, your father, your mother and everything that belongs to you, but you will suffer no less in that which is dear to you for having married without consulting me, and your torment will not end, nor those of your princess, until you have submitted to my orders."

As she finished speaking, she disappeared, along with the princess, the room and the palace, and he found himself in his apartment, naked except for a chemise, sword in hand. He was so astonished and so beside himself with anger, that he did not think that it was freezing cold, for it was the middle of winter. At the noise he made, his guards entered his room and begged him to go to bed or allow himself to be dressed. He made the latter decision and went to the queen's room.

For her part, she had passed the night in the cruelest of all anxieties. She had not been able to sleep on going to bed, and in order to try to succeed in that she had wanted to talk about her chagrins with little Camion; but she had shaken her case in vain; Camion was no longer in it. She feared having lost her in the gardens, and had got up after having torches lit in order to search for her, but it was futile; she had disappeared completely, and the queen had returned to bed in a frightful chagrin. When her son came in she let it burst forth.

He was so afflicted himself that he did not perceive the queen's tears. Seeing him so agitated, she said to him: "Doubtless you've come to announce something frightful to me?"

"Yes, Madame," said the prince, "for I've come to tell you that I want to die if I cannot recover my princess."

"What, my son? Do you love that unfortunate princess already?"

"What, your Camion?" said the prince. "Can you suspect me of it, Madame? It's my dear whale that has been stolen from me; it's only for her that I can't live, and it's Marmotte, cruel Marmotte, who has taken her."

"Oh, my son," said the queen, "I am much more afflicted than you, for if someone has stolen your whale, someone has also stolen Camion from me; she had dis-appeared from her case since yesterday evening."

They told one another then about their reciprocal adventures, and bewailed their common misfortune to-gether. The king was informed of the cries and despair of the queen and the chagrin of his son. He came to the apartment where that tragic scene was unfolding, and as he had a good deal of intelligence he immediately thought of having posters put up regarding Camion, of-fering a large reward for anyone who brought her back. Everyone thought that expedient marvelous, and even the queen, in spite of her great dolor, was obliged to agree that one could never imagine such a singular thing without having a transcendent mind.

The posters were made and distributed, and the queen was calmed by the hope of soon having news of the little princess. For Zirphil, the loss of the princess interested him as little as her presence; he resolved to go in search of a fay of whom he had heard mention; he asked the king and queen for permission, and departed, only accompanied by a squire.

It was a long way from that land to the one where the fay was, but time and obstacles could not stop the amorous impatience of young Zirphil. He passed through countries and realms without number; nothing in particu-lar happened to him, because he did not want it to; for, being as handsome as amour and as brave as his sword, adventures would have been presented to him if he had wanted to go in search of them.

Finally, after a year of traveling, he arrived at the commencement of the desert where the fay had her dwelling. He dismounted and left his squire in a little cabin with orders to wait for him and not to be impatient.

He went into the desert, which was frightful by virtue of its solitude; only owls lived here, but their cries did not frighten the magnanimous soul of the prince.

One evening, he perceived in the distance a light that made him believe that he was approaching the grotto, for who else but a fay would reside in that horrible desert? He walked for a long time during the night; finally, at daybreak, he discovered the famous grotto, but a lake of fire separated him from it, and all his valor could not save him from the flames that spread out to the right and the left.

He searched for a long time for what he could do, and his courage nearly abandoned him when he saw that there was not even a bridge; despair served him better; beside himself with chagrin and amour, he decided to end his life in the lake if he could not traverse it.

He had no sooner made that strange resolution than he executed it and threw himself headlong into the flames, but only felt a mild heat, which did not inconvenience him, and passed to the other side without difficulty.

Scarcely was he out of it when a young and beautiful salamander emerged from the lake and said to him: "Prince Zirphil, if your love is as great as your courage, you ought to hope for everything from the fay Luminous; she loves you, but she wants to test you."

Zirphil made a profound reverence to the salamander in order to thank her, for she did not give him time to speak; she plunged back into the flames, and he continued on his way. He finally arrived at the base of a rock of prodigious height, which seemed to be entirely ablaze, so brilliant was it. It was a carbuncle so large that the fay was comfortably lodged inside it.

As soon as the prince approached, Luminous emerged from the rock. He prostrated himself before her; she had him get up and enter the grotto.

"Prince Zirphil," she said to him, "A power equal to mine has balanced the good fortune with which I endowed you at birth, but you ought to expect everything of my cares. However, it will require as much patience as courage to vanquish the malevolence of Marmotte; I cannot tell you anymore."

"At least, Madame," said the prince, "Do me the favor of telling me whether my beautiful whale is unfortunate, and whether I shall see her again soon."

"She is not unfortunate," said the fay, "but you can only see her after having crushed her in the mortar of King Merlan."

"O Heaven!" cried the prince. "She is in his power, and I have to dread, not merely the amour that he has for her, but also the horror of crushing her with my own hands!"

"Arm yourself with strength," said the fay, "and don't hesitate to obey; all your happiness depends on it, and that of your wife."

"But she'll die if I crush her," said the prince, "and I would rather die myself...."

"Go," said the fay, "And don't argue. Every moment you lose adds to Marmotte's fury. Go to the abode of King Merlan. Tell him that you are the page I promised him, and count on my protection." Afterwards, she showed him, on a map, the route that it was necessary to follow in order to reach the abode of King Merlan; then she dismissed him, after having told him that the ring that the whale princess had given him would enable him to see everything that he had to do when the king ordered difficult things.

He set forth, and after a journey of a few days he arrived in a pastureland terminated by the sea, on the edge of which a small ship of mother-of-pearl garnished with gold was moored. He looked at his ruby and saw himself inside, boarding the ship; he went aboard, and after he had detached it, the wind pushed it out to sea.

After a few hours of navigation, the ship stopped at the foot of a castle of rock crystal built on piles. He leapt down and went into a courtyard that led to a magnificent vestibule and apartments without number, all the walls of which were rock crystal, admirably engraved, creating the most beautiful effect in the world. Men with the heads of fish of all species lived in the castle. He had no doubt that it was the dwelling of King Merlan; he quivered with anger, but he constrained himself in order to ask a turbot, who seemed to be the captain of the guard, how he could see King Merlan.

The turbot-man gave him a sign gravely to approach, and he went into the guard-room, where he saw a thousand armed men with the heads of pikes, who formed a hedge as he passed by. Finally, he reached the throne room, after having pierced an infinite crowd of fish-men. They did not make a lot of noise, for they were mute; the greater number had the heads of whitings; he saw several of them who appeared to be the most considerable, by virtue of the crowds surrounding them and the self-important manner they adopted toward others.

He reached the king's cabinet, from which he saw the council emerging, composed of twelve men with the heads of sharks. Finally, the king appeared himself; like the others, he had the head of a whiting, but he had fins on his shoulders, and from the waist downwards he was a veritable whiting. He could speak, and his attire only consisted of a sash of dorado-skin, which was quite brilliant. He had a helmet in the form of a crown, from which rose the tail of a cod, forming its plume. Four whitings were carrying him in a Japanese porcelain bucket as large as a bath-tub; it was full of sea-water; his greatest magnificence was to have it filled twice a day by the dukes and peers of his court; that employment was much sought-after.

King Merlan was very large, and looked more like a monster than anything else. When he had spoken to a few of those who had brought him petitions he perceived the prince. "Who are you, my friend?" he said to him. "By what hazard has a human come here?"

"Sire," said Zirphil, "I am the page that the fay Luminous promised you."

"I know what he is," said the king, laughing and showing his teeth, like those of a saw. "Take him to my seraglio and let him teach my crayfish to talk."

Immediately, a troop of whiting surrounded him and took him where the king had ordered. As they went past the apartments again, all the fish, even those in greatest favor, gave him abundant signs of amity. He was taken through a delightful garden, at the end of which was a charming pavilion of mother-of-pearl, with large coral branches ornamenting the walls.

The whiting favorites introduced him into a similarly-ornamented hall, the windows of which overlooked a magnificent pool. He was made to understand that it was his dwelling, and, after having shown him a small bed-room that opened in a corner of the hall, which he understood to be his, the whitings withdrew and he remained alone, quite astonished to find himself a prisoner of sorts in his rival's abode.

He was reviewing the state of his affairs when he saw the door of his room open and ten or twelve thousand crayfish, conducted by one larger than the others, came in and arranged themselves in straight lines, which almost filled his apartment. The one marching at their head climbed up on a table that was beside him and said to him:

"Prince, I know you, and you owe a great deal to my cares; but as it is rare to find gratitude in humans, I shall not tell you what I have done for you, in order not to destroy the sentiments that you have inspired in me; know, then, that these are King Merlan's crayfish, that they alone can speak in this empire, and that you have been chosen to teach them fine language, social etiquette and the means of pleasing their sovereign. You will find them intelligent, but it is necessary, every morning, that you choose ten of them to be crushed in the king's mortar, in order to make a broth."

The crayfish having stopped speaking, the prince spoke. "I did not know, Madame, that you had been good enough to take an interest in my regard; the fact that I feel gratitude for it already might help you to lose the bad idea that you have conceived of humans in general, since, on the assurance you have given me, I feel capable of being touched by it; but what worries me greatly is knowing what it is necessary to do in order to reason with the persons whose education you have been good enough to confide to me; if I were sure that they are as intelligent as you, I would have little difficulty, and I would be honored by that task, but the more they seem to me to be possible to teach, the less courage I would have to punish them for that of which they are probably not culpable; having lived with them, how will I deliver them to a torture…?"

"You are an obstinate and great talker," said the crayfish, "but we shall be able to reduce you." Then she rose up above the table and, leaping to the floor, took on the true form of Marmotte, to the life—for she was that wicked fay.

"O Heaven!" cried the prince. "So this is the person who boasts of being so interested in my days, the one who has rendered them unhappy? Oh, Luminous," he went on, "You have abandoned me...."

He had not finished speaking when Marmotte precipitated herself through the window into the reservoir and disappeared. He remained alone with the twelve thousand crayfish.

After having thought for a while about what he was going to do to teach them to live, for which they were waiting in great silence, it came to his mind that he might well find among them the beautiful and unfortunate whale, since the frightful Marmotte had ordered him to crush ten of them every morning.

Why crush them, he thought, *if not to enrage me?* "No matter," he exclaimed, getting to his feet, "Let us at least try to recognize her, in order to die of dolor before her eyes." Then he asked the crayfish whether they would be kind enough to let him search among them to see whether there might be one of his acquaintance.

"We don't know anything, Sire," said the first one to speak, "but you can seek information until it is time for us to return to the reservoir, for it's absolutely necessary for us to spend the night there."

Zirphil then began his search, but the more he searched, the less he discovered; he only remarked from a few words that he extracted from those he questioned that they were as many princesses transformed by the malevolence of Marmotte. It gave him an inconceivable chagrin to be obliged to choose ten of them for the king's broth.

When evening came, they made him perceive that it was necessary to return to the reservoir, and it was not without difficulty that he resolved to deprive himself of the pleasant amusement of seeking the princess. In the entire day he had only been able to speak to a hundred and fifty of them, but as he was at least sure that she was not among those, he decided to take ten from that number.

He had no sooner chosen than he got ready to carry them to the king's kitchens, but he was stopped by the most astonishing bursts of laughter that seized the victims that he was about to immolate. He was so surprised by that, that he could not speak for some time; finally, he interrupted them to ask what was so pleasant about what he was about to do. They redoubled their laughter, with such noisy bursts and so wholeheartedly that he could not help mingling his laughter with theirs, in spite of the chagrin he felt.

They tried to speak, but they could not; they interrupted one another to say: "Oh, I can't do any more!" or "Oh, I'm going to die!" or "No, there's nothing so funny!" and laughing.

Finally, he arrived at the palace, laughing like them with the full force of his lungs, and when he had shown a pike-head that was in charge of the kitchen what he was holding in his hands, he was brought a green porphyry mortar garnished with gold, into which he put the crayfish and got ready to crush them. Then the bottom of the mortar opened and a brilliant flame emerged, which dazzled the prince and retreated as the bottom closed again. He could not see anything any longer, including the crayfish, which had disappeared. That astonished him, and yet caused him joy, for he was afflicted by the thought of having to crush such joyful crayfish.

The pike appeared annoyed by the adventure, and wept bitterly. The prince was as astonished by that as he had been by the laughter of the crayfish; he could not determine the reason, because the pike-head could not speak.

Greatly troubled by his adventure, he returned to his pretty apartment, where he no longer found the crayfish; they had returned to the reservoir.

The next morning, the crayfish cane in without Marmotte; he searched for the princess, but did not find her again. He chose ten of the most beautiful; the same thing happened; they laughed, and the pike wept when they disappeared with the flames. For three months in succession he always saw the same thing; he did not hear any mention of the King of the Merlans, so he was only anxious about not seeing the beautiful whale.

One evening, when he was returning home from the kitchen, he was traversing the palace gardens, and as he went past a palisade that surrounded a charming arbor, in the middle of which was a little fountain, he heard talking. That astonished him; he had believed all the inhabitants of the realm to be as mute as those he had seen. He walked more slowly, and heard a voice saying: "But my princess, as long as you don't reveal yourself, your husband will never recognize you?"

"What do you want me to do?" said another voice, which he recognized as one he had heard so many times. "The cruelty of Marmotte obliges me not to make myself known without risking my life and his. The sage Luminous, who is guiding him, hides my face from him in order to conserve us both; but it's absolutely necessary that he crush me, that's an irrevocable decree."

"But why must he crush you?" said the other. "You've never wanted to tell me your story. Your confidante Citronette would have told me, if she hadn't been chosen last week for the king's broth."

"Alas," said the princess, "The poor woman has already suffered the torture that I'm awaiting; I would have liked to be able to take her place, for she's surely in the grotto now."

"But tell me," said the other voice, "since it's such a beautiful night, why you're subject to Marmotte's vengeance? I've already told you who I am, and I'm burning with impatience you know your better."

"Although it renews my dolor," said the princess, "I can't refuse to satisfy you. Also, it involves talking about Zirphil, and I deliver myself joyfully to everything that can remind me of him."

One can easily judge the pleasure that the prince felt at that fortunate moment. He slipped gently into the arbor but, as it was very dark, he could not see anything; he therefore listened intently, and this is what he heard, word for word:

"My father was the king of a country neighboring Mount Caucasus. He reigned as best he could over a people of incredible unruliness; there were perpetual revolts; the windows of the palace had often been broken by stones thrown at them. The queen, my mother, who was very intelligent, composed harangues for him to appease the seditions, but when one had succeeded one day, there was a new impetus the following day. The judges were weary of condemning people to death and the executioners of hanging them; finally, there came a point so violent that, seeing all our provinces united against us, my father decided to go into the country in order not to see such disagreeable things. He took the queen with him and left one of his ministers, who was very wise and less cowardly than my father, to govern the kingdom.

"My mother was pregnant with me, so she had difficulty arriving at the foot of Mount Caucasus, which my father had chosen as his habitation. Our malevolent subjects lit fires of joy at their departure, and the next day, they killed our minister, saying that he wanted to be ruler, and that they preferred the king. My father was not touched by their preference, and remained hidden in his little house, where I was soon born. I was named Camion, because I was very small. The king and queen, very weary of the honors that had cost them so dear, wanting to hide my birth, raised me as a shepherdess.

"After ten years, which seemed to them to be ten minutes, so content were they with their retreat, the fays that inhabited the Caucasus, indignant at the wickedness of the men who populated our realm, resolved to bring order to it.

"One day, when I was with my sheep in the meadow adjacent to our garden, I was accosted by two old shepherdesses, who begged me to give them shelter for the night. They seemed so exhausted and sad that my soul was moved by compassion. 'Come,' I said to them. 'My father, who is a pastor, will be glad to receive you.' I ran to the cabin to warn him of their arrival; he came to met them, and received them with much generosity, as did the queen, my mother. I brought my ewes back and I drew milk from them for our guests. In the meantime, my father prepared them a nice little supper, and the queen, who, as you already know, was very intelligent, conversed with them marvelously.

"I had a little lamb, which I loved madly. My father summoned me to give it to him, so that he could put it on the spit. I was not accustomed to resist his will, so I brought it to him, but I was so afflicted by it that I went to weep next to my mother, who was so occupied in talking to the good women that she did not notice. 'What's the matter with little Camion?' asked one of them, who saw that I was in tears.

"'Alas, Madame,' I said, 'it's my father, who is going to roast my little lamb for you.'

'What!' said the one who had not yet spoken. 'It's for us that this harm is being done to pretty Camion!' Then she got up, and waved a wand, and instantly, a magnificently served table emerged from under the ground, and the two old shepherdesses became two ladies, so beautiful and so glittering with gems that I stood there, motionless. I didn't even pay attention to my little lamb, which was bounding around the room and making a thousand leaps, rejoicing the company greatly. Finally, I ran to him, after having kissed the hands of the beautiful ladies, but I was astonished to see all his wool changed to silver cannetille, and all covered in pink ribbons.

"My father and my mother were occupied in serving the fays, for you have deduced that they were two of them. They lifted up the king and queen, who had prostrated themselves.

"'King and Queen,' said the one who appeared to be the more majestic, we have known you for a long time, and your misfortunes have moved us to pity. Don't believe that grandeurs dispense one from the woes attached to human life; you must know from experience that the more elevated one's rank is, the more sensitive one is to their experience. Your patience and your virtue have put you above your misfortunes; it is time to give you the recompense. I am the fay Luminous, and I have come to ask you what might suit Your Majesties. Speak,

273

and have no fear of putting our power to the proof. Confer together; your wishes will be granted; but above all, don't talk about Camion; her destiny is separate. The fay Marmotte, envious all that she promises of brilliance, has obscured her for some time, but she will sense the price of her happiness more when she has known the misfortunes of life; we shall protect her by softening them, which is all we are permitted to do. Speak; afterwards we can do everything for you.'

"After that speech the fays fell silent. The queen turned toward the king in order to tell him to respond, for she was weeping on learning that I was destined to be unhappy; but my father was in no better state to talk than she was. He made pitiful cries, and I, seeing them weeping, quit my sheep in order to weep with them. The fays waited with a great impatience and in complete silence for our tears to end.

"Finally, my mother pushed my father slightly, to make him perceive that they were waiting for his response. He therefore took his handkerchief away from his face and said that, since it was decided that I would be unhappy, none of the benefits that were offered to him could be agreeable to him, and he refused the good fortune that was promised to him, since it would always be poisoned by the idea he had of what I had to dread. Seeing that the poor man was not going to say another word, the queen added that she begged the fays to take away their lives on the day when destiny made me feel its rigor, and that the only favor they demanded was that of not witnessing it.

"The good fays, moved by the extreme dolor that reigned in the royal family, spoke in whispers for a while; then Luminous, who had already spoken, said to the queen: 'Console yourself, Madame; the misfortunes by which Camion are menaced will not be so great that they cannot end happily, for as soon as the husband we have destined for her has obeyed what destiny will order him to do, she will be happy with him forever, and our sister's malignity will not be able to do anything to him or to her. It is a prince worthy of her that she shall give her, but all that we can tell you that it is absolutely necessary that you lower your daughter into the well every morning and that she bathes there for half an hour. If you observe that rule exactly, perhaps she will avoid the evils by which she is menaced; it is in her twelfth year that this destiny must be accomplished; if she reaches thirteen without feeling the effect, there will be nothing more to fear. That is all with regard to her; as for you, wish and we can grant your wishes,'

"The king and queen looked at one another, and after a short silence, the king asked to become a statue until my thirteenth year was accomplished, and the queen limited her wishes to asking that the well where I had to bathe would always be appropriate to the season. Charmed by that excess of tenderness, the fays added that the water would be scented with orange blossom, and that every time that, and as many times as, the queen threw that water over the king, he would resume his natural form, and would become a statue again when he wished. Then they took their leave of us, after having praised the king and queen for their moderation, and promised to aid them every time they had need of it, on burning a sprig of the cannetille with which my lamb was covered.

"They disappeared, and I felt chagrin for the first time in my life on seeing my father the king become a large statue of black marble. The queen dissolved in tears, and so did I, but finally, as everything ceases, I

stopped crying and no longer occupied myself with anything but consoling my mother, because I felt that I was
full of reason and capable of sentiments.

"The queen spent her life at the foot of the statue,
and after having bathed as I had been ordered to do, I
went to get milk from our ewes, which we ate to sustain
ourselves, for the queen did not have the strength to
want anything else, and it was only out of amity for me
that she wanted to conserve a life that seemed so bitter to
her.

"'Alas, my daughter,' she said to me sometimes,
'what use have our grandeur and our elevation been to
us?'—for she was no longer hiding my birth from me—
'would it not have been better to have been born in a
lower rank, since the crown entails such great chagrins?
Only virtue, my dear Camion, enables me to support
them, with the aid of my tenderness for you; but there
are moments when my soul seems to want to separate
itself from me, and I confess that I feel relief in imagining that I might die. It is not for me that you ought to
weep,' she added, 'but your father, whose dolor, even
greater than mine, brought him to want almost to cease
to live. Never forget, my dear daughter, the gratitude that
you owe him.'

"'Alas, Madame,' I replied, 'I am incapable of ever
forgetting him, and I am even less likely not to remember that you wanted to live in order to help me.'

"I was bathed every day, and my mother was very
annoyed always to see the king an inanimate statue, but
she dared not recall him to life, fearing to give him the
dolor of being witness to what must happen to me; the
fays not having specified it, we were in mortal anxiety in
that regard. The queen, especially, imagined frightful
things, because her ideas, having a vast field in which to

expand, set no limits on her fear. For myself, I was only slightly embarrassed by it, so true is it that youth is the only time when we enjoy the present.

"My mother said to me incessantly that she had a desire to revive the king; I had the same thought. Finally, after six months, seeing that the fays' bath had embellished me considerably and ornamented my mind, which was being formed from day to day, she resolved to satisfy it, at least, she said, to give the king the pleasure of seeing me, so she ordered me to bring her water from the well. In fact, after the bath I sent up a vase full of the marvelous water, and the statue was no sooner sprinkled with it than my father became a man. The queen threw herself at his feet to beg his pardon for having troubled his repose. He lifted her up and embraced her tenderly; peace was soon made, and she presented me to him.

"I was ashamed to tell you that he was charmed and surprised," said the voice, interrupting itself, "for how can you believe that I, the ugliest of crayfish, am a beautiful princess?"

"Of course I believe you," said the one to whom she was speaking. "I can boast of being as charming as one can be beneath this vile shell. But continue, I beg you, for I'm waiting impatiently for the end of your story."

"Well, then," said the other voice, "the king was delighted with me, gave me a thousand caresses, and asked the queen whether she had any news. 'Alas,' she said, 'who can come to give me any in this desert? Moreover, uniquely occupied in mourning your metamorphosis, I scarcely seek to inform myself about a world that is nothing to me without you.

"'Well,' said the king, 'I will give you some myself; for don't believe that I have always been asleep. The fays who watch for us have enabled me to see my

277

subjects punished. Of my entire kingdom thy have made a vast pond, and all the inhabitants are fish-people. A nephew of the fay Marmotte, whom they have established as king, persecutes them with an unequaled cruelty; he eats them for the slightest fault, but at the end of a time that is unknown to me, a prince will come who will be king in his stead, and it is in that great kingdom, which will be reestablished, that Camion will find all her happiness. That is all I know. It's not a bad way to have passed the time,' he added, laughing, 'to have known those things. The fays came to inform me every night, and I would perhaps have known more of you had left me longer, but in sum, I'm delighted to see you, and I don't know whether I'll become a statue again so soon, given the pleasure I have in being with you.'

"We spent some time very happily. The king and queen were a little sad, however, when they thought that I was approaching thirteen years of age. As the queen bathed me with great care she hoped that the prediction would not come to pass, but who can boast of going against destiny?

"One morning, when the queen had already got up and was picking flowers to decorate our cabin, because the king liked them very much, she saw an ugly beast emerge from beneath a tuberose plant, very similar to a marmot. That animal threw itself upon her and bit her nose; she fainted because of the pain the wound caused her, and after an hour my father, having not seen her return, went to search for her. Imagine his astonishment on seeing her nearly dead and covered in blood!

"He uttered frightful screams; I went to his aid and we carried the unconscious queen back and put her to bed; she did not recover consciousness for another two hours. Finally, she began to show signs of life, and we had the pleasure of seeing her, a moment later, in very good health, save for the pain of the wound, which was causing her to suffer a great deal. She asked immediately whether I had been to bathe, but we had been so occupied that I had forgotten. She was very alarmed; however, seeing that no accident had happened as yet, she was reassured, and told us about her adventure, which surprised us greatly.

"The day passed without any other chagrin; the king had taken a rifle and had searched everywhere for the accursed beast without finding it. The next day, at daybreak, the queen woke up and came to find me in order to repair the previous day's fault. She lowered me into the well as usual, but alas, O fatal and exceedingly unfortunate day, at that same instant, the sky, although serene, made a frightful thunder heard; the air lit up, and a fiery dart emerged from a blazing cloud, which fell into the well. My mother, frightened, let go of the rope that held me and I fell to the bottom, without any other harm than feeling that half my body was nothing but an enormous fish, of the kind known as a whale.

"I swam around for a while, and called to the queen with all my might. She did not reply; I was afflicted, and I was weeping bitterly, as much for her loss as my metamorphosis, when I felt an unknown power forcing me to descend to the bottom of the water. Having touched it, I entered into a crystal grotto, where I found a kind of nymph, rather ugly, so much did she resemble and oversized frog. However, she smiled at my approach and said to me: 'Camion, I am the nymph of the bottomless well; I have orders to welcome you and to make you accomplish the penitence that is destined to you for having failed to bathe. Follow me and don't argue.'

"How, alas, could I have done otherwise? I was so troubled and so desperate at finding myself dry that I did not have the strength to speak. She took me by the tail and dragged me, not without suffering, into a green marble hall that was near her grotto, and put me in a golden vat full of water, where I began to recover my spirits.

"The good nymph appeared delighted by that. 'My name is Citronette,' she said; 'I am commissioned to take care of you; you can give me any order you wish. I know the past and the present perfectly; as for the future, it is not given to me to penetrate it. So, command, and at least I shall be able to help you pass the time of your penitence without tedium.'

"I embraced the good Citronette at those words, and set about telling her the events of my life; then I asked her what had become of the king and the queen.

"She was about to reply to me when a frightful marmot as large as a human being came into the hall and chilled me with horror. It was walking on its hind legs and leaning on a golden wand, which gave it a certain grace. It approached the vat, where I would have liked to be able to drown myself, so frightened was I, and it lifted the wand and touched me with it.

"'Camion,' it said, 'you are in my power, and nothing can get you out of it but your obedience and that of the husband my sisters have destined for you. Listen to me, and lose that fear, which is not befitting to a great courage. Since our childhood I have wanted to take care of you and to marry you to my nephew, King Merlan. Luminous and two or three of my sisters had already taken possession of that right; I was annoyed by that, and I let my ill humor fall on you; unable to do anything against them, I resolved to punish you for their stubbornness, and I endowed you with being a whale for at least half your life. My sisters protested so much against the injustice that I reduced my vengeance by three and a half quarters, but I reserved for my complaisance making you marry my nephew. Luminous, who is imperious, and, unfortunately, above me, did not want to hear of that accommodation, because she had already destined you for a prince that she protects. It was therefore necessary again to cede to her opinion, in spite of my resentment. All that I was able to obtain is that the first one who delivers you from my paws will be your husband.'

"It paused. 'These are their portraits,' it said, showing me two golden lockets. 'You will know them by that, but if one of them comes to deliver you, he must give you his faith in marriage in the vat, and in order to get out of it, is necessary that he flays your whale's scales one by one; otherwise, you will always remain a fish. My nephew would not worry about that, but Luminous's protégé might find it very onerous, for he gives me the impression of being a very delicate little gentleman. Employ your cleverness, therefore, to make him flay you, and after that, you will no longer be unfortunate, if that is what it is to be a beautiful whale, very fat and well-nourished, and having water up to your neck.'

"At those words, to which I made no reply, I was very afflicted, as much by my present state as by the flaying through which I had to pass.

"Marmotte disappeared, leaving us the two picture-lockets. I was bewailing my chagrins and my situation, without thinking of looking at them, when the good and pitiful Citronette said to me: 'Come on, it's necessary not to be afflicted by evils that one can't remedy. Let's see whether I can't help you to console yourself. First of all, don't weep so much, for I have a tender heart, and I can't see your tears without having a desire to accompany them with mine. Let's dissipate them by looking at these portraits.'

"As she finished speaking, she opened the first locket and showed it to me; we both uttered the screams of Melusine on seeing a vile head of a whiting, albeit painted with all the advantage that it had been possible to give it; in spite of that, nothing so ugly had ever been seen in human memory. 'Take that object away,' I said to her. 'I can't bear the sight of it any longer. I'd rather be a whale all my life than marry the horrible whiting.'

"She didn't give me time to finish my imprecations against the monster. 'Look at this young darling,' she said. "Oh, that one could flay us at his pleasure; we wouldn't be so distressed by it!'

"I looked quickly, to see whether what she said was true, and was convinced of it only too soon. A noble and charming physiognomy was presented to my gaze; tender and delicate eyes embellished a face full of mildness and majesty; an impression of intelligence reigned therein that completed the graces of the delightful painting; long black hair, naturally curly, gave it an air that Citronette took for nonchalance, but which I didn't scorn when I found nothing in it but charm and tenderness.

"I therefore gazed at that lovely face with a pleasure that I didn't perceive. Citronette noticed it first. 'In good faith,' she cried, 'that's the one we'll choose!'

"That folly drew me out of my reverie, and, blushing at my ecstasy, I said: 'What's the point of flattering myself? Oh, my dear Citronette, this seems to me to be another of the cruel Marmotte's tricks. She has exhausted her art in order to give me the regret of never finding a similar object in nature.'

"'What!' said Citronette. 'Reflections on this portrait already? Truly, I hadn't expected it so soon.' I

blushed again at that bad joke, and became very embarrassed at having revealed too naively the effect that the
beautiful painting produced on my heart.

Citronette read my thought again. 'No,' she said,
embracing me, 'don't repent of that confession; I find
your good faith charming, and to console you, I'll tell
you that Marmotte is not deceiving you and that there is
a prince in the world who is the veritable original of that
picture.'

"That assurance gave me a momentary joy, but an
instant later I lost it, thinking that the prince in question
would never see me, since I was in the bowels of the
earth, and that Marmotte, by means of her power, would
sooner enable my dwelling to be pierced by her monstrous nephew than aid a prince that she hated because
he had been destined for me without her consent.

"I did not hide what I was thinking from Citronette;
any pretence would have been futile, for she read the
most secret of my thoughts with a surprising facility; I
preferred, therefore, to honor her with them, she merited
it by her attachment to me, and I found a great consolation in that; for I experienced from that day on that when
one's heart is filled by an object, one is glad to be able to
talk about it. In fact, I was in love from that moment on,
and Citronelle, with a great deal of intelligence and clari-
ty, rid me of the confusion and disturbance that the
commencement of a grand passion imports into a soul.

"She softened my dolor by allowing me to talk
about it, and gently changed the subject of the conversation, which almost always revolved around my tenderness and my chagrins. She told me that the king had
been transported to the abode of King Merlan, and that
the queen, at the moment when she had lost me, had become a crayfish.

"I could not understand that. 'One does not become a crayfish,' I said.

"'Do you understand any better how you have become a whale?' she said. She was right, but one is often astonished by things that happen to other, although one has the greatest subjects of astonishment oneself. My scant experience enabled that. Citronette often laughed at my innocence, and was surprised to see me so eloquent in my tenderness, for it is true that I was, on that chapter, and I found that the passion in question bears great enlightenment into the mind.

"I no longer slept; I woke the obliging Citronette a hounded times by night in order to talk to her about my prince. She had told me his name, and told me that he hunted almost every day in the forest above the place where I was buried. She proposed to me that she try to lure him into our abode, but I did not want to consent to that, although I was dying of desire for it. I was afraid that he might die for want of respiration; we were accustomed to it, and that was different. I feared that it might be too bold a step; furthermore, I was desolate at appearing to him as a whale, and I would have died if he had aversion for me like the one that the sight of the King of the Merlans had inspired in me.

"Citronette reassured me by telling me that, in spite of the whale's tail, my face was charming. I believed it sometimes, but more often I was anxious about it, and after having looked at myself, I did not find myself good enough to believe that I could inspire amour in the man who had enabled me to know it so well. Because of that, my self-esteem sustained my virtue. Has anyone any other that is veritable, alas? It is very rare to find a virtue pure enough not to be founded on any such motive.

"I spent my days imagining means of seeing him and making myself visible to him, which I destroyed as soon as I had imagined them. Citronette was a great help to me at that time, for it is necessary to admit that she had an infinite intelligence and even more kindness and generosity.

"One day, when I was even sadder than usual—for amour has the property that it often bears tender souls to sadness—I saw the frightful Marmotte come in with two individuals that I did not recognize at first. I got it into my head that it was her frightful nephew that she had brought me; I uttered cries of fright. 'But when she's flayed," said the vile Marmotte, 'she won't scream any louder; see whether one is doing her any great harm!'

"'My God, my sister,' said one of the persons who had come with her, whom I recognized joyfully for those I had once seen in our hamlet; let's leave your talk of flaying and say to Camion what we have to tell her.'

"'Gladly,' said Marmotte, 'but it's on the conditions that you know.'

"The good fay, without listening to her or replying to her, then addressed herself to me, 'Camion,' she said, 'we are too distressed by your condition not to think of remedying it, in as much as you have not merited it. My sisters and I have resolved to do everything in our power to ameliorate it. This, then, is what we have imagined. You are going to be presented at the court of the prince for whom I have destined you since childhood, but, my dear child, you will not appear such as you are, and it is ordered that you return three times a week to spend the night in your vat, for until you are married....'

"'And flayed,' the vile Marmotte interjected, laughing. The good fay turned toward her, shrugging her shoulders, and resumed immediately:

285

"'Until you are married, you will be a whale here. The rest, we cannot tell you. You will be instructed in due course, but above all, keep your secret, for if a word escapes you that tends to reveal it, neither I nor my sisters will be able to do anything for you, and you will be delivered to my sister Marmotte.'

"'That is what I am waiting for,' said the evil fay, 'and I already see her in my power, for a secret kept by a girl is a phenomenon.'

"'That is her affair,' said Luminous—she was the one who had already spoken to me. 'At any rate, my daughter,' she said to me, 'you shall become a little enamel doll, thinking and speaking; we will conserve all your features, and I give you a week to examine whether what I am saying is agreeable to you. We will come back then, and you will tell me whether you consent to it, or whether you would prefer to wait here for the event that will bring you one of the two husbands that we have destined for you.'

"I did not have time to respond; the fays left after those words, and I remained confounded by all that I had just seen and heard. I remained with Citronette, who made me envisage that it would be a good fortune for me to be an enamel doll. I sighed when I thought that my prince would never have a liking for such a toy, but in the end, the desire to see and know him prevailed over that of pleasing him, and I decided to accept the course of action that had been proposed to me, all the more so as Zirphil—thus he had been named to me—might well be anticipated by King Merlan, and that idea made me die of dolor.

"Citronette told me that he hunted every day in the forest above me, and every day I made her take on the form of a stag, a hind or a wild boar in order to bring me

286

news, which never failed to correspond to what my heart thought, for she depicted him to me a hundred times above the portrait of him that I had, and my imagination embellished him even further, to the extent that I was resolved to see him or die.

"I only had one more day to wait for the fays, and Citronette had gone into the forest as a wild boar in order to ward off my impatience, when I saw her return followed by the exceedingly lovable Zirphil. I cannot describe my joy and my astonishment; there are no terms adequate to express them. But what transported me above all was that the charming price seemed enchanted by me; perhaps what I felt was too strong not to aid me to deceive myself, but in sum, I believed that I saw in his eyes that he felt what he had made me know.

"Citronette, more attentive to my happiness than to respecting our ecstasy, extracted us from it by begging him to flay me or marry me. Returning to myself then, and sensing the danger of my situation, I joined in with her, and by virtue of our cries and our tears he resolved to give me his faith. I had no sooner accepted it than he disappeared, without knowing how, and I found myself in my ordinary form, lying in a good bed; there was no longer any question of being a whale, but I was still in the bowels of the earth, in the green hall, and Citronette had lost the power to emerge from it and to transform herself.

"I waited for the fays with a frightful tremor; my tenderness had been redoubled by the knowledge of its object, and I feared that my charming spouse might be caught up in the fays' vengeance, not having waited for them to be witness to my marriage. Citronette did her best to reassure me, but I could not vanquish my dolor and my fear.

"Marmotte appeared with the daylight; I did not see Luminous or her companion. She did not seem as irritated as usual; she touched me with her wand without speaking to me, and I became a charming little doll, which she put in her toothpick-case and transported herself to the abode of the queen, my husband's mother. She gave her to me, with an order to have me marry her son, or to expect all the woes that she was capable of inflicting on them. She told them that I was her god-daughter and that my name was Princess Camion.

"I did in fact, acquire a considerable amity for my mother-in-law; I found her charming, in being the mother of Zirphil, whom I adored, and my caresses obtained hrs. Every night I was transported to the green hall, and I enjoyed the pleasure of spending them there with my husband, for the same power acted on him and transported him as well as me into that subterranean dwelling. I did not know why I was forbidden to tell him my secret, since I was married, but I kept it, in spite of the impatience he was in to know it.

"You will see," said the person who was speaking, sighing, "how one cannot avoid one's destiny. However," she said, interrupting herself, "it is beginning to get light, and I sense that I am utterly fatigued by being out of the water; let's resume the road to the reservoir and tomorrow, at the same time, if we aren't chosen for the broth of the unworthy King of the Merlans, we'll resume the thread of the story. Let's go."

Zirphil is not hear any more, and resumed the route to his own apartment, very afflicted by not having told the princess that he was so close to her; but the fear of augmenting her woes further by that indiscretion consoled him for not having risked it. The dolor of seeing her ready to perish at his hands, however, determined him to interrogate the crayfish again in order to discover their history.

Prince Zirphil went to bed, but it was not to sleep; he could not close his eyes all night. Having found his princess again, to see her as a crayfish ready to be sacrificed to the broth of King Merlan seemed to him to be a torture even worse than the death to which he thought she was reserved. He was sighing and agitating cruelly when a loud noise became audible in the garden; at first he could only hear it confusedly, but on listening carefully he distinguished flutes and marine conches. He got up and looked out of the window; then he saw King Merlan, accompanied by the twelve sharks that composed his council, advancing toward the pavilion.

He went to open the door promptly, and the troop came in; the king, in his tank, first had all the sea-water drawn out by the peers of the realm who were accompanying him, and after having rested for a moment and had the members of the council take their places, he addressed himself to the young man.

"Whoever you are," he said, "you have apparently resolved to make me die of hunger, for you send me a broth every day that I cannot swallow; but young man, I want to tell you that if you are in accord with enemy powers in order to poison me, you have made a bad decision; as the nephew of the fay Marmotte, I am beyond any reach, and my life is secure.

The prince, astonished to see himself suspected of such a base sentiment, was about to respond proudly, but as he raised his hand his gaze happened to fall on his ring, and he saw Luminous therein, who was putting her finger over her mouth in order to signal to him to keep quiet. He had not yet taken it into his head to consult it, so much had his dolor occupied him. He did, in fact, keep quiet, but an indignation appeared on his face that the sharks noticed; they mimed applause, which meant that they had not thought him capable of it.

"Oho!" said he king. "Since this myrmidon appears so annoyed, it's necessary to make him work before us. Let someone go to my kitchen and bring back the crayfish mortar; I want to regale the council."

Immediately, a pike-head went to fetch what the king had demanded. In the meantime, the twelve sharks took a large net, which they threw into the reservoir through the window, and brought out three or four thousand crayfish.

During the interval that the council employed in fishing and the pike-heard went to fetch the king's mortar, Zirphil reflected, and sensed that the most critical moment of his life was approaching, which was to decide absolutely his good or ill fortune. He armed himself with a resolution proof against anything, and, turning all his thoughts toward the fay Luminous, he begged her to be favorable to him. He looked into the ring at that moment, and saw the beautiful fay, making signs to him to use the pestle courageously. That animated him, and relieved him of some of the dolor he felt in regard to that impending cruelty.

Finally, the unfortunate mortar appeared. Zirphil approached it with a good grace and prepared dutifully to obey the king; but the same thing happened that had previously happened in the kitchen; the bottom of the mortar opened and the flame devoured hem. The king and his accursed sharks were greatly amused by that spectacle, and did not delay in refilling the mortar.

Finally, only one of the four thousand remained; she was beautiful and delightfully plump. The king ordered that an attempt be made to shell her, in order to see whether he could eat her raw. She was given to Zirphil in order for him to try; he was tremulous at that new torture, but he was much more so when he saw the poor crayfish put her two paws together and, her eyes full of tears, say to him: "Alas, Zirphil, what have I done to you to want to do me so much harm?"

Moved by those words, his heart pierced with dolor, looked at her sadly. Finally, he took it upon himself to ask the king to let someone else crush her.

The king, jealous of his authority and entirely resolved, was inflamed by anger at that humble plea, and threatened Zirphil with being crushed himself if he did not shell her.

The poor prince took her back from one of the sharks, to whose hands he had confided her, and with a little knife that he was given, he approached the trembling crayfish. He looked at his ring and saw Luminous laughing, and speaking to a veiled person whose hand she was holding; he did not understand that at all, and the king, who did not give him time to reflect, shouted at him to finish it. The prince inserted the knife into the shell with so much force that the crayfish cried out in pain; he turned his gaze away from hers, and could not help weeping; in the end, he continued, but to his great astonishment, he had no sooner finished shelling than he saw in his hands the villainous Marmotte, who leapt to the ground, uttering bursts of laughter so noisy and disagreeable, while mocking Zirphil, that it prevented him from feeling ill, for he had been ready to faint.

The astonished king cried: "What! It's my aunt!"

"Truly, it's her," said the persecuting beast, "but my dear Merlan, I've come to give you some terrible news."

291

Merlan went pale at those words, and the council assumed an air of contentment that finished disconcerting the king and his frightful aunt.

"It's all over, my darling," Marmotte continued. "You're going to return to your damp realm, for this little dimwit you see has turned out to have a constancy proof against anything, and he has triumphed over all the ambushes I've set for him to prevent him from stealing the princess I had destined for you."

At those words, King Merlan fell into an excess of fury that cannot be described; he voiced extravagances that demonstrated clearly that he had very keen passions. Marmotte tried in vain to calm him down; neither pleas not threats did any good; he broke his tank into a thousand pieces and remaining dry, he fainted.

Marmotte, beside herself with wrath, turned to Zirphil, who had remained a tranquil spectator to that tragic scene, and said to him: "You've won, Zirphil, by the power of a fay to whom I'm obedient, but you're not yet at the end of your troubles; you can't be happy until you've returned to my hands the case that contained the accursed Camion. Even Luminous is in accord with that, and I've obtained from her that you'll go on suffering until that time.

With those words, she loaded King Merlan on to her shoulders and hurled herself into the reservoir with the sharks, the palace and all its inhabitants. Zirphil found himself alone at the foot of a great mountain, in a country as arid as it was deserted, without finding any vestige of a habitation, nor even the great reservoir. Everything had disappeared at once.

The prince was even more afflicted than astonished by such an extraordinary event; he had become familiar with prodigies; he was only sensible any longer to the chagrin that the persecution of the fay Marmotte caused him.

"I can't doubt," he said, "that I've crushed my princess. Yes, I've crushed her, and I'm no happier for it. Oh, barbaric Marmotte! And you, Luminous, you left me without help, after having obeyed you at the expense of everything it might cost a heart as sensitive as mine."

His dolor and the scant repose that he had had since the previous night, which he had spent in the labyrinth, cast him into a weakness in which he would probably have perished if he had not had enough courage to desire to live.

"If I could only find the wherewithal to sustain myself," he said, "but in this horrible solitude, I won't even find a single fruit that might refresh me."

He had no sooner pronounced the final word than his ring opened, and a little table emerged laden with excellent dishes. It grew large enough in a moment to become appropriate to the person for whom it was destined. He found everything there that could flatter his taste and his eyes, so elegantly organized was the meal. In sum, nothing was lacking; even the wine was delicious. He rendered thanks for it to Luminous, for who else could have protected him so appropriately? He ate, drank, and recovered his strength

When he had finished, the table lost its form, and went back into the ring.

As it was late, he made little headway in climbing the mountain, and lay down under a wretched tree, which hardly had enough foliage to protect him from the insults of the air.

"Alas," he said, as he lay down, "that is how men are made; they forget past benefits and are only sensible to the present harm. At present I'd trade my table for a bed less hard."

A moment later he sensed that he was in a very good bed, but he could not see anything, for it seemed that the obscurity had become more intense; that was because of the good curtains that surrounded the bed, preserving him from the cold and the damp. He went to sleep after having thanked the gods and attentive Luminous again.

When he woke up, at daybreak, he found himself in a cot of yellow and silver taffeta, which was placed in the middle of a similarly-colored satin tent, and embroidered all over with bright silver letters, which formed the name *Zirphil*, and all those letters were supported by ruby whales. Everything necessary that could be imagined was in that pretty tent.

If the prince had been in a more tranquil situation he would have admired that elegant habitation, but he only looked at the whales, got dressed and emerged from the tent, which was folded up and went back into the ring, as it had emerged therefrom.

He set forth toward the top of the mountain, having no more difficulty in finding what he needed to eat or sleep, since he was certain of having either as soon as he formed the wish. He only had the anxiety of finding Luminous again, for the ring was mute on that subject, and he found himself in a land so unfamiliar and so deserted that he had no alternative but to allow himself to be guided by hazard.

After having sent several days climbing constantly without discovering anything, he arrived on the edge of a shaft carved into the rock. He sat down next to it in order to rest, and started crying out, as he was accustomed to do: "Luminous! Can I not find you, then?"

The last time he pronounced those words, he heard a voice that emerged from the shaft, which said: "If that is Zirphil, let him speak to me."

The joy that he had in hearing that voice was even less than that he felt in thinking that he recognized it. He launched himself toward the rim and said: "Yes, I'm Zirphil; but you, are you not Citronette?"

"Yes," she said, and with that, she emerged from the well and came to embrace the prince.

The pleasure that the sight of her gave him is inexpressible; he bombarded the nymph with questions about her and the princess. Eventually, after the enthusiasm of the first moment, they spoke more reasonably

"I'll tell you, then," she said, "everything you don't know, for since you crushed us, we've enjoyed a happiness that was only troubled by your absence, and I waited for you here, on the part of the fay Luminous, in order to instruct you as to what remains for you to do in order to become the possessor, without trouble and without dread, of a princess who loves you as much as you love her; but as it still requires some time for you to achieve that happiness, I'll tell you what remains for you to know of the marvelous story of your lovely wife."

Zirphil kissed Citronette's hands a thousand times, and followed her into her grotto, into which she took him, where he nearly died of pleasure and dolor when he recognized the place where he had seen the divine whale for the first time. Eventually, after sitting down and having a meal that emerged from his ring, he asked the good Citronette to take up the story where the princess had suspended it.

"As it is here," she said, "that Luminous will come to find you, you can learn everything that you want to know in the meantime, for there's no need for you to run after her. She has confided you to my care, and a lover is less impatient when one talks to him about the one he loves.

"The fay Marmotte was unaware of your marriage; she had transformed our friend into an enamel doll, believing that you would be put off by her figure. Luminous conducted that affair herself, knowing that nothing would take the princess away from you if you married her, or if you destroyed her enchantment by flaying her. You married her, and you know everything that has happened since. By night, she resumed her form, and came to lament the chagrin she had in spending the days in the pouch of your mother, the queen, for Marmotte had obtained from Luminous that the princess would suffer until you had fulfilled your destiny, which was to flay her, so angry was she to know that you had married her and that King Merlan, her nephew, could no longer become her husband.

"As she was no longer a whale, it was very difficult to have her flayed, but Marmotte, fertile in expedients, had imagined having you crush her, and had forbidden the princess to tell you anything about that, under the penalty of your life, and had promised her the greatest felicities afterwards.

"'How will he ever bring himself to crush me?' she said to me sometimes, while waiting for you. 'Oh, my dear Citronette, if it were only my life that Marmotte was threatening, I would give it to her without difficulty, in order to spare my husband he chagrins that are in preparation for him; but it is my husband's life that is threatened, the life that is so dear to me. Oh, Marmotte, barbaric Marmotte! Is it possible that you take pleasure in making me suffer so cruelly, when I have not given you any reason for it?'

"She knew the time prescribed for your separation, but she could not tell you. The last time you saw her, you know that you found her all in tears; you asked her the reason; she gave the pretext of your attention for little Camion, and made a crime of it; you appeased her feigned jealousy; but the fatal hour when Marmotte would come arrived; you were transported to your father's palace and the princess and I were changed into crayfish and put in a little rush basket that the fay put over her arm. Then, mounting a chariot pulled by two snakes, we went to the palace of King Merlan. The palace in question had once been that of the king, the father of the princess; the city, having been changed into a lake, formed the reservoir where we lived so frequently since, and all the fish-people were the unruly subjects of that good king.

"It's necessary to tell you, Sire," said Citronette, interrupting herself, "that at the moment when the princess fell to the bottom of my well, the fays that had come to help them before appeared to that unfortunate prince and the queen, his wife, in order to console them for the loss of the princess, but the unhappy couple, knowing that it was into their kingdom that Camion would be relegated, chose to come here rather than be distanced from her, in spite of what they had to dread of the ferocity of King Merlan, whose aunt had had him crowned king of the fish-people. The fays did not disguise anything from them of the destiny of the princess, and the king, her father, asked to be the guardian of the kitchens and Merlan's mortar.

"As soon as the fay had struck him with her wand, he became a pike-head, as you saw him during his function, and you ought no longer to be surprised to have always seen him weeping bitterly when you brought the crayfish in order to crush them; for, as he knew that his daughter was due to suffer that torture, he always thought that it was her that you were bringing, and that unfortunate prince did not have an instant's repose, for his daughter had nothing that could enable him to recognize her.

"As for the queen, she asked to be changed into a crayfish, in order to be with the princess; that was done.

"In our regard, on our arrival in Merlan's abode, the fay presented us to him, and ordered him to have a crayfish broth made every day. After that order, we were thrown into the reservoir. My first concern was to search for the queen, in order to soothe the chagrins of the princess slightly, but either because of the order of destiny or ineptitude on my part, it was impossible for me to find her. We spent our days afflicting ourselves while searching for her, and our best moments were those in which we recalled the circumstances of our unfortunate lives.

"You finally arrived; we were introduced to you, but it was forbidden to us to make ourselves known to you before you interrogated us, and we dared not infringe that law, irritated as we were to suffer its rigor for trivia. The princess told me that she nearly died of fright on seeing you in conversation with the cruel Marmotte; we saw you interrogating our companions with a mortal impatience, deducing easily what decision you had made, but you did not reach us soon enough. We also knew that it was necessary to be crushed, but we had learned that we would immediately reestablished in our original estate, and that the wicked Marmotte would have no further empire over us.

"On the eve of the day when you were due to begin subjecting us to that torture, we were all lamenting our destiny, and we had assembled in a cavity of our reservoir when Luminous appeared. 'Do not weep, my children,' said the amiable fay. 'I have come to inform you that you will not be exposed to suffer that which threatens you, provided that you go to your torture cheerfully, and that you do not respond to any questions that your conductor asks you. I cannot tell you anymore; I'm pressed for time; but remember what I have prescribed and you will not have to repent of it; let those to whom destiny is most cruel not lose hope, everything will be well.'

"We all thanked the fay, and we appeared before you firmly resolved to keep our affairs secret. You spoke to some, who only gave you vague replies, and when you had chosen ten of us we went back to the reservoir, where the assurance of our imminent deliverance gave us a natural gaiety that served the projects of our protectress very well. What Luminous has said in the last place gave the beautiful Camion a liberty of spirit that rendered her charming in the eyes of the queen, her mother, and to me, for the queen had finally recognized us and the three of us did not quit one another.

"The queen and I were chosen one morning; we did not have time to bid adieu to the princess; an unknown power acted upon us at that moment, and we had a state of mind so cheerful that we nearly died laughing at the pleasant things that escaped us. We arrived in the kitchens, carried by you. We had no sooner touched the bottom of the fatal mortar than Luminous came to our aid in person, and, rendering me my natural form, transported me to my ordinary dwelling. I had the consolation of seeing the queen and our companions also resume theirs, but I don't know what became of them. The fay embraced me and told me to wait for you and tell you all these things when you came to search for the princess.

"I waited for this moment with impatience, as you can believe, Sire," Citronette said to the prince, who was listening to her. "Finally, I came to sit at the entrance to my well yesterday, when Luminous appeared. 'Our children will be happy, my dear Citronette' she said to me, 'Zirphil has to return the case to Marmotte in order to complete his labors, for he has finally flayed her.

"'Oh, great queen,' I cried, are we fortunate enough no longer to have any doubt of it?'

'Yes,' she said, 'that's very true; he thought he had only flayed Marmotte, but it really was the princess, and Marmotte had hidden in the hilt of the knife that served for that species of sacrifice; at the moment when he had finished shelling the crayfish, she made the princess disappear and took her place in order to intimidate him again."

"What!" cried the prince. "It was my charming wife to whom I did so much harm? What! I had the barbarity to make her submit to such a cruel torture! Oh, Heaven, she will never forgive me, and I fully deserve that."

The unhappy Zirphil spoke so impetuously, and was so greatly afflicted, that poor Citronette was quite afflicted herself at having given him that cruel news.

"What," she said, finally, seeing him plunged in those reflections. "You didn't know?"

"No, I didn't know that," he said. "What determined me to flay that unfortunate and exceedingly charming crayfish was that I saw Luminous in my ring speaking to a veiled person, and even laughing with her; I flattered myself that that was my princess, and I thought that she had passed into the mortar like all the others. Oh, I shall never console myself for that stupidity."

"But Sire," said Citronette, "the charm depended on flaying her or crushing her, and you had not done either one; in any case, the person to whom Luminous was speaking was the queen, the mother of the princess; they were waiting for the end of the adventure, in order to seize your wife, to preserve her for you; it was necessary that it happened."

"No matter," said the prince. "If I had known, I would have pierced my heart with that frightful knife."

"But think," said Citronette, "that if you had pierced your heart, the princess would have remained in the power of your enemy and your frightful rival forever, and that it is far better to have shelled her than to have died in order to leave her unhappy."

In fact, that reasoning, taken from the truth of the matter, appeased the prince's dolor, and he consented to take a little nourishment in order to sustain himself.

They had just finished their small meal when the vault of the hall opened and Luminous appeared, sitting on a carbuncle drawn by a hundred butterflies. She got down, aided by the prince, who bathed the hem of her robe with a torrent of tears.

The fay lifted him up, and said to him: "Prince Zirphil, it is today that you are to collect the fruit of your heroic labors. Console yourself, and finally enjoy your happiness. I have vanquished the fury of Marmotte by my pleas and your courage has disarmed her. Come with me to receive your princess from her hands and mine.

"Oh, Madame," cried the prince, throwing himself at her knees, "is it not a dream that I am hearing? Can it be that my happiness is veritable?"

"Do not doubt it, Sire," said the fay. "Come to your kingdom to console your mother for the absence and death of the king, your father; your subjects are waiting for you in order to crown you."

In spite of his joy, the prince felt a grief that moderated it at the news of the death of the king, his father; but the fay, in order to extract him from his affliction, had him climb up alongside her, and permitted Citronette to put herself at their feet. Then the butterflies deployed their brilliant wings and set forth for the realm of King Zirphil.

On the way, the fay told him to open the ring, and he found inside the case that it was necessary to return to Marmotte. The king thanked the generous fay a thousand times over, and they arrived in the kingdom where they were awaited with so much impatience.

The queen, Zirphil's mother, came to welcome the fay as she descended from her chariot, and all the people, informed of the return of the prince, made a din of acclamation that extracted him from his dolor slightly. He embraced the queen tenderly and they all went up into a magnificent apartment that the queen had destined for the fay.

They had no sooner entered it than Marmotte arrived in a chariot lined with Spanish leather, drawn by eight winged white rats. She was guiding the beautiful Camion with her father and mother, the king and queen.

Luminous and the queen went toward one another and embraced; the prince went respectfully to kiss her paw, which she held out to him, laughing, and he presented her case to her. Then she permitted him to kiss his wife and she introduced him to the king and the queen, who embraced him with a thousand transports of joy.

The members of the numerous and illustrious assembly were all talking at the same time; joy reigned everywhere. Camion and her charming husband were the only ones who did not say a word, they had so many things to say; their silence had a certain touching eloquence that moved everyone; the good Citronette wept with joy as she kissed the hands of the divine princess.

Finally, Luminous took them both by the hand and advanced with them toward the queen, Zirphil's mother.

"Here, Madame," she said, "are two young lovers who are only waiting for your consent to be happy, to complete their good fortune; my sister, the king and queen here present, and I all beg you to grant it.

The queen responded to that politeness as she had to, by embracing the two spouses tenderly. "Yes, my children," she said to them, "live happily together, and suffer that in yielding my crown to you, I share with you a happiness to which I would like to have contributed."

Zirphil and the princess threw themselves at her feet, from which she lifted them up, and she embraced them again; they implored her not to abandon them, and to aid them with her advice.

Then Marmotte touched the beautiful Camion with her wand; her garments, which were already magnificent, became silver brocade, embroidered with diamonds, and her beautiful hair spread out and coiffed her so perfectly that the kings and queens confessed that she was dazzling. The case that the fay was holding changed into a crown made entirely of brilliant diamonds, so beautiful and so artfully wrought that the chamber and the entire palace received a new brightness therefrom. Marmotte placed it on the head of the princess.

The prince appeared in his turn with garments exactly matching Camion's, and from the ring that she had given him emerged an exactly similar crown.

He married her here and then, and they were proclaimed king and queen of the beautiful country.

The fays gave the royal feast, in which nothing was lacking. After having spent a week with them and heaped them with benefits, they departed again, taking the king and queen, Queen Camion's parents, back to their realm, whose inhabitants they had punished, and which they had repopulated with a new people, faithful to their masters.

As for Citronette the fays permitted her to come and spend some time with her beautiful queen, and, knowing that it was her only desire, consented that Camion would have the pleasure of seeing her whenever she wished.

The fays finally left, and no one was ever as happy as King Zirphil and Queen Camion were. They made one another's felicity; the days seemed moments to them. They had children, which rendered them even more fortunate. They lived until extreme old age, always loving one another with the same ardor and always desirous of pleasing one another. After them, their realm was divided, and after various changes, it became, under one of their descendants, the flourishing empire of the great Mogul.

FRENCH CLASSIC FANTASY

Honoré de Balzac. *The Last Fay*
Gabrielle-Suzanne Barbot de Villeneuve. *The Naiads * Beauty and The Beast*
Chevalier de Béthune. *The World of Mercury*
Jean Carrère. *The End of Atlantis*
Charlotte-Rose Caumont de La Force. *The Land of Delights*
Félicien Champsaur. *Pharaoh's Wife*
Jacques Collin de Plancy. *Voyage to the Center of the Earth*
Gaston Danville. *The Perfume of Lust*
Paul Féval. *Anne of the Isles*
Charles de Fieux. *Lamékis*
Judith Gautier. *Isoline and the Serpent-Flower*
Nathalie Henneberg. *The Green Gods*
Gustave Kahn. *The Tale of Gold and Silence*
Edmond Haraucourrt. *Dieudonat*
Marie-Jeanne L'Héritier de Villandon. *The Robe of Sincerity*
André Lichtenberger. *The Centaurs; The Children of the Crab*
J-M. & Randy Lofficier. *The French Fantasy Treasury 1-3*
Charles Lomon & P.-B. Gheuzi. *The Last Days of Atlantis*
Maurice Magre. *The Marvelous Story of Claire d'Amour; The Call of the Beast; Priscilla of Alexandria; The Angel of Lust; The Mystery of the Tiger; The Poison of Goa; Lucifer; The Blood of Toulouse; The Albigensian Treasure; Jean de Fodoas; Melusine; The Brothers of the Virgin Gold*
Camille Mauclair. *The Virgin Orient*
Hippolyte Mettais. *Paris Before the Deluge*
Henriette-Julie de Murat. *The Palace of Vengeance*
Charles Nodier. *Trilby * The Crumb Fairy*
Edgar Quinet. *The Enchanter Merlin*
Henri de Régnier. *A Surfeit of Mirrors*
Restif de la Bretonne. *The Fay Ouroucoucou* (2 vols.)
J.-H. Rosny Aîné. *Pan's Flute*
Marie-Anne de Roumier-Robert. *The Voyage of Lord Seaton to the Seven Planets*

www.ingramcontent.com/pod-product-compliance
Lightning Source LLC
Chambersburg PA
CBHW060428030726
47495CB00003B/782